Wartime in the Dales

By Diane Allen

For the Sake of Her Family
For a Mother's Sins
For a Father's Pride
Like Father, Like Son
The Mistress of Windfell Manor
The Windfell Family Secrets
Daughter of the Dales
The Miner's Wife
The Girl from the Tanner's Yard
A Precious Daughter
A Child of the Dales
The Yorkshire Farm Girl
Wartime in the Dales

DIANE ALLEN

Wartime in the Dales

MACMILLAN

First published 2024 by Macmillan
an imprint of Pan Macmillan
The Smithson, 6 Briset Street, London EC1M 5NR
EU representative: Macmillan Publishers Ireland Ltd, 1st Floor,
The Liffey Trust Centre, 117–126 Sheriff Street Upper,
Dublin 1, D01 YC43
Associated companies throughout the world
www.panmacmillan.com

ISBN 978-1-5290-9306-3

1 3 5 7 9 8 6 4 2

A CIP catalogue record for this book is available from the British Library.

Typeset by Palimpsest Book Production Ltd, Falkirk, Stirlingshire
Printed and bound by CPI Group (UK) Ltd, Croydon, CR0 4YY

Visit **www.panmacmillan.com** to read more about all our books
and to buy them. You will also find features, author interviews and
news of any author events, and you can sign up for e-newsletters
so that you're always first to hear about our new releases

For Pam Windle, a true friend

Chapter 1

'Maggie Shaunessy, if I have to tell you again to get yourself back into this house, I'll have no option but to let your father know. He'll take his belt off to you when he gets home,' Nancy yelled down the cobbled back street of the row of terraced red-brick houses that the Shaunessys called home. It was nearing dusk and Nancy worried that the slightest light shown from their humble home would at the least get the air-raid warden knocking heavily on their door or, even worse, show the Luftwaffe where Liverpool docks were, even though war with Germany had not yet been declared. All houses around the docklands had been given their orders not to show any light as they prepared for England to join the war that was inevitably coming.

'Just another five minutes, Mam. We want to finish this game of hopscotch,' eleven-year-old Maggie shouted back at her mother as she and Lizzie Taylor threw their stones into the squares chalked onto the cracked pavements of Marsh Lane.

'Now, Maggie, you come *now*.' Nancy folded her arms over her double-crossed apron and scowled as her daughter took no notice of her.

'And you can get yourself in, Lizzie Taylor, and you can both do as your mothers say,' Annie Taylor said as she came out of her house next door to Nancy's after overhearing.

Both women leaned against their doors and looked at one another.

'If I'd have said another five minutes to my mother, she'd have gone and slapped my legs and pulled me in by my ears. They have no respect as we had,' Annie said, folding her arms as well.

'I threaten her with her father's belt, but he'd never lay a hand on her. It's more likely to be me with a quick flick of my tea-towel around her legs. That usually does the trick,' Nancy said and smiled at Annie. 'Is Jack still at the docks, like my old man?'

'That he is. They're busy, run off their feet with all that's going on in the world. I can't say I'm not worried, now we all have to carry gas masks and adhere to the blackout rules. There's a war coming our way; you can tell by the way the government's panicking.' Annie sighed. 'Bloody Jerries, you'd think they would have had enough last time.' Then she turned to the girls. 'Hurry up and finish the game, you two!'

'What do you think about this scheme they're talking about? This Operation Pied Piper malarkey where we're supposed to happily send our children to live with an unknown family in the country because of the bombing that they're expecting to come our way?' Nancy asked anxiously. 'I can't see my Maggie wanting to do that and besides, they could be going to anyone. I would never sleep of a night for worrying about her.' She looked up at the two girls as they ran hand in hand together back to their homes.

'It's better than being bombed to hell, Nancy. My Jack says we'll be targeted because of the docks and we're right next to them here in Bootle. It only takes a stray bomb. They'll not be bothered who they knock off – children, old folk . . . It'll make no difference to them if they think it's going to make them win the war.'

Annie put her hand on Lizzie's head as she came and stood next to her.

'You'd be all right if you two were kept together. It would be a nice holiday in the country for you, don't you think, girls? It would only be for a week or so,' Annie said, smiling as the girls looked at one another and grinned. They were both thinking of the countryside which on high days and holidays they visited with their parents.

Maggie and Lizzie giggled.

'Yes, we could feed the hens and go for walks and all sorts; it would be a right adventure,' Lizzie said, glancing up at her mother. But Maggie said nothing as Nancy looked at her and knew what she was thinking. She could not leave home, she was a home-bird, and she loved being with her mother and walking around the busy docklands with her father.

'We'll see. It hasn't got that far yet. Germany might

come to its senses and that Hitler might back down, no need to worry at the moment,' Nancy said and ushered Maggie into the hallway of their small terraced house. It was bath night and the tin bath in front of the kitchen fire needed filling before the men of the family returned from the docks. 'I'll see you in the morning, Annie. Monday soon comes around – washing day. Let's hope that the weather keeps dry.'

'Yes, it comes all too soon; I'll wash our bedding if nothing else in the morning. Goodnight. Let's hope for better news in the morning. Perhaps Hitler will have his own washing day and not have time to invade anywhere if he's anything like us two. I wonder if he uses Dolly Blue in his washing.' Annie laughed as she closed the door behind her and Lizzie, leaving Maggie looking up at her mother with a lot of questions to be asked.

'Mam, I don't want to go and live in the country on my own. Why are folk talking about it all the time?' Maggie said as soon as they were in the kitchen.

'Well, love, people are worried that Liverpool is going to be bombed, as well as all the big cities in England. That's what the barrage balloons have gone up for, which your da showed you when you went to the docks with him the other day. They make it harder for any aeroplane to drop its bombs. But the government wants you to be safe, that's why they're making plans for some children to go and live in the country, just for a while,' Nancy explained as she filled the bath with warm water from the boiler in the outhouse. 'Don't worry about it, nothing

4

has been done yet and your da hasn't said anything at all about you having to go.'

'Well, I don't want to go. I want to stay here with you and my da and our Raymond. They're not going to bomb our house, we've done nothing wrong,' Maggie protested as her mother indicated for her to get a move on and undress.

'No, I know, love, it hasn't come to that yet. Now hurry up, you don't want your da and Raymond to catch you with nothing on and they'll be back from the docks before long.' Nancy sighed as she watched her daughter strip naked and climb into the tin bath. She didn't want her to go anywhere, but at the same time, she needed her to keep safe. Hitler would not be bothered about who lived in fourteen Marsh Lane when it came to dropping his bombs on Liverpool Docklands, but how did you tell your eleven-year-old that?

'Don't forget to wash behind your ears. That carbolic soap is not good at making lather but at least you'll be clean,' Nancy said as she placed Maggie's nightclothes on the chair next to her. 'You look like a skinned rabbit, our Maggie. There's not an inch of fat on you,' she said, laughing as the girl climbed out of the bath and dried herself.

'It's better than being a fatty, like Ruth Moore. She's always being picked on at school,' Maggie said as she quickly dried herself and pulled on her winceyette night-dress.

'That's because her mam and da run the fish shop. It's what they live on every day. She'll lose it once she gets a little older and wants to attract the lads. Now, here's your cocoa. Drink that up quickly and then away to your bed,' Nancy said as she towelled Maggie's long dark hair as dry as she could.

'Why would she want to attract a lad, Mam? I hate them, especially the ones that go to St Joseph's. They shout names at you and stick out their tongues.'

'Aye, well, you'll understand when you're older. Now, look sharp. Your father and Raymond are back – I can hear the backyard gate opening. Let me get this bath out of the way and make them some supper,' Nancy said, dragging the partially filled tin bath to the back door, making way for her son and husband to come into the kitchen and take their baths before tipping it up on its end and emptying the water across the cobbled yard.

'My turn next, is it?' Raymond said as he stepped into the kitchen and took off his donkey jacket. 'We should be able to swim like a fish with the number of baths you make us have.' He grinned at his younger sister.

'Nothing wrong with keeping clean. Anybody would think you were allergic to bath water,' Nancy said as she poured a full kettle of boiling water into the bath and watched her son strip off in front of them both without a care in the world. 'Supper won't be long. Fish paste sandwiches unless you've brought something back with you from the docks?'

'You'll not be getting much from the docks in the future, Mother. There's talk of blockades, and U-boats out on the hunt between here and America. However, I have managed to get my hands on some bananas; they're in my bait bag. Maggie, you can take one to school with you in the morning,' Dan Shaunessy, the head of the house, said as he untied his sturdy boots and put them to one side after another hard day's graft unloading and loading the cargo ships in Stanley Dock. Even on a Sunday, the docks were busy and no regard was given to folk's religion.

Maggie went to her father's bag, which often came back with a treat in it from some exotic location. It was a perk of the job. Just as Ruth Moore had fish and chips most nights, the Shaunessys lived on whatever was scavenged from the docks.

'Bananas are better than nothing. A bit green they are, mind,' Nancy said as Maggie pulled them out of her father's bag and showed them to her mother.

'You'll be glad of anything I bring back in a bit. Things are getting worse,' Dan said. 'Half the ships that used to come into port from Europe are no longer arriving. As long as our American friends can keep supplying us, that's all that matters.' He looked across at his son for confirmation.

'Aye, it's a bit bad out there and it's going to get worse yet,' Raymond said as he sat down at the kitchen table after standing stark naked in front of his mother and young sister before drying himself and dressing.

'Maggie, I think it's past your bedtime. And Raymond, I think it's time you stopped bathing in front of your sister. She's at that age now.' Nancy shot a warning glance for the men to stop their worrying conversation in front of her before telling her husband to empty the bath water out into the yard once he had bathed. 'Come on, get up the stairs. It'll soon be morning and school time.'

'But, Mam, it's still light,' Maggie protested, pulling a face.

'Bed, my lady. Now go,' Nancy said forcefully, watching as Maggie reluctantly left the family kitchen and made her way to her small bedroom directly above it.

There Maggie lay in her bed and listened to the grown-ups in her family discuss the world's problems in muffled voices. She tossed and turned and worried about what had been said about being evacuated and the looks on her parents' and Raymond's faces. She didn't want to be sent to the country, away from her friends and family. She had never left her family home or even Liverpool. To be without her mam and da was unthinkable. She fretted and tried to pick up on what was being said down below in the kitchen. Eventually, she was so tired that sleep won the battle of the night and she found herself drifting off to the drone and smell of the family home that she could never envisage leaving, especially on her own.

'What are those women doing, Nancy, giving out those leaflets? They're from the WVS so they're bound to be nosy old biddies. Just look at them in their grey tweed coats with their badges on their arms. Nobody like us can afford to dress like them, middle-class do-gooders.' Annie let go of Lizzie's hand and watched as she and Maggie went running through the school gates. The bell rang and all the children in the yard went trooping in past the teacher, who said good morning to each pupil.

'I don't know what they're about but they're heading our way and I don't have time to waste my breath on them this morning. Let's head off, Annie. You have your boiler on and I want to get my clothes out before all the washing lines down our street are taken,' Nancy said. She started to head home but stopped in her tracks as one of the women approached her and shouted.

'Ladies, ladies, just a minute of your time, please. It's important. We are from the Women's Voluntary Service and are under the government's instructions to inform and impress the importance of their latest decision regarding the safety of your children.' The taller of the two women smiled and held out her hand, which was holding a pile of leaflets. 'Please take one. Because war is likely to be declared with Germany soon, there are plans to move children living in towns and cities that could be targeted to the country in the next few days. I'm sure that you've both heard about it and want your children to be safe.'

'She'll be just as safe at home. We'll take care of that. Besides, we're not at war yet,' Nancy said sharply. She looked at the picture of the perfect family printed on the leaflet, with a mother smiling as she supposedly felt happy with her decision to send her children away from home.

'I'll take one,' Annie said, looking at it. 'I saw in the paper that Jack was reading this morning that Germany has invaded Poland and is now threatening France. They'll soon be threatening us if they're not stopped. Jack said we wouldn't stand a chance with the planes and bombs they have this time.' For once, Annie seemed worried as she started to read the leaflet.

'You're not thinking of sending Lizzie to the country? You don't know who she'd be with and she's never been away from home, just like my Maggie. Both would be so unhappy. My Maggie was fretting about it last night, I could tell.' Nancy looked in disbelief as Annie read the whole leaflet.

'I'd rather she was unhappy for a week or two than lying dead under our bombed-out house. Jack was saying that the docks are bound to be targeted. We discussed it last night and I think if there's an assurance that she'll go to a good family, we would send her.'

'Let us assure you that no child will be at risk where we send them. As you say, better homesick for a day or two than being pulled out of rubble maimed or even worse,' the smaller of the women said, with worry on her face. 'Liverpool and all the ports will be targeted; I beg you to think of your child's safety.'

Nancy shook her head and read the leaflet. 'You want them gone by the end of the week and carrying only this amount of luggage? No toys allowed even! Maggie still takes her teddy to bed with her, although she's eleven.' Nancy gasped and could feel her heart beating fast. She had talked about this with Dan when they lay in bed and he, like Jack, had taken the view that Maggie would be better off in the country. All the dockers feared for their families and homes if Germany decided to bomb the ports and houses around them.

'Yes, but you can write regularly and perhaps even go

to visit if possible. New clothes could be posted, along with her much-loved teddy, once she's settled.' The woman pressed her hand on Nancy's sleeve. 'At least she would be safe.' She stepped back and looked at both women. 'I really do urge you to send your girls to safety and I hope to be able to register them and billet them. Give me their names and details in the morning. The special trains are due to leave Lime Street station on Saturday and all the names need to be on the list, and don't forget their gas masks. You can never be too careful.' Both women in their smart uniforms walked away, leaving Nancy and Annie looking at one another.

'It'll break my heart, and Maggie's too, Annie, but what else can we do? I'd never live with myself if I lost her through not listening to sound advice,' Nancy said, sighing.

'If they're billeted together, they would have one another. They'd be all right then,' Annie said quietly. 'I think we'll have to do it, Nancy. It would break my heart too if I lost my girl and it was my fault.'

'I know, you are right, but there's going to be one hell of a lot of tears.' Nancy sniffed as she wiped the first one of many away.

Chapter 2

'This list is a bit basic. I'm going to put in an extra change of top clothes.' Nancy looked at the list that the WVS ladies had given her as she brought out the only suitcase that they had in the house and started to fill it.

Change of underclothes, nightclothes, plimsolls, stockings, toothbrush, comb, towel, soap, facecloth, handkerchief and a warm coat. She read and checked off each item as she folded and placed it in the suitcase with love, along with the extra things that she knew Maggie would need: a tin of Spam and another of corned beef, and a packet of Rich Tea biscuits just in case she was to go hungry. There was no knowing where her daughter was to be living and Nancy was not going to let her go hungry for the first few days.

'I don't want to go, Mam. Please don't send me away, I'm frightened,' Maggie wailed as her mother closed the clasps of the suitcase and looked at her.

'You'll be all right. Stick with Lizzie and then you've

got one another. I'll write every day and you won't be there long anyway. It's for your own safety, Maggie. We would never be able to live with ourselves if this house was bombed and we lost you for the sake of not sending you on holiday to the country.'

'But it isn't a holiday, Mam; I might never see you again. I don't know where I'm going and you don't know either! Please, I don't want to go.' Maggie pulled on her mother's arm as Nancy buttoned up her coat and hung her gas mask in its cardboard box around her neck.

'You'll be safe. Now come on, that's Annie and Lizzie knocking on the door. They're waiting for you.' Nancy tried not to show that her heart was breaking as she smoothed Maggie's hair. 'It's because we love you that we have to do this.' She kissed her daughter's brow. 'Now, best foot forward and no more tears.' Nancy picked up the small leather case and walked out of the kitchen down the narrow passage to the front door and opened it to her best friend and neighbour.

'I was starting to think that you'd changed your mind and that Lizzie was going on her own,' Annie said as she looked at Nancy and then the tear-stained face of Maggie.

'I don't want her to go, but Maggie understands that it's for the best. Now, let's get this over and done with before I decide differently.' Nancy smiled at Lizzie, who had not shed one tear and was regarding the whole affair as an adventure. A few weeks in the country with perhaps no school would be a brilliant experience as far as she was concerned.

'Come on, Maggie; stop your bawling. We'll have a

grand time together. There will be cows and lambs and all sorts to see and do. It's the country!' Lizzie grabbed Maggie's hand and held it tight. 'We'll stick together, we'll be all right, I promise.'

Nancy closed the door to the family home behind her and heard Maggie draw breath as she looked longingly at it as they walked down the street, making their way to the busy Lime Street station and, from there, no one quite knew.

The streets became more and more filled with parents and their children carrying cases and bags with their belongings in them as they neared the Victorian ironclad station. Buses had been billeted from all over Liverpool for those unable to walk the distance and there was a mass of suitcases and children crying, hanging on to their mothers' arms for dear life as the buses parked up and unloaded their unwilling passengers. Some, however, were hardly carrying anything and some, like Maggie and Lizzie, had more than they needed. It was a journey of despair and mothers and children all knew it.

'There aren't many fathers seeing their children off,' Annie said. 'We always get the dirty jobs. Although I know our Jack was broken-hearted when he kissed Lizzie when she was still asleep before he went to work.'

'Dan has gone for a walk. He needed to be on his own, he said, and didn't want to be here to wave goodbye. He said what he needed before he left. He's a man of few words but I know he's hurting just like us.' Nancy entered the railway building and followed the signs for *Evacuated Children* to the end of three platforms where steam engines were waiting to take their precious loads. At each platform end, the women from the WVS were organizing name tags and assuring mothers that their children would be cared for and that they would know where they had been billeted as soon as possible.

Maggie felt a bit brighter. If all these children were going to the country, it must be all right. There were most of her friends, and hundreds more queuing and boarding the trains that were standing filling the air with steam and smoke and smelling of the coal that drove them. She had never been on a train before, so that was an adventure in itself.

'I hope we go on that green one,' Lizzie said as her mother queued to have her label put on her alongside Nancy and Maggie.

'I'd just like to know where they're going,' Nancy said as she watched Maggie get her name tag with all her details placed upon it pinned to her coat. Maggie looked up and felt like crying again as she noticed the worry on her mother's face. She clutched Nancy's hand tight as all four were directed down a platform to where a claret-coloured train was letting off steam and was making ready to leave the station. Children climbed on board, leaving their mothers peering through the windows waiting for the very last minute to say their farewells.

'You remember you are loved very much and I'll write every day and make sure that you're all right. You've got to be a brave girl; once it's safe to come home, we'll send for you.' Nancy clutched Maggie close to her and fought back the tears as she hugged her tight. 'Now, go on, get on the train. Look, there's a window seat free just for you and Lizzie if you hurry,' Nancy said, watching as Lizzie climbed on first and secured the seat and waited for Maggie to join her. 'Go on, quickly. I love you, my darling.'

'I love you too, Mam,' Maggie sobbed but then she picked up her suitcase and put a brave face on and joined Lizzie to look out of the window. No sooner had she done so than the guard began walking along the platform, weaving in and out of the heartbroken mothers, slamming the train doors closed and then blowing his whistle for the train to move slowly away. The steam from the engine blew down on the grieving mothers hiding their tears as they ran along the platform edge and waved for as long as they could to say goodbye to the ones they loved.

Nancy and Annie linked arms, dried their tears and comforted one another. 'Well, we can't bring them back now. I only hope that we've done right. Your Maggie was truly heartbroken and I don't think I'll ever forget the windows full of unhappy faces looking out. It pulled on the heartstrings,' Annie said to Nancy before turning to the station guard, who also looked heartbroken. 'He'll know where the train's bound. Let's ask him, then we have a rough idea of where they are in the country.'

'Good idea. I'll ask.' Nancy walked over and tapped the guard on his shoulder. 'Excuse me, can you tell my friend and me where that train is bound? Our children are on it and we would like to have some idea of their end destination.'

'That train belongs to the LMS; it's bound for Skipton in the Yorkshire Dales. I've got my only lad on it so I know how you're feeling.' The guard got out his handkerchief and blew his nose. 'It's the best and safest place to go, that's why my lad is on it. That'en goes into Wales and the other goes to Lancashire, so your children will be well out of the way. But it hurts, doesn't it, losing them and not knowing if you're ever going to see them again?'

'Yorkshire? That's miles away!' Nancy and Annie looked at one another in disbelief.

'Yes, but the safest place, as I say. So don't fret and just hope that they all get billeted to good families that will look after them. My missis is a bag of nerves and heartbroken. She couldn't bear to wave him off. They'll be all right. Better in Yorkshire than left for bloody Hitler to kill. Have you seen a newspaper today? He's invaded France and we're giving him an ultimatum that he's to withdraw in the next twenty-four hours. Believe me, you'll not regret sending your children to the country. I certainly won't,' the guard said, leaving both women standing on the platform feeling gobsmacked.

'Yorkshire! And we're about to go to war. Oh, my Lord!' Nancy sighed and looked at her best friend. 'Please, good Lord, keep them safe, and us too in that case.'

Maggie sat back in her seat and watched out of the train window as it left Liverpool and the built-up sprawling towns of Merseyside. She didn't feel like talking to Lizzie, who seemed to be overtaken by the chattering bug as she kept gazing out of the window at the passing countryside.

However, Lizzie had plenty of other people to talk to as the carriage was filled with four boys, as well as another girl, who, like Maggie, sat quiet and sombre, worrying about leaving home. The four boys didn't seem to care that they were leaving home and Maggie looked at them with slight disdain. They were all badly dressed in near-ragged clothes, with shaven heads and scabby knees, and, worst of all, they didn't smell very nice. But that didn't stop Lizzie from talking to them.

'I'm going to learn to milk cows and play with lambs. It'll be lovely,' she said as the crowded inner-city streets and buildings made way for green fields and woods and streams. Maggie and Lizzie peered out of the window and squashed their noses next to the glass. Neither had ever been out of Liverpool before and they were awe-inspired as the train left the grime of the station behind and raced through the outskirts of the city. The smell of the steam was new to both of the girls and their bare legs itched slightly on the hardwearing striped material of the train seats.

'Well, I'm going to hunt tigers and bears and learn to shoot a proper gun,' said the oldest of the boys with a grin. 'You can stick with your lambs; everybody knows sheep are a bit thick.'

'Sheep aren't thick; it's you that's thick. Everyone knows there are no tigers and bears in this country. They're in Africa. Anyway, you're too young to have a gun so you can't shoot anything.' Lizzie sat back down next to Maggie. 'Come on, Maggie, we're going to have plenty of adventures. Cheer up.'

'I want to go home. I'm not bothered if Hitler drops his bombs on us, I want my mam and da.' Maggie glared across at the lads that were making fun of her, pulling faces and pretending to cry.

Then the other girl in the carriage started to cry and Lizzie turned to her. 'Don't you start as well. Look, we're all in it together, and we'll all be all right if we stick together,' Lizzie said, not wanting to admit that she was as frightened as the rest of them. But then they all started to think of the family and the lives they had left behind them, and when the reality that they might never see their parents again hit them all, a silence fell over the carriage as the train made its way deeper into the countryside. They passed hedges, remote stations that they had never seen the likes of before, and eventually the wild open moorlands and the fields of Yorkshire. They were entering a whole new world, very different from the one that both girls had been brought up in.

'The train is stopping! It's stopping!' one of the lads shouted as the feel of the brakes being applied was felt throughout the train. 'We must be here!' All of them gazed out of the window and looked at the station that they had arrived at. There were three women and two men on the platform and they watched as children were made to file in an orderly pattern from the first three carriages. Nobody came near the carriage they were in and a sigh went up from all of them.

'Well, nobody has come for us; they must not want us to settle at Settle,' the oldest of the lads said, making the girl in the corner cry yet again as the train jerked back into action, leaving the sleepy market village behind and making its way further into the Dales. The same happened again at the next two stations and still, nobody was needed from the carriage they all sat in.

'Surely, it will be our turn now?' Maggie said as the train rolled into a larger town and a warden could be heard opening the carriage doors into the corridor of the train.

'Now then, you gang, last but not least. Only the best children for Skipton,' he said, smiling as he watched the carriage of children queue with two more full carriages all clutching the few possessions they had with them. 'Line up and then the ladies on the platform will take you to the waiting room where you will be billeted to your new homes. Did everybody get everything, gas masks and cases?' he asked, looking at the cross-section of city children that were going to find it hard to mix in with country children, and getting no reply. 'Right then, this station is called Skipton. The town has a market and a castle for those of you who will be staying here, but some of you might be lucky enough to live on farms. Now, that will be a novelty for you.' The tall man in a grey suit smiled at the raggle-taggle band of children and felt nothing but sympathy for them as they were miles from home without any family. 'Right, all of you jump down off the train. Those ladies will show you to the waiting room and they have drinks and sandwiches for you before you are told where to go and with whom.'

'Will there be any toffees, mister?' the youngest of the four boys asked just before he alighted from the train.

'Aye, there will be some toffees waiting for you, son, and a whole lot more,' the warden said. He smiled as the troupe were met and taken to be fed and logged in the waiting room, which was doubling up as a reception and billeting hall, with local people waiting to see and choose who they could take.

Maggie and Lizzie stood on the platform and looked around them at the country station, with flowering geraniums in planters and tended gardens and station staff staring at them, as well as the women of the WVS who encouraged the group to go into the waiting room, where at the far side a long trestle table was laid out with sandwiches and cakes. It all looked too inviting to turn down, no matter that their stomachs felt knotted in turmoil at the thought of leaving home and not knowing what the future held, so Lizzie and Maggie filled the LMS embossed white plates they were handed with a selection of what was on offer.

'Oh, bless them. How could their parents let them out of their sight?' said one of the ladies that were pouring orange squash into tumblers as the line of children passed by.

'I don't know but some seem to be carrying hardly anything and look a little ragged. Just look at that little lad – his eyes are nearly popping out of their sockets as he looks at the table filled with food. I don't think he could crush any more scone in his mouth if he tried,' the other serving lady said and watched as all the children, hungry from their journey, ate and drank.

'If this is what we're going to be fed like when we're

living here, I don't think I'll ever want to go home,' Lizzie said as she tucked into another egg sandwich and grinned.

'Mmm . . . it is good. But I'd still rather be at home with my mam,' Maggie said, glancing at the adults who were all looking at them with pity. 'Who do you think will choose us? I hope that it's somebody kind.' She looked over at the woman serving the orange squash and thought that she had a particularly kind face and she wouldn't have minded going home with her.

'I don't know, but we'll soon find out. Look, that man is getting ready to check all our names against our tags. He has a clipboard by the looks of it and will have the place we're to be billeted too, I bet,' Lizzie said. She sat back in her chair and watched as the young lad she now knew as Archie, after seeing his name tag, filled his pockets with a handful of home-made toffee wrapped up in greaseproof paper.

Maggie grinned. 'Well, he's making sure he's not going to go hungry wherever he's going to. I only hope that we're billeted together. Link your arms into mine when we walk out of here, and then they'll hopefully know that we want to be together.'

'Yes, I wouldn't want to be with him. He's got more holes in his pullover than there is a jumper, and he smells,' Lizzie said as the accounting officer asked if everybody had eaten enough and, if so, could they line up to be taken to the nearby community hall so as not to fill the waiting room for awaiting train passengers. There, they would be introduced to whoever would provide them with a new home for the length of time they were to be there.

22

'Here goes. Please let us get a nice home together,' Maggie said and held Lizzie's hand tightly as the labels on their coats were checked and they were told to walk out of the station to a long, low hut that had SKIPTON RAILWAYMEN'S CLUB above the door and a lot of people waiting outside for their arrival. 'I feel sick,' Maggie said, and felt her legs shaking as she entered the hall and looked at all the expectant faces.

'Me too. I wish I hadn't had so many sandwiches now,' Lizzie whispered. She smiled at the people who looked at them all and went quiet as a tall man dressed as a vicar came and stood next to her with the billeting officer.

'Ah, Vicar, we're so grateful that you and your wife will be taking one of our children. Now, let me see, we thought that you might make Archie here welcome in your home,' the billeting officer said, urging the vicar to move on to the young lad with bulging pockets that stood next to Maggie. 'He's aged ten and he comes from a very large family that he has had to leave behind in Wallasey.'

The vicar looked Archie up and down and shook his head. 'No, no, my wife specifically said not to bring a boy home. Neither of us is used to children so we could never handle a boy, but we could make a girl welcome. Now, this girl looks from a good home and appears to be well cared for,' the vicar said and looked at Lizzie. 'Yes, she would fit in well with us. She could help my wife with the numerous events that we hold and would not look out of place in the vicarage. My wife has always wanted a daughter to spoil.' The vicar smiled at Lizzie and looked at the billeting officer before turning back to the girl.

'What's your name, child? I am Reverend Arthur Brown and I'd like to make you welcome in my home at the vicarage in Gargrave.' He ignored the fact that the billeting officer was trying to tell him that she and Maggie would like to stay together if possible.

'I'm Lizzie Taylor, sir, and this is my friend Maggie. We are best friends and would like to stay together if you please, sir,' Lizzie said quietly.

'I'm afraid I can't take two of you but I can assure you that you will want for nothing at the vicarage and perhaps you will be able to see your friend at school each day anyway.' The vicar stopped smiling and turned to the billeting officer and whispered, 'This girl is perfect for the vicarage. Where was she billeted for?' Then he turned again to smile at Lizzie.

'Hawith Hall, Vicar. Lord and Lady Bradley said they would take two children, so I had placed Lizzie and Maggie there together,' the billeting officer said, noticing the worry on the girls' faces.

'You see, my dear, you would be able to see your friend Maggie each and every day. The Bradleys are only a field or two away from the vicarage. Perfect!' The vicar held out his hand for Lizzie to take. 'Lizzie Taylor, please come home with me and we will endeavour to make the vicarage a home for you. My wife won't be able to contain her happiness at having a daughter to look after for a while.'

Lizzie looked at Maggie and didn't want to leave her

even though they would be, as usual, next-door neighbours. She looked with pleading eyes at her friend to rescue her from the vicar but Maggie, knowing that her friend would have a good home with him, released her hand and let her go.

'There now, don't cry. We have a lovely room waiting for you and we have a dog and a cat.' The vicar bent down and comforted Lizzie as he saw the tears falling. 'And your friend Maggie . . . I assure you, Hawith Hall is only a stone's throw away. All will be well. Now, give me your suitcase and we will go and see Mrs Brown, who will, I am sure, be delighted to meet you.' The vicar picked up Lizzie's case and took her hand as the billeting officer changed his list. He wasn't going to argue with Reverend Brown and he was just glad that another of his wards had found a home.

Maggie watched as her friend turned around in the doorway and glanced back, wondering if she would ever see Lizzie again despite the assurance the vicar had given them. She heard Archie sob and turned to him to give him comfort.

'Nobody ever wants me. Even my mam was glad to get rid of me and often tells me she wishes she'd never had me.'

Maggie took pity on the small underfed lad and put her arm around him. 'Yes, somebody will soon come for us. The Bradleys will not have forgotten about us, I'm sure,' Maggie said positively as she watched other children being led away to their new homes, leaving her and Archie standing alone in the room with the billeting officer and Archie still crying.

'Don't worry, children, you do have a home to go to tonight. It would seem that the Bradleys, as usual, are making us wait.' The officer glanced at his watch and then sighed deeply as the sound of a car drawing up outside the hall could be heard. 'See, this will be them now.'

Maggie looked up and Archie stopped crying as a tall, short-haired, immaculately dressed man in a grey suit carrying a chauffeur's cap under his arm entered the room.

'Sorry, there were cows on the road. It's milking time and the Brewsters' herd held me up,' the man said and looked at Maggie and Archie. 'These two for the hall then?' he said to the officer, who looked displeased.

'Yes, this is Maggie and Archie. I thought the lord and lady would grace us with their presence, but obviously I was wrong,' the officer remarked snidely. 'They are charming children and I'm sure that everyone will make them welcome at Hawith, or so I hope.'

'Aye, they'll be all right with us. There are plenty of us to keep an eye on them and they'll not go hungry. You'll be better with us than in Liverpool, littl'uns,' he said as he lifted Maggie and Archie's possessions up. 'Come on then, let's go back to the madhouse. I'm needed all night as there's a party to be held tonight at the hall and I'm busy ferrying folk about.' He winked at Archie. 'I bet you've never ridden in a car like mine before.' Maggie and Archie walked behind him quietly and wondered if they truly were going to a madhouse and what sort of a party it was as they crossed the hall and headed out into the dying light of the evening.

'Wow!' Archie said as he looked at the black Rolls-Royce parked up outside the club and watched as the chauffeur placed their luggage into the boot.

'Aye, you two are the lucky ones. You'll be going back to Liverpool right little toffs,' the chauffeur said and opened the door for them both to climb into the poshest car either of them had ever seen. If this was the car, what was their new home to be like? Maggie thought as she sat back deep into the corner of the leather seats and looked at Archie almost lost in the shadows. If it was all that posh, would they be able to care about her and Archie? she wondered. Lord and Lady Bradley had obviously not bothered to come and pick them up and see them like other hosting families. Perhaps Lizzie had the better home with the vicar and his wife as at least she knew whom she was staying with. Only time would tell, she thought as she watched fields and hedges go past and night replace the evening. Money wasn't everything, her mam always said, it's family that you remember. She held back the tears.

Chapter 3

Maggie lay in her bed and looked around her. The sun was shining in through the window and it felt warm on her skin. The sheets smelled clean and ironed and all around her were pieces of furniture that her mother would have called antiques but her father would have called old-fashioned. She had barely seen anything on arriving at her new home as it had been dark, although she had noticed that there was a lengthy drive to Hawith Hall and that it was large with pillars and stone steps at the front. Still, they had not been allowed to enter by the front door. The chauffeur, who she now knew to be called Jeff Robinson, had bundled both her and Archie out of the car and taken them directly into the kitchen quarters, where they had been given a drink and another lot of food before a maid called Alice had taken them up what she called the back servant stairs to their bedrooms. There Alice had watched her wash in the jug of water on the washstand and then undress before telling her to climb into bed and that if she heard a lot of noise from downstairs, not to be worried as there were guests in the house. Once in bed, Maggie had lain for a little while thinking about the family she had left behind and the long journey to the poshest house she had ever seen, but then sleep and weariness had overcome her and she had felt her eyes gradually becoming heavier and heavier, before she eventually drifted off to sleep. Alice need not have worried about her hearing any noise from the guests downstairs as she had been too exhausted to hear anything, but now, after a good night's sleep, she was more alert as she propped herself up in bed and surveyed the room. A woman dressed as a Victorian servant feeding some hens stared at her from a plain wooden frame, and she looked at her and thought how beautiful she was even though she was clearly a servant. Had she gone to sleep with the curtains undrawn? she wondered. She could have sworn she remembered Alice, the maid, drawing them before she got into bed. She swung her legs out of bed, sat on the edge and looked at her clothes neatly folded and waiting for her upon a small padded bedroom chair. Somebody had already been in her bedroom that morning but she had been too dead to the world to hear them, she thought as she walked across to the window on the bare wooden floor and looked out at the view. She gasped, holding her breath as she stared out across the parkland that Hawith Hall stood in. Landscaped when the hall was built, there were aged oak trees and a stream and a lake with a fountain in the middle, while the wide spotless steps leading from the hall led down to the gravel path that she remembered treading on last night. It was a scene from a fairy-tale book. She thought she could just make out the spire of a church through the trees and the roofs of a village in the distance. Lizzie must be there, she thought, sighing and hoping that she wanted for nothing either where she was placed. She turned suddenly as she heard a gentle knock on the door, and saw Alice entering the room.

'Ah, our sleeping beauty awakes,' Alice said quietly and smiled as she came over to her. 'I came in earlier, but I think if Hitler had dropped a bomb directly on our house, it probably would not have woken you. Bless, you were so tired.' She placed her hand on Maggie's shoulder. 'Now, you wash. There's some water in the jug that I brought up before, it should still nearly be warm, and then if you get dressed while I make your bed, then I'll take you down to the kitchen for some breakfast. Your brother, Archie, is already there. He's a bit of a live wire.'

'He's not my brother,' Maggie said quickly. 'I hardly know him. We were just on the same train together and then we found we were to come here.' Maggie dropped her head and remembered the selections that had taken place and now realized how an animal must feel when it was looked at and poked and prodded at an auction.

'Oh, I should have guessed. He didn't seem like your brother, although he didn't say that he wasn't when I told him you were still asleep. Anyway, he's tucking into a good breakfast; the cook is making sure of that, even though it's nearly ten and if anybody else had asked for breakfast at that time, she would have gone mad. She

30

can be a dragon but she's got a heart of gold really,' Alice said as she pulled the bed-sheets back and ran her hand over the bed, making sure there had been no night-time accidents, as in Archie's bed, before plumping up the pillows and making the bed while Maggie got dressed.

Maggie said nothing as she pulled her nightdress over her head, stepped into her skirt and jumper, and pulled up her socks and knickers before putting her brown sandals back on her feet. She quickly took a wash in the bowl, pouring in the water from the jug and using her face flannel and soap that had been unpacked the previous night, before brushing her long dark hair.

'Tonight and tomorrow you need not wash in your room if you don't want. Further along the corridor, a bathroom and toilet are shared between the servants that live here, and you and Archie while you are with us. Now, we'll go down and see to you having some breakfast and then Lord and Lady Bradley would like to meet you both before they go to lunch with some of their friends. That is, if Lady Bradley is feeling well enough. The number of bottles thrown out this morning could sink a battleship,' Alice said quietly and then smiled at Maggie. 'But that's none of our business. I'm afraid you'll have to get used to the comings and goings at the hall, as all of us have. Let's say the house is never quiet.' She opened the bedroom door for Maggie to follow her.

'How many live in this house?' Maggie asked as they passed several bedroom doors before they got to the door that led them from the servants' quarters down the stairs and into the main rooms of the Bradley family.

'There are only four in the family: Lady Rebecca and Lord Maurice, and when they're both home, there's Michael, their son, who is courting a young lady, and Charlotte, their daughter, so there's always one or the other of them here. Plus, of course, there are four live-in servants: myself, Mrs Perceval, the cook, Baxter, the butler, a snooty old devil, and Millie, the parlourmaid. You'll meet them all over the day, plus there's the chauffeur who brought you last night, and because his lordship won't get rid of his horses, we have old Tom, the groundsman, who lives in the farmhouse with his wife Ethel. None of us bites, but we're not used to children running around the hall so just take care, especially with the cook. She can be a bit temperamental under pressure,' Alice said, smiling as they reached the bottom of the stairs and opened a door to the busy well-run kitchen of the hall.

'Well, young miss, have you an ever-empty stomach like this one? Never have I seen a lad eat as much as he's put down his throat this morning,' Ada Perceval said as she bustled past Alice with her handful of cabbages that had just been brought in from the kitchen garden and nodded in the direction of Archie. 'There's porridge in the pot, Alice, help yourself, and some toast that Millie has just made is on the table with some tea. That's if that'en hasn't eaten it all. Although it is nearly lunchtime. I hope all my days aren't going to be like this now we have children back in the house.' Ada picked up a sharp knife to slice the cabbage after washing it and frightened Archie with the scowling look on her face.

Alice pulled a chair out from across the opposite side of the table from Archie and beckoned Maggie to sit down as she gave her a plate and cutlery and poured her a cup of tea from the stoneware teapot. She pulled the rack of toast nearer to Maggie and out of the reach of Archie.

Maggie looked across at Archie. He had an expression of contentment on his face as it had been the first time he had had his belly full for years and he couldn't quite believe his luck. He glanced across at Maggie taking a slice of toast. The smells of the busy kitchen were like heaven and the fuss that was being made of him was something he never thought he'd get used to.

'Can't believe that we're here. I had a bed all to myself and a room and I've had more breakfast than I've ever eaten. In fact, I never have breakfast unless I can pinch a bit of bread before I go to school,' Archie said and watched as Maggie politely ate her toast and drank her tea. She smiled at Alice as she placed a bowl of leftover porridge in front of her.

'Mam always makes me breakfast, but never like this. Sometimes I have an egg and soldiers if we have some but usually it's just a slice of toast,' Maggie said quietly and looked at the lad in his ragged jumper and washed-out shirt and shorts.

'My mam is too busy looking after the babies; there's quite a few of us and we've had a lodger since my dad left us so she hasn't time for me,' Archie said, watching all around him as the cook opened the oven door to reveal a shoulder of mutton cooking. He couldn't believe that there was so much food and he was going to be able to eat it.

All heads raised and the kitchen came to a halt as Baxter, the butler, came into the kitchen and coughed to gain everyone's attention.

Archie sniggered and whispered across the table to Maggie, 'He's a penguin,' and then went quiet as Baxter glared at him.

'I'm afraid, ladies, that we are to await some worrying news to be announced on the wireless at eleven this morning; we have permission to listen to the news as it is going to have consequences for all our lives. Alice, could you present the children upstairs to their lordships later in the afternoon? They have asked for some time to digest the news that I think we all know we are going to hear from our prime minister,' Baxter said, noticing the worry on the kitchen staff's faces.

'Yes, that's no problem; I'll take them up this afternoon,' Alice said and smiled at both children as they looked at the adults with fear in their eyes.

'Mrs Perceval, they are also staying at home now, so they would like their Sunday lunch at one thirty as usual,' Baxter said and looked at the fiery cook as she began muttering under her breath. Ada Perceval always said what she thought but she was none the worse for that. In fact, he admired the woman for her forthright ways.

'Just as well that the meat is in the oven and the potatoes are peeled. Sometimes I think they imagine I'm a mind reader,' Ada said, wiping her hands on her apron.

'You'd better get the wireless plugged in and warmed up as it will soon be eleven. Although none of us wants to hear what's to be announced, despite knowing it's coming,' she went on, turning to the two children, who were now looking even more worried. 'No matter what is said, we will just have to make the best of it and be thankful that we're in the countryside.' Ada pulled a chair out to sit next to Archie as Baxter placed the large box of a radio on the table and found the Home Service on the cream and brown dial. They all gathered around with bated breath to hear what the announcement was to be.

Archie looked across at Maggie. He had never heard a wireless before up close and was amazed at the voices that sounded so clear coming from it.

'Aye, Lord, this is going to be bad,' Mrs Perceval said at the announcement that the prime minister was about to address the nation.

The group of servants and children went quiet as Neville Chamberlain gave his speech:

I am speaking to you from the Cabinet Room of 10 Downing Street. This morning the English Ambassador in Berlin handed the German Government a final note, stating that unless we heard from them by eleven o'clock that they were prepared at once to withdraw their troops from Poland, a state of war would exist between us. I have to tell you now that no such undertaking has been received and, consequently, this country is at war with Germany.

'Well, that's no surprise, but all hell will let loose now,' Mrs Perceval said and pushed back her chair as the wireless was turned off.

'Language, please, Mrs Perceval. We have children present. There is no need for hysteria,' Baxter said, sitting back in his chair and sighing.

'We are at war, you old stuffed shirt. You'll hear a lot worse before this comes to an end.' Ada Perceval went back to her kitchen sink, shaking her head and muttering.

'Are you two all right?' Alice said. She looked at both down-crested children and knew they were thinking of their homes and families and the danger that they both knew they were all in in Liverpool.

Both nodded but Maggie wiped back a tear and whispered to herself, 'Please keep Mam and Dad safe and tell Hitler not to bomb my home.'

Chapter 4

'Well, my dear, that confirms what we all feared: we are now at war with Germany,' Maurice Bradley said and walked across to help himself to an early drink of whisky.

'Yes, it does.' Rebecca Bradley sighed. 'Oh, my dear, I'm so fearful for us all but especially for Michael. Why he had to join the forces I still can't understand.' She wiped a tear away from her eye with her lace handkerchief and held her hand out for a small glass of sherry to soothe her nerves. Her husband passed it to her and then stood with his arms behind his back next to the fireplace and appearing worried. He gazed around the room as he leaned against the ornate Adam fireplace. He loved his genteel way of living, his ability to live and dress like a gentleman, but he feared those days were nearly at an end.

'We're not the only ones with sons that will be risking their lives, or daughters come to that! We will just have to keep a stiff upper lip and take what's thrown at us. I'm thankful that we live where we do as at least we'll not be the main attraction for those bloody Jerries. Lord knows what they'll be capable of this time round.'

'Oh, Maurice, don't say that. You know how I worry. At least we're doing our bit, for the two children we have staying with us; at least they'll be safe. Saying that, we'd better let Alice know that we can see them now. The boy sounds wretched. I believe Baxter said that he had wet the bed last night; I hope that he doesn't make a habit of it. I suppose I should have known better than to agree to have two children from the back streets of Liverpool under our roof.' Rebecca emptied her glass and passed it back to her husband and hinted for a refill, which he ignored as he rang the servants' bell that hung at the side of the fireplace.

'Let's get the children seen to before another drink, dear. It would not be a good idea for you to be worse for wear when they first meet you.' Maurice looked up as Baxter entered the room.

'We will see the children now, Baxter, if Alice would be so kind as to bring them to us,' he said. He sighed and tried to look as if he really wanted the extra burden of evacuees on his plate. He smiled at his wife as she composed herself and looked again like the true lady of the manor as she sat in her favourite wing-backed chair and waited for the children to be presented to her.

Maggie felt her stomach churning as she followed Alice across the tiled floor of the entrance hall and stood outside the white-painted doors of the drawing room. Archie looked even scruffier than the day before and there was a dribble of egg yolk running down his shirt, which he did not seem to care about as he scratched his head and stuck his fingers up his nose until Alice told him to stop it and that he should show manners when talking to the Bradleys, to which he just shrugged his shoulders. Maggie, however, knew that these folk were posh and if she was to have a happy billet with them, she should act properly, the way her mother had told her to.

'Ah, so these are our two guests, Alice. Now, what are your names, children?' Rebecca Bradley smiled at them both and looked them up and down, scrutinizing every stitch of clothes upon them and trying not to show disdain at the outward appearance of Archie.

Alice pushed Maggie a little forward and urged her to talk.

'I'm Maggie Shaunessy and I'm pleased to meet you,' Maggie said, wondering whether to curtsey or not and thinking better of it.

Maurice Bradley looked at her and said quietly, 'Charming,' under his breath.

'And you, my dear boy?' Rebecca said and looked at him hard.

'I'm Archie Brannigan. It's a swanky shop that you've got here, missis.' Archie let out a long, low whistle as he looked around him.

Both of the Bradleys could not help but smile at that and then they regained their composure as they looked at both children.

'Well, Archie and Maggie, welcome to our home. We will make you as welcome as we can under the circumstances. I'm sure that you will have heard that we are now officially at war with Germany, but we don't want you to worry. You'll be quite safe here in the Dales,' Maurice Bradley said, taking a quick drink from his whisky glass as if to swill away the bitter taste of war. 'Now, you will be in Alice's hands for most of the time that you are living with us. You have the freedom of all the grounds and our houses. When it comes to the house, we have many guests that come and go so I have agreed with Alice to keep you more in the servants' quarters than the house itself. It is simpler that way for everyone involved.' Maurice looked at Archie and was glad that he had said that from the very beginning – the last thing he wanted was a back-street city urchin running around the place. 'Now, Alice, if there is anything that they need, you let me or Lady Bradley know. Both children are to start school shortly at Gargrave. However, perhaps tomorrow you should take them into Skipton and get more suitable clothing for attending school.' Maurice Bradley looked directly at Archie; the girl was clothed adequately but the boy needed some help in that department. He could not have the locals gossiping that he was living at the hall dressed so poorly.

'Yes, sir, I'll see to that. We can make it a day out, a treat for all of us.' Alice smiled at both her charges and placed her hand on the small of each child's back to urge them out of the room.

'Oh, and Alice, perhaps a bath is in order. I also think that there may be some of Michaels' old clothes in his room that might fit Archie if you have a look,' Lady Rebecca said, smiling and giving a knowing glance at her trusted maid.

'Yes, ma'am, that is what I was going to arrange for tonight. A good scrub will make everyone feel better,' Alice said as she watched Archie scratch his head once more. There were headlice in his hair for sure. The sooner they were treated, the better, else the whole house would be affected.

'There, you've met the lord and her ladyship and they're not that scary, are they?' Alice said to them both as they made their way back down the servants' stairs to the kitchen. 'They're just ordinary people once you get to know them, except that they have plenty of money and a big house.'

'You are right there, missis. I've never known such a swanky place and I can hardly tell what they both say, they both sound as if they've a gobful of toffee when they talk,' Archie said. He couldn't wait to get back into the kitchen where he felt more at home.

'Well, you sound different to us as you have a Liverpudlian twang to your voice. I take it your family is from Ireland, Maggie, with a last name of Shaunessy? It really gives the game away!' Alice asked as she looked at Maggie, who had gone quiet.

'Yes, my nana was from Dublin, and my da still talks in Irish sometimes when he forgets his Scouse accent.' Maggie's eyes filled with tears. She missed her mother and her da and even her brother Raymond, no matter how he plagued her. The hall was going to be no home; it was just a place of safety. There would not be much love shown to either of them while they were there. She was going to miss her mother's soft Irish drawl and her father's hard

41

Scouse voice that everyone respected at the docks. Here she knew that they were to be neither seen nor heard in the posh part of the hall. They were children lodgers that nobody wanted – that was the top and bottom of it. Still, they would be attending school most of the time so at least then she could spend her days with Lizzie and they could remember the times when they played on the streets together, and perhaps they could make one or two new friends if lucky. She sniffed loudly and tried to smile as the heat of the kitchen hit their faces. At least they would be fed and dressed, which would be a real treat for Archie; he had landed on his feet good and proper.

'Well, what did you think of our Lord and Lady Bradley? They're not bad as employers. At least they have kept most of their staff on, unlike some of the other big houses. I remember when there was nearly double the staff here, mind, but that was in the old days.' Mrs Perceval sighed and looked up from her seat where she was resting with her feet balanced on a footstool. 'You can both think yourselves lucky that you're here. At least you'll be fed and you'll be able to do what you please. There will be no being made to help on the farm or help in a shop here. I reckon a lot of you evacuees will be in for a shock as it's not all sunny days and nothing to do here in the Dales.'

Archie and Maggie looked at Mrs Perceval as she got up from her seat without giving them a chance to tell her what either thought of their benefactors, and shouted at Millie the maid as the suet pudding for lunch could be heard to be boiling dry on top of the stove.

'They are indeed lucky, Mrs Perceval. They are even to be treated to a trip into Skipton in the morning and to be bought new clothes to start school in.' Alice smiled at both children and folded her arms.

'Aye, well, he couldn't go to school looking like that. His lordship would have a fit at somebody going to school from here in rags,' the straight-talking cook said and then went over to the sink as Archie bowed his head, hurt by the comments made about him.

'Never mind, we'll have a lovely time. We'll get the shopping done and then we'll go and have tea at the castle tea rooms with the allowance that I'm allowed to spend on you, and Jeff can take us in the car if he's free,' Alice said and Maggie could not help but notice a blush come to her cheeks as if she should not have mentioned the chauffeur. 'You'll like that, won't you?'

Archie nodded and Maggie said quietly, 'Yes,' as she noticed Mrs Perceval shake her head.

'Now, why don't you both go and look around the grounds? You can't be hungry yet, so we'll serve lunch to Lord and Lady Bradley and we'll all have ours while you have a look around. Then you can come in and have a sandwich and a drink just to put you on until dinner tonight.' Alice placed her hand on both children's backs and pushed them in the direction of the kitchen door that led out on to the gravelled back drive. 'There are some horses in the stable – Tom will let you near them, although they are his pride and joy – and some carp in the fountain for you to look at, and plenty of fields for you to run in. It is all completely different to where you have been brought up, of that I'm sure.' Alice opened the back door, letting the September light flood in across the bleached-clean flagged kitchen floor. 'Now, go and do what you want but be back in just over an hour else it will throw the kitchen routine out.'

Maggie stood and looked at Alice, as she smiled at her and shooed her hands at both her and Archie. She did not know where to go or what to do. Everywhere was alien to her. There were no streets to play on, no shops, and no smell of the sea; what was she supposed to do? She sighed and felt like crying as Alice closed the kitchen door behind them both, and then she looked at Archie as he stomped across the yard to where he knew the car had been garaged the previous night. She sniffed and wiped the solitary tear away from her eye. She would bury her feelings and try and make the best of it.

'Where are you going?' Maggie shouted after him as he headed for the garage and the farm buildings across the yard, standing in the shadow of the large house that was Hawith Hall. The yard was gravelled and kept immaculately free of weeds and clutter. There was a large hay barn with a cart tipped up by the wall and just before the gate that led to the stables was where the garage was. She could see that the car was parked outside and Jeff looked like he was cleaning it.

'I'm going to have a nosy around this gaff. Are you coming?' Archie shouted back and waited for Maggie to catch him up. 'Alice said there were horses here somewhere. I've always liked horses. I make a fuss of the rag 'n' bone man's when he comes up our street.'

'I like horses but I'm frightened of them,' Maggie said. 'My mam says you have to watch your fingers else they'll bite into them if you feed them.' She looked at Archie. She was beginning to change her mind about him. He might look like a rag-bag of clothes, mucky and unloved, but he was a kind soul and if her father hadn't got a job at the docks, she too would be dressed like Archie.

'Not if you hold your hand out flat with some food on it. Old Bridges that comes up and down our street shouting for rag 'n' bone learned me that and he let me ride on his horse's back. He used to tease me and say that I'm so small I'd make a good jockey and that I'd win the Grand National.' Archie's face lit up remembering the time that he'd enjoyed helping the rag 'n' bone man on his street.

'You have to train and all sorts to be a jockey and you have to have a lot of money. Racehorses cost a lot and just eat up your money. I've heard my brother say that when he's come out of the bookie's after placing a bet,' Maggie said as she walked by the side of Archie, both stopping outside the garage where Jeff the chauffeur was polishing the Rolls-Royce, so much that his face reflected in the paintwork as he wiped and buffered the precious car.

'Now then, you two, have you both settled in? You'll be looked after if I know Alice.' Jeff leaned back on the car's bonnet and looked at the two children and smiled as he held the cleaning cloth in his hand.

'Yes, thank you, sir,' Maggie said, watching as Archie

45

walked around the car and inspected it in detail now that he could see it in the light of day.

'Don't you put your hands on her, my lad. It's taken me all morning to get the shine on her. I don't want any mucky fingerprints now; she's my pride and joy,' he said sharply before turning to Maggie. 'No need to call me sir, Jeff will do. No need to stand on ceremony with me, my lass. Now, what are you both up to? Going for a stroll, are you, to get out from under Mrs Perceval's feet? She's got a fair tongue on her when she wants. Now that is one person you have to respect, or else your lives will be worth nothing. She runs the show if you ask me.' Jeff grinned as Archie went back to stand next to Maggie.

'Archie wants to see the horses. Alice says there are stables here,' Maggie said, glancing at Archie, who had decided that he wasn't keen on the flashily dressed Jeff whether he drove a Rolls-Royce or not.

'Aye, they're over there around the end of the house and through that gate. Old Tom will be with them. He thinks more of them than he does his wife. Watch what you're doing; don't be getting yourselves into any bother, or spooking his horses, else there'll be hell to pay. Now, I've to go and pick a guest up from the station. Tell Alice I'm asking after her when you go back into the hall. I haven't seen her this morning and she's a grand lass,' Jeff said before putting his chauffeur's hat on and climbing into the car.

'I don't like him. He's swanky,' Archie said and wrinkled his nose up before wiping it on his sleeve.

'He seems to think we will get ourselves into bother

with everybody, the way he was talking. Folk are not like this at home. They never worry about what you're up to unless you're doing something that you really shouldn't be doing. I think I'm going to miss home.' Maggie sighed as she looked up at the three storeys of the Georgian hall which she would never have dared to believe she would be living in. The place was massive, with windows that shone in the September sunshine and carved columns at each of the doors. It was a million times different to her back-to-back terraced home in Liverpool.

'I'm not. My belly has never been as full and I've got a bed to myself. But I suppose I'll still miss home in a way, although I'm used to being told to behave myself – folk do it all the time.' Archie sighed as he opened the gate into the stables and felt his heart soar at the sight of two large Clydesdale horses that were tethered to an iron ring on the wall. 'I never want to go home, especially now I've seen these. Just look at them! Aren't they the grandest things you've ever seen?' Archie gasped as he walked over and whistled long and low as the two giant Clydesdales munched contentedly from hay racks, and paid no attention to the lad that was standing in awe of them.

Maggie watched as Archie walked up to them without any fear and patted their necks. She was not as confident. She could hear the sound of their mouths eating the hay, looked at the huge feathered feet, and remembered her mother's words of warning.

'Tha can look, but that's all. Don't you be feeding my

lasses any rubbish from the big house or go scaring them.' A voice came from the darkness of the stable and then an elderly man that barely reached the horses' withers appeared from out of the stable. He was dressed in corduroy breeches, held up by braces, over a checked shirt, he had a flat cap on his head, and his face was as tanned as the leather of the harnesses that were on the pair of horses. 'This'en Blossom and the other is Gertie. Gentle giants they are but mind their feet and back legs as they don't like not being able to see who's behind them.' Old Tom came and looked at the two children that he guessed were the evacuees he had been told were coming to live at the hall and stood by the horses' sides and patted them, watching Archie as he too patted the horses' necks and talked to them. 'You like a hoss then, lad? Even though you're from the city?' Tom smiled as he watched Archie pull a handful of grass from the hay rack and offer it to one of them to eat.

'I do, mister. They are grand, aren't they?' Archie said and smiled.

'And you, young miss, what do you think? These are my pride and joy, along with the hunter of Lord Bradley's that is a little bit grander than these two and needs its own stall. Now, come and say hello, let them get to know your smell and show that you're not frightened of them,' Tom said, looking at Maggie and seeing that she was not as sure of herself as the lad that she was with.

Maggie stepped forward gingerly, put her hand out to touch the huge shoulder of the first horse, and then stepped back as the horse turned and snorted at her.

48

'It's all right, lass, she's just saying hello,' Tom said as he watched Archie, who appeared happy and at home as he patted his two horses.

'I'm not used to horses. I've never been around them except for the ones working on the docks with my da and he tells me to keep clear of them,' Maggie said as she stepped back again.

'Aye, well, he's right to make you wary. So your father works on the docks at Liverpool by the sound of your accents? You are a long way from home but you'll be cared for here at the hall. Now, how about I lift you up and you can sit on Blossom's back for a while? She's really gentle and she will just keep on eating while you get used to sitting up there.' Tom smiled and held his arms out to lift Maggie onto the wide back of the gentle horse.

'I don't know. I might fall and it's a long way down,' Maggie said worriedly.

'You are a sissy, Maggie. I'd like to sit on one of 'em's backs. Can I, Old Tom? Please can I?' Archie asked in excitement.

'I'll Old Tom you! It's Mr Parker to you, no matter what they in the big house call me, you young scallywag.'

'Sorry, Mr Parker.' Archie hung his head and then looked up again with a grin on his face.

'Aye, go on. Do you want a hand up or can you manage yourself by standing on the mounting block just there next to Gertie?' Tom stared at the lad with cheek and watched as he climbed up the three steps of the mounting block and then held on to the horse's mane. He swung his leg over its back and sat proud as punch on top.

'Go on Maggie, you'll love it,' Archie said as he looked down at her standing timid but wanting to join him.

'Here, I'll lift you onto Blossom. She'll not even know that you're on her back because you look as light and as delicate as a piece of swan's down.' Tom looked at Maggie and noticed her dark hair and her clean dress with a hand-knitted cardigan over the top of it. She came from a better home than the cheeky Archie, but was still not that wealthy, he surmised, as she stepped forward and decided to pluck up the courage. 'That's it, just put your legs on either side and hold on to that tuft.'

Maggie's heart was in her mouth as Tom lifted her high in the air and she tried to keep her skirts down, remembering her mother's advice never to show her knickers to anyone, as he lifted her without any effort onto the broad back of Blossom. She held tight to the mane and felt the warmth of the animal underneath her. She smelled the hay and the horse as she held on with all her might and managed a smile at both Archie and Tom. She was on the top of the world on a horse in Yorkshire, a long way from home, but it felt exciting, just for once, as she looked at Archie and smiled.

'Just look at that! Old Tom's got both of them children being led around the yard by him on the back of his horses. I never thought I'd see that.' Millie the kitchen maid peered out of the window and chuckled and was joined by Mrs Perceval and Alice in her pristine black and white uniform. The three of them watched for a minute or two, taking time out from the busy kitchen lined with walls of pans and crockery of all kinds. Herbs freshly picked from the garden by Tom were hung above the fireplace and it smelled of home-made pies and all things good to eat.

'He used to do the same with Master Michael and Miss Charlotte, but now he's a lot older. Daft old sod, he never has the time of day for us but just look at him with those two,' Mrs Perceval said and tutted as she went back to see to the lunch for upstairs.

'Everything happens for a reason. He and his wife have never been blessed with children, and now he's showing someone else some love. That Archie could do with some love being shown him and all, bless,' Alice said, smiling at their happy faces as they were paraded around the yard yet again. 'I should warn you, though, don't put your head too near Archie's as I'm sure that he's got nits. I only hope that he hasn't passed them on to anybody else. I'm about to tackle them tonight when he has a bath and some of Michael's old clothes given to him. He's like a scruffy rag doll at the moment.'

'Oh, Lord, Alice, you could have told us earlier,' Millie wailed, starting to scratch her head and wriggle about in her brown maid's uniform thinking that she had lice.

'You've not been near him, unlike me. Anyway, it will be sorted by tonight once I've found something to deal with them,' Alice said. 'Just don't sit near him, or Maggie, come to that, as they've been together since they came.'

'Nits! That is all I need in my kitchen! You can take their sandwiches and drinks outside, Alice, and get them washed and bathed as fast as you can. The last thing I wanted was children in my kitchen but no one, as usual, listened.' Mrs Perceval growled and shook her head, pushing a plate of egg sandwiches and two iced fairy cakes to one side. 'There's some lemonade in the pantry; take it out to them and they can eat in the yard. Tell them it's a picnic!'

Alice shook her head. 'I wish I'd never said anything. The poor lad can't help it. Lord knows what his home is like.'

'Mucky, I'd say. A pee'd bed and nits, that's just what we want,' Millie whispered and watched as Alice took Archie and Maggie's dinner out to them.

'Well, Tom has made you welcome. I've been watching you from out of the window. You both look as if you've enjoyed yourselves.'

'It was grand, Alice. I like it here. Mr Parker says I can come to the stables any time as long as he's about,' Archie said, his gaze following the old man as he led his team back into the stables.

'And you, Maggie, I saw you on the back of the horse. You seemed a bit uncertain at first but then you started to smile, I noticed.' Alice poured the lemonade into two tumblers for the pair of them.

'I was frightened at first, but then I got used to it. I was so high up and it was such a long way to fall but Mr Parker made sure we were safe and the horses are lovely.' Maggie took a long drink of her lemonade and watched as Archie scoffed one of the sandwiches without hesitation. Archie looked up as he saw Tom walking across to them carrying a brown ridged bottle in his hand.

'I'm thinking you might need some of this before the day is out.' Tom just winked and gave Alice the bottle and watched her as she read the label.

Pig Oil, Lime and Sulphur for Horse Feather Mite.

'Made it myself. Does wonders for horses; should cure your problem 'cause I can't see his lord and ladyship having anything for the likes.' Alice quickly put the bottle in her apron pocket.

'Thank you, it's just what I needed,' Alice muttered swiftly while both children ate their lunch and enjoyed the fresh air, unsuspecting that one of them, if not both, was going to be shampooed with it later in the day.

'It's got paraffin in it so don't go near naked flames. Otherwise, it will work wonders,' Tom warned her and sauntered off, whistling.

'Right, once you've had lunch we'll take a walk, then we'll hunt through some of Michael's and Charlotte's clothes up in the loft from when they were younger and then it'll be a bath for the pair of you,' Alice said firmly.

'I hate baths; do I need to have one?' Archie said.

'Yes, you do,' Alice replied sharply.

'I'm not sharing with her,' Archie said, pulling a face at Maggie.

'No, and I'm not sharing with you.'

'Neither of you is sharing. Maggie, we'll run yours first and then a new one for Archie, and I need to inspect your hair – we don't want any unexpected visitors,' Alice said and blushed.

'Nits. You mean nits. I'm always having my head shaved to get rid of them,' Archie said.

Maggie gasped. 'I'm not having my head shaved! You'd better not have given me nits, Archie Brannigan! I can't be seen without my lovely hair!' she yelled, staring at Archie.

'Shh, Maggie, we won't be shaving any heads. There's a different way of getting rid of them, or at least I hope there is.' Alice sighed. When she had come to work as the maid to Lady Bradley she hadn't envisaged being the mother to two children and putting a paraffin mixture on their heads, but things had never run smoothly since she had arrived, so this was just one more worry for her in her life at the hall. A life she could not walk away from if she wanted to because of an invisible tie that only she knew of and, to be honest, two evacuees were the least of her problems.

Chapter 5

Maggie kept looking at Archie's hair. It already made you look twice at him, as it was a basin cut given to him by his mother and there were marks where the scissors had accidentally snipped into his skin. However, that morning Alice had covered it with a greasy layer that smelled of paraffin. She was only thankful that no sign of nits had been found in her hair. She always made sure that her locks were brushed well and plaited, unlike Archie's. She wondered if he had ever had a brush or comb put through his hair in his life.

'We will just leave it on until tonight and then it should have done its job. You'll look shiny and new like a bobbin when you attend school tomorrow,' Alice said as she pulled a woollen cap that she had found that once belonged to Master Michael over his plastered head.

'I stink, and I don't want to go into Skipton for some new clothes. These will do just fine.' Archie looked down at his new apparel that had been hunted out of drawers and cases that had once been Master Michael's. They were better than what he had arrived in although a little too big and slightly worn.

'Nonsense. If Lady Bradley is offering to spend some money on you, then we'll have you looking smart and cared for. You can't let the hall's name down now you're living here.' Alice, for once, was short with her words as she bundled both Maggie and Archie out of the back door.

'Maggie, have you got a hanky? You never know when you might need one. We're off to Whittaker's for your clothes and then we'll have a walk around Skipton, watch the barges on the canal and perhaps visit the castle before we have tea with Mr Robinson, Jeff, when he comes to pick us up,' Alice said. She steadied her plain felt hat upon her head before holding hands with both children as she crossed the yard to where Jeff was standing next to the car with a cigarette in his mouth.

Maggie nodded her head and looked at Alice as she walked up to the car, and noticed that Jeff placed his hand on Alice's arm as he opened the back door for her and Archie to climb in.

'I hope that you told Alice here that I was asking after her yesterday?' Jeff said, looking hard at Maggie and then frowning as he caught a whiff of Archie's head.

'I did,' Maggie said and shifted along the red leather back seat to make room for Archie.

'She did, Jeff, but there's hardly any need to send that message through Maggie. After all, you're always only at the garage when not out driving,' Alice replied sharply and pushed Archie in next to Maggie.

'I needed you to know that I was thinking of you,' Jeff said and then added, 'That kid stinks! Keep the windows open, I've to take his lordship to the station in the morning. What the hell has he got on his head?'

'That's none of your business,' Alice said sharply and then reached for the winder to lower the window as she agreed with Jeff, Archie did smell. But it was worth it for one day to get his head clear of lice. She then walked away from the car and spoke to Jeff in a low voice so the children couldn't hear.

'I know I stink but at least I've stopped itching,' Archie said and bowed his head, nearly in tears. 'I wish I could stop here and just have another day with the horses. I hate school at the best of times and this will be a fresh one and I'll not know anybody. And today I don't want to go for some new clothes. And why do I want to go and look at barges? We have big ocean-going ships and I don't even stand and look at them.'

Maggie felt like putting her arm around Archie but thought better of it. She had not slept all night thinking about her home, her mam, her da, and even her brother. She'd have loved to be home with them instead of sitting in the back of a posh car and getting a new set of clothes, and she felt like joining Archie in tears. 'It'll be all right. Once we start school, you'll soon make some new friends and we're looked after here,' Maggie said, watching Alice speaking to Jeff and noting that both looked happy with one another as they walked back to the car and climbed in. Maggie patted Archie's bony knee and smiled. She was only a little older than him but she had to be brave.

'Now, keep your window down, Archie, and don't take any notice of Mr Robinson. He just got out of bed the wrong side this morning.' Alice turned and looked at both children as she climbed in the car and sat in the front seat. Both looked glum and upset even though she was determined to give them a good day. 'Skipton here we come!'

The car fell into silence as it made the short drive to Skipton. Maggie looked around her at the open green fields and the cows and sheep that were grazing in them. This was a different world from the one she grew up in; it was beautiful but a bit daunting. She was also feeling a little like Archie, that she was not good enough for the place they had been allocated and no amount of new clothes would make her accent or ways change. Besides, her mam had sent her with the best clothes she had. She didn't need any more, they were good enough.

Jeff parked on a cobbled street and people stopped and stared at the car that was not a common sight in the market town of Skipton and then at Jeff opening the doors to two raggle-taggle children and their maid.

'I'll not come with you to the outfitter's; I'll meet you in the tea room next to the castle at one. I'll stay in the car and will happen buy a newspaper to read while you look around,' Jeff said coolly, not making a fuss at all about Maggie and Archie.

'Right, we won't be long. The Singing Kettle at one it is then,' Alice said and took hold of both Archie's and Maggie's hands. Both felt uncomfortable holding her hand as they had wandered the streets of Liverpool without care or worry, so there was hardly any need for their hands to be held on this small high street.

Maggie looked all around her as she walked quickly along the cobbled pavements, not getting a chance to look in any shop windows. There was no point anyway as she had no money and neither did Archie. To hear Alice and Jeff talk, you'd have thought Skipton was huge, but in Maggie's eyes there was nothing to it. A single high street ran through the centre of the town with the parish church at one end and the stalls of the market jostling for position on either side of the road. It was larger than the small village of Gargrave, but it would have been swamped and gone unnoticed if it had been part of Liverpool.

'Right, here we go. This is where we'll get you both some clothes. Maggie, her ladyship says that you are to have two new cardigans and two new dresses, while Archie, we'll get you socks, undergarments, trousers, shirts and jumpers. Thank heavens the Bradleys are paying. I wouldn't like the bill.' Alice sighed as she pushed open the shop's door and made the bell ring. 'You should both be grateful that at least nobody will be able to comment about your dress when you attend school. You are luckier than some children that have come as evacuees; some will not have a penny spent on them.' Alice spotted a portly woman who came quickly to see what she could sell the Bradleys' maid.

Maggie looked around the shop. It smelled of cotton and polish and there were wooden counters with displays of folded underwear and any clothing that a child could wish for.

'Ah, Mrs Fraser, a full set of underwear for the boy, please, times two. No underwear for the girl but we need two good dresses and two cardigans, something that will keep her warm until the winter months, and of course shirts, jumpers and trousers for the boy. Perhaps you have something suitable in the sale? The pattern or fashion won't matter,' Alice said and then glanced at Maggie and Archie as they stood and listened and looked around them.

Maggie remembered her mam making the dress that she was in and how she had lovingly sewn it together with fabric that thcy had both chosen from off the market on her grandmother's old treadle sewing machine until late into the evening. The clothes that she was to attend school in were going to have no love stitched into them; she wasn't going to have any attachment to them at all. They were just going to be goods unwanted by other buyers, although newly bought. She watched and didn't say anything as Alice held a checked pinafore dress up next to her and made sure that it was the right length.

'With a red jumper underneath that it would nearly do you until the weather really does turn and by then you may be back home,' Alice said, standing back as Maggie held it up to herself and looking at her up and down before turning to the shopkeeper, Mrs Fraser. 'You say you have two and jumpers for underneath? That will be better than a dress and cardigan. The pinafore is a bit long, but I'm sure Maggie will soon grow into it.' Alice smiled; it looked good enough to her so there was no need to ask if Maggie liked it. The main thing was that it fit into the budget that she had been given. 'I'll take two of each and for the boy, Archie, two of those vests, age nine to ten, even though he is, I believe, nearly eleven, and underpants to match, two pairs of grey woollen socks and then what have you in the sales in his department?'

'You do right buying the clothes now because I understand there's soon to be clothes rationing brought in. That will make a mess of our business. I don't know how this government thinks people are going to live, with all the restrictions they want to enforce upon us because of this war.' Mrs Fraser sighed and then reached for a box from high up on the wooden shelves. 'We have some corduroy trousers in a tan colour; they haven't been that popular, so I can sell you two for the price of one and they would look smart with a grey V-neck jumper that is part of our lower-priced range, and with a checked shirt underneath that would be right smart. I suppose the Bradleys won't want them to look uncared for.'

'No, definitely not,' Alice said. 'We have all got to keep our appearances up no matter what. They look just fine. Archie is going to look very smart.' Alice smiled at the lad who was gazing around the shop and not taking any notice of what he was going to be wearing.

Mrs Fraser quickly placed all the clothes in a pile and totted the bill up before wrapping them in plain brown paper. 'Poor things, so far from their homes and what homes by the looks of the lad?' She said this in a low whisper but still loud enough for both Archie and Maggie to hear. 'There might be nowt left of their homes once they go back but then again, I'm in fear of bombs being dropped here on Skipton. There is after all the railway station and the cotton mill that those bombers might target. Although a ministry man and an ARP warden have been visiting all the shops this morning. I've to put this up on all my windows in case of bombs falling and the glass in the windows smashing. Look at the stuff! Now, that's not going to do much for my sales – strips of brown paper that have to be soaked in water! Scrimp they called it. We will all be scrimping and saving after this war is over, I can tell you.'

Alice looked around at her two wards with their heads hung low. 'I'm sure we'll all be safe, both in Liverpool and here. It's better to be safe than sorry. Now we've made our purchases we're going to look around the castle and then have some lunch.' Turning back to the shop-keeper, she said, 'Mr Robinson will pick the parcel up and the invoice for the big house. He should be with you shortly.'

'I thought Lord Bradley would have got rid of him by now, what with the mysterious way his wife died and the fact that everyone knows that you can't trust him as far as you can throw him,' Mrs Fraser said. 'He's been the talk of Skipton! He thinks too much of himself does that one and he's always chatting the women up.'

'I really can't comment, Mrs Fraser. He's always a perfect gentleman with me and, to be honest, it is none of my or your business,' Alice replied very sharply and put her hand on both Maggie's and Archie's shoulders and guided them to the shop's door.

'I didn't mean to pry. I'm sure he's a good man. It's just that folk talk; they have nothing else better to do,' Mrs Fraser said quickly, rushing to open the shop's door. 'Will the hall be taking any more evacuees? After all, the place is large enough to take quite a few.'

'I don't think so,' Alice said and walked out onto the street, grabbing Maggie's and Archie's hands again. 'Thank you and good day.'

'Well, we will be here to dress them if they do. Thank you for your business,' Mrs Fraser said. She watched as the three walked down the street before shouting to her husband to keep the door open because the shop smelled of whatever the lad had on his head.

'That woman is an intolerable busybody. If she didn't run such a good business, I would not have gone near her,' Alice said to both Maggie and Archie.

'Is Mr Robinson's wife dead?' Archie asked and looked up at Alice.

'Yes, she was found dead at the foot of their stairs about six months ago. It was an accident; the poor man has been devastated ever since her death.' Alice guided them across the busy main road and around the corner, up to the entrance of the castle, glancing at the clock on the church tower as it struck eleven.

'Oh, she must have fallen,' Archie said and then went quiet.

'Do you think my home will be bombed? Will my mam and da be all right?' Maggie asked, feeling the tears welling up in her eyes after thinking about what Mrs Fraser had said.

'No, and the silly old woman should have thought about what she was saying. Now, don't let her spoil your day. We'll just walk through the castle gates and have a quick look around and then we'll meet Jeff for some lunch. Come on, stop sobbing. You and your family will be all right, I promise you.' Alice bent down and wiped Maggie's tears. 'Now, aren't you two going to look smart at school? The smartest two in the class, I bet.'

'Yes, but nobody will want to sit next to me if I smell like I do now,' Archie said as he was feeling like retching from the concoction on his head. 'I don't want to go to the tea room. Everyone will pull a face at me and stare at me looking and smelling like this. I want to go home. My real home, back to the streets I know and where nobody looks at me like they do here.' He had realized that people judged him more in the country by his looks and what he said.

'Yes, and I want to go home, back to my mam and da, and my school where it doesn't matter what you look like and dress like,' Maggie wailed. Although Alice had been nothing but kind to her she wanted home and the thought of bombs falling on her beloved family had made her realize that she might never see any of them again.

Alice pulled on their arms as they protested.

'I don't want to go around this castle! Who's bothered about looking around a castle?' Maggie said between her sobs as Alice sat down with them under the shade of the large yew tree that grew in the middle of the castle's courtyard, leaning back on its twisted trunk and surrounded by the mullion windows and high walls of the castle. 'It's just a big posh house; I'd rather be back home. There was nothing like it on the streets of Liverpool.' Everything was so posh in the Dales and the houses were old and the people, like the houses, were drab and fusty. She sobbed and Archie sat next to her and held back his tears too. Her mam and da might already be dead for all she knew, sprawled in the debris of their home or her da blown up while he was working on the docks. Maggie's imagination ran riot recalling the shopkeeper's words.

'Do you want to go back? You can't go home home, but we can go back to the hall. At least we've got your clothes for school.' Alice sighed. She had looked forward to an excuse for a posh tea at The Singing Kettle and to be able to enjoy the company of Jeff Robinson away from the hall and out of eyesight of the rest of the servants. She knew how much everyone would tittle-tattle if they knew her feelings for the recently bereaved Jeff but her heart was touched by the predicament of her two evacuees and she couldn't bear the sight of them crying. She too remembered when she had first gone into service and had missed her home so much.

'Yes, Alice, please can we go back to the hall? At least people won't look at us like they do here and talk about us as if we're not there,' Maggie said, looking at Archie. She had thought he wasn't bothered about being away from home but when tested he seemed to be as broken-hearted as she was.

'Yes, please, Alice. I'd rather be with Old Tom and his horses than walk around Skipton and I want this stuff washed off my head. I can't stand it so I'm sure my nits won't have survived.' Archie wiped his eyes and left tracks down his face as he pleaded with Alice. He wanted to be somewhere he felt safe and although he had said he wanted to go home, he preferred to be with Tom and his horses.

'All right then, we'll walk back to the car and hope that Jeff – Mr Robinson – is there and that he's picked your clothes up from the shop. The tea shop will have to wait for another day,' Alice said and shook her head. 'I'd never have turned a free tea down at your age. I'm surprised at you, Archie Brannigan, you love your food.'

'I do, but I wouldn't enjoy it today and folk would just look at me. I wish that you had shaved my head like my mam usually does and then it wouldn't have mattered.'

Maggie felt sorry for poor Archie. The people he had met so far had looked him up and down and judged him too quickly. But he was like any young lad that was being brought up on the back streets of Wallasey; she was used to him. Back home nobody would have thought twice about him having a shaved head but here things were different. Coming to stay at the hall, posh as it was, had its drawbacks. You weren't part of a family and a certain standard obviously had to be maintained. She knew there and then that until they were back home with their parents both of them would miss feeling the love of their families, no matter how rough and ready in Archie's case.

Jeff was leaning over the roof of the car talking to a farmer that had just tethered his horse and cart next to him. In the back of the cart was one of the evacuees that

66

had come on the train with Maggie and Archie. He was still dressed in the clothes that he had come in and looked like a rabbit in headlights when he saw Alice, Maggie and Archie coming towards him.

'What, are you lot back already and wanting to go home?' Jeff exclaimed, with the farmer listening in to the conversation. 'It's a good job I've picked their clothes up for you. That Mrs Fraser couldn't get rid of me fast enough, whatever was wrong with her.'

'Yes, it's all too much for them. We'll go home, Jeff, and have tea at The Singing Kettle another day hopefully!' Alice said, and watched as Maggie and Archie climbed into the back seats.

'You're spoiling them. You don't let them say what they want to do; they are nobbut from off the back streets. I've got this'en riding in the back. He's sleeping above the stable and he's to pull his weight on the farm if he's to stay,' the farmer said and nodded his head at the lad that looked petrified. 'I'm going to be having him picking any loose stones up in my fields this afternoon, he's got to earn his keep.'

'Nay, he needs to be looked after better than that,' Jeff said. 'You'd not want to be miles away from the ones you love with a family you don't know.'

'That's just what I did when I was a lad. I was taken on as a farm lad on the other side of the dale to my family and it didn't hurt me,' the farmer said. 'But I suppose you'll have to mollycoddle them that are with you; it'd look bad for them snobs at the hall if they didn't. Riding in a bloody Rolls-Royce! I've seen it all now and him with nits. You'll not be doing that for much longer, not when petrol is rationed.' The farmer roughly got hold of the lad's arm and pulled him down out of his cart. 'More money than sense,' he muttered and marched off down the high street with the young lad in front of him.

Archie turned and whispered to Maggie. 'I'm glad that we're not with him. At least we're looked after and fed.'

'Yes, I think we're lucky but it still hurts to think of home, although at least we are looked after,' Maggie whispered back.

'Right, let's go home, and if you're missing your parents so much, I suggest we write a letter to them this afternoon. Let them know where you are and that you're being looked after and then they can write back to you,' Alice said and smiled as Jeff placed his hand on her knee as he climbed into the car next to her.

'My mam won't. She can't write and I'm not that good at it,' Archie said and hung his head.

'I'll help and somebody, I'm sure, will write to you,' Maggie said and thought about what she wanted to say to her mam and da. A letter home would make her feel so much better. They would know where she was then and hopefully, please God, they would come and visit her or, even better, send for her to go home.

With letters written and a supper of scrambled egg on toast followed by yet another bath, it was time for bed.

Maggie looked at Archie's spotlessly clean head and realized for the first time how blond his hair was, and that under the grubbiness he was quite a bonny lad, as she wished him goodnight from down the corridor between their bedrooms. She looked at the pile of clothes all folded on her chair and waiting for her to put them on in the morning when school was on the agenda. She felt her stomach churn with anticipation of a new school and new children to make friends with. The one good thing was that she could catch up with Lizzie because she was bound to be there. There was no Alice to put her to bed tonight as she said she had something else to do, so Maggie pulled back her sheets, blankets and eiderdown. Dusk was just falling outside but the heavy drapes of the windows made the room dark as she lay down in bed.

If she was home, she'd be able to hear the soothing voices of her mam and da and Raymond coming up from the kitchen and the constant noise of wagons and horses and carts going back and forward to the docks on the road outside. It was night-time when it was worst; just before she went to sleep the tears began to fall. She wanted her mother to be there to kiss her and even chastise her for being late to bed, but instead there was nobody.

Chapter 6

'It's all right this blinking lot sending out leaflets and telling us all what to do, but it's different for them in London. How the heck are we going to get back and forward if petrol is soon to be on ration? And as for food . . . well, I dread to think,' Mrs Perceval spouted as she looked at the leaflet that Lord Bradley had come down and given her. Not a wise thing to do first thing in the morning when breakfast service was underway and there was the extra pressure of two children to feed before school.

'But it'll be a lot worse for them in London, Mrs P. They're in line for bombings. We're not here, or I hope not,' Millie said as she cleaned the cooker top after the fried kippers and bacon.

'Aye, well, in this leaflet they say no washing to be left out after dusk, especially white sheets, else the bombers can see it from up above and know they're near housing. Have you ever heard anything so daft? Our washing is always in before the night air gets to it anyway. I just hope that them upstairs don't decide to take on any more evacuees or turn this place into a nursing hospital for wounded soldiers because it won't be them that are doing all the work, that is a certainty. You won't get me to stay if they do.'

Millie shook her head at the cook moaning as usual but everyone knew that if it came to it, she would lay down her life for Lord and Lady Bradley and the house that she had originally started in service in as scullery maid. 'Hey up, look at these two posh folks, all squeaky clean and ready for school.' Millie smiled and watched as Archie and Maggie, followed by Alice, entered the kitchen.

Cook turned and gazed at the two children. 'Aye, very smart. He could have done with a fresh pair of shoes, Alice; Baxter said when he was polishing them that they were nearly worn through. But aye, smart enough. There's a boiled egg and soldiers for them both on the table, but I don't know how long I'll be able to do that for now there's the threat of rationing,' Mrs Perceval moaned and nodded over to the scrubbed kitchen table.

'Thank you. We shouldn't be ever short of eggs as Tom has a flock of hens down in the bottom field, or will we have to sell them to folk that haven't any?' Alice said and regretted immediately asking as the cook turned and replied.

'I don't know, I know nowt, but I know there's going to be a lot of changes in this kitchen, if I can only get my hands on some things that they're suggesting.' Mrs

Perceval watched as Maggie and Archie pulled their chairs up to the table and took a drink of tea before cracking the tops of their eggs open. 'Jeff will be chuntering this morning, just like his lordship was, as there will be no having the odd trip out in that car that he loves. The old Ford will have to come back out of the garage; it doesn't sup as much petrol. And just look, we have to put this tape all over the windows. What a mess the hall is going to look, not to mention the work involved!' She sighed and then watched as Baxter the butler entered the kitchen.

'Are you still moaning, Ada?' Peter Baxter said and winked at Millie and Alice. Everyone knew that Ada knew how to moan but they also knew it was only when she was worried.

'It's Mrs Perceval when we're in company and well you know it. Yes, I am, it's always more work and no thanks,' she moaned.

'So, it wasn't you that was asleep in that chair yesterday afternoon and snoring loud enough to raise the rafters when all else was quiet?' Peter Baxter grinned and winked at both Maggie and Archie who also had grins on their faces.

'I might have closed my eyes for forty winks in the afternoon but I don't snore and don't you be saying that I do. Anyway, you sometimes go to sleep after reading the newspaper so you can't lecture me.'

'There will be a lot worse off than us, that's for sure. The only way to get through this war is to all pull together and help one another out,' Baxter said and then tousled Archie's hair as he stood next to him and wondered why everyone gasped as nobody had told him of the nit situation, not daring to. 'First day at school for you two today. I'm sure you will enjoy it. It's only a small village school so everybody knows one another.' Baxter smiled and then looked at Alice. 'Are you walking them there, because you'd better get a move on?'

'Yes, we're going now, Mr Baxter. It looks like both have finished their breakfast. Come on now. You've both got your name tags and gas masks, I hope? Mrs Perceval has made you some sandwiches for your lunch. You can come back here to eat them or perhaps join friends in the playground or by the stream; it's still warm enough for you to do that.' Alice picked up two packets of egg sandwiches wrapped up in greaseproof paper and waited for Maggie and Archie at the kitchen door. 'Tomorrow morning, once you know your way, you can walk to school by yourselves. I'll go with you this morning to introduce you to the teacher and to see you get there on time.'

Maggie looked at Archie. Was he feeling as fearful as she was? She couldn't tell as he walked out of the kitchen into the September sunshine. He said nothing, placing his hands in his new corduroy trousers which seemed a little too large for him, just like her pinafore, but at least their clothes were warm, she thought as they walked down the drive from Hawith Hall to meet the country lane that led into the village of Gargrave.

Tom poked his head out of the stable door and shook it. 'Poor little buggers,' he whispered as he watched the group go out of the yard. He and his wife Ethel had talked about them over their supper. She was all for having an evacuee to stay with them when local families had been asked but he'd put his foot down. Ethel had a bad heart and she didn't want to be chasing about after a young'un. Now he'd seen the two that had come to stay at the hall, he was regretting his decision. She'd have loved the pair of them and he knew it. Perhaps a ride on the horses and to get the lad involved in looking after them would show that he cared, and no doubt Ethel would be sending the lass something she'd make her, a knitted doll or something like what she spent her time making for local charity events. They'd do their best to make them feel settled at the hall because the Bradleys, he knew, would not make them that welcome. They had their own family and valued their privacy.

'This is the gatehouse where Jeff lives and Tom and his wife live up this lane in the estate's farmhouse,' Alice said. She stopped for a minute for Maggie and Archie to look at the traditional gatehouse that stood at the bottom of the drive to Hawith Hall that had once been gated to keep the drive private.

'It's not as big as the hall, but it's still bigger than our house. Some of the houses on our row have six or eight living in them. Does Jeff live on his own since he lost his wife?' Maggie asked, imagining Jeff's wife falling down the stairs and wondering if she had come back to haunt it.

'Yes, he does. He's not got any family, although I know he would make a wonderful father if he had.' Alice smiled and felt warm inside. She had not listened to the idle gossip about Miss Charlotte being involved with Jeff when it filled the kitchen. In fact, there had always been talk and gossip about Jeff, Baxter even suspecting at one time that Rebecca Bradley, the mistress of the house, had more than a passing interest in the handsome man. All Alice was bothered about was that Jeff was now her fella and she would defend him no matter what the scandal.

'You are sweet on him, aren't you, Alice?' Archie blurted out and grinned.

'I don't know what you mean, young man,' Alice said, starting to walk quickly towards the village.

'She is. I saw her smile at him in that way women do and he touched her knee yesterday.' Archie grinned and then kicked a stone down the road, scuffing yet again his already heavily worn shoes.

'Archie, shush, you're making Alice blush,' Maggie said. She looked up at Alice, who was indeed blushing. Her secret was out. It hadn't taken long for two town children to notice that there was a love affair growing between them. 'It's nice to have a good friend, isn't it, Alice? I'm looking forward to seeing my friend Lizzie today,' Maggie said and then put her hands in her pinafore pockets. At least somebody was happy at the hall and she was glad it was Alice.

The children dragged their feet as they approached the small Dales village of Gargrave, both worried about joining a country school where they knew nobody.

Passing over the bridge that spanned the still busy canal, Maggie looked at the stone-built cottages with slate or stone roofs, with the last remnants of summer roses still flowering around some of the front doors. The people standing out on the street turned their heads and looked at the group as they walked along the pavement to where the school stood on the main road leading to Skipton and Settle. Some smiled and others turned their heads and gossiped about the influx of townie children to their small community. Maggie felt her legs go to jelly as she rounded the corner to hear the school bell ringing and saw the black-painted railings of the schoolyard that held children from the age of five to fourteen prisoners within its walls.

'There, here we are now,' Alice said and smiled as she opened the school's gate and ushered Archie and Maggie into the playground. All the other children looked at the three of them as Alice held their hands and approached the school. Maggie felt sick as she walked into the Victorian-built school through the main entrance. There was a corridor that led to various class-rooms that you could see into, as the top half of the boarded walls were windows. It smelled of paper, ink and a strange mixture of cooked cabbage and of children and their habits. It was much like the school that she had left behind in Liverpool but a lot smaller.

'Now, who have we here? Two more new faces to our school?' A woman in a machine-knitted turquoise cardigan and tweed skirt bent down and read first Archie's name tag and age and then Maggie's.

'Ah, so you're Maggie. Lizzie was expecting you yesterday; she'll be glad that you're here. She made sure that I kept the desk and chair next to her in my class free for you. I'm Mrs Sanderson and I'll be your teacher, Maggie.' Vera Sanderson smiled and then looked at Archie.

'Lizzie is here and she's waiting for me!' Maggie gasped.

'Yes, my dear. I'll take you to your classroom and to her in a second. You, young man, will be in Mr Smith's class, just down the hall, the second door along. Perhaps this young lady will take you there? She knows the way well as Alice used to attend school here. Didn't you, Alice?'

'Yes, I did, and I couldn't wait to leave but now I wish I could come back and learn more and pay more attention to what I was being taught,' Alice said and tried to smile.

'If I had a penny for every time that was said to me, I'd be a rich woman. Now, that sounds like the bell has stopped being rung, so it's time for everyone to come into registration,' Mrs Sanderson said. She stood up and watched as her pupils and others came streaming in through the doors. 'Quietly now, in an orderly fashion. Go to your desks and get ready.' She calmed down two older boys that were arguing over what comic was best between *The Hotspur* and *The Champion*.

Maggie watched as Archie followed Alice to his classroom and Mrs Sanderson put her hand on her shoulder and guided her towards her own. There Maggie immediately saw Lizzie with a huge smile on her face, waving her hand to sit at the desk next to her. Maggie made her way over to sit at the desk but didn't dare say anything to her best friend as the teacher moved to the front of the class and rapped her desk with a ruler.

'Quiet now, children. Let's calm down. Now, let me introduce you to the latest pupil to join us in these difficult times. Her name is Maggie Shaunessy and I want you to make her welcome in our school.' Mrs Sanderson looked straight at Maggie and urged her to stand up. 'Now tell us a bit about yourself, Maggie, and then I will take the register.'

Maggie felt nervous. All eyes were on her as she started to stutter the few words that she had not had any chance to rehearse.

'My name is Maggie Shaunessy. I come from Liverpool and live at fourteen Marsh Lane, Bootle. I live there with my mam, my da and my brother Raymond. I go to All Saints Catholic school and this is my best friend.' Maggie turned and looked at Lizzie, hoping for reassurance, but she got none as Lizzie put her head down and said nothing. 'I'm only here because Hitler is going to bomb the docks and we live near to them and my da and brother work at them.' Maggie hesitated, not knowing what else to say as everyone still stared at her until her teacher stepped in.

'Maggie is living at Hawith Hall. Now, isn't she lucky, girls and boys? We would all like to live there but please make her welcome at this school. She's a long way from home and has joined us for her safety. Now, let me add her name to our registration and then please call out when I shout your name.'

Maggie sat back down and felt a pang of homesickness as she heard two boys at the back of the class mimic her Scouse accent and snigger. Lizzie gave her a sneaky glance, smiled and mouthed across to her that they'd speak at

78

playtime before answering to her name being called. Maggie looked around her. This school was not like hers in Liverpool: there were no prayers as soon as the day started, no pictures of the Holy Mother and the burning heart. Her da would be glad of that as he had never wanted her to go to a Catholic school but her mother had insisted, no matter how she and her da had protested. She was glad that she had not said anything about her school in the letter that she had written the previous night as her mam would have been worrying about her soul, as she often did when she played with non-Catholic friends. Maggie looked up as the teacher placed a pen and ink on her desk and an exercise book, instructing her to put her name and class upon it. Please don't let the first lesson be arithmetic, Maggie thought as they were all instructed to open their books and to look at the blackboard. She sighed a sigh of relief when Mrs Sanderson wrote *A Day in My Life* on the board and turned to the class.

'Now, to get to know each other better, I want you to write about your lives until playtime and then afterwards I will need you all to read your words aloud to the class. A decent number of words, Jonathan Truelove, not just two lines,' Mrs Sanderson said, directing her words to the boy at the back as he grinned and opened his exercise book. 'And no talking until playtime.'

Maggie put her head down and started to write. It might be a Proddie school but it was just as strict as hers in Bootle when it came to working. She picked up her pen and wrote about her days at her true home with her mam and da. Tears ran down her face with every word written as she remembered playing on Marsh Lane with Lizzie. At least they were back together now and they had so much to share at playtime. She couldn't wait to speak to her friend and catch up.

'Oh, Maggie, I'm so glad that you're here. I couldn't wait for you to join us. Yesterday when you weren't at school I wondered if you'd gone to a different one but then Mrs Sanderson said you were starting today and that you could sit next to me.' Lizzie, once out of the school and in the playground, gave her best friend a big hug and held her tight.

'We had to get new clothes yesterday before Lady and Lord Bradley would let us start school. They're right snobs but it's all right there,' Maggie said as she linked her arm through Lizzie's and walked to the side of the school where they leaned on the wall and watched children of all ages play around the yard. Maggie could see Archie with a group of boys and hoped that he would be all right; she didn't recognize any of them from their train ride from Liverpool.

'Well, I hate it, I hate it, I hate it and I want to go home,' Lizzie sobbed. 'I'd have been all right if we'd stopped together, but the vicar had to come and split us up. I've written to my mam and told her I'm living with a vicar and his wife; she'll not be happy. She'll say it's a sin, I know she will. Let's hope that she gets me placed with you or sends for me back home,' Lizzie wailed, wiping away the tears.

'I thought you hated the nuns that taught us and that you had to go to our school. I've not prayed once since we came here. Do you think I'll go to hell?' Maggie asked and then hugged Lizzie close.

'Reverend Brown is as bad as the nuns. He's always making me pray for my soul and on the first day we came he had me brushing out the church and putting out hymn books on the pews. My mam would have gone mad that I was in a Proddie church, let alone living with a vicar.' Lizzie breathed in and looked at her best friend. 'You might go to hell now but you won't once you confess when we're back home. I miss my mam and I hate it here,' Lizzie blurted as a group of village children gathered around them.

'It'll get better now we have one another. I only live up the lane from you, and I can see the church from my bedroom window. I'll think of you every night and perhaps say a prayer just to be on the safe side.' Maggie looked at the three girls that were watching them both as they approached.

'You two talk funny and my mother says we shouldn't bother with you, that you're townies and probably have nits or worse,' the oldest girl said. She stared at both Maggie and Lizzie and looked them up and down while her friends sniggered. 'We don't want you Scousers in our village.'

'Well, we don't want to be here but we are and there's nothing you can do about it,' Maggie said. She wasn't going to have her and Lizzie picked upon as she remembered her mother's words of advice: that no matter what anybody said to her, she was just as good as them.

'Oh, this one's got more of a mouth on her,' the girl said and grinned at her friends. 'This one did too, but we soon shut her up. She pulled on Lizzie's pigtails and leaned near her.

'Leave her alone! Let go of her hair!' Maggie said and came in between them, not understanding why Lizzie was not standing her ground with them. Back home in Liverpool she would not have put up with their behaviour for a minute but all the fight seemed to have gone from her.

'Hurr? What's hurr? You don't talk like us, you don't act like us and we don't want you here,' the bully said, before realizing that Mrs Sanderson was watching the confrontation. She backed off, sauntering across the yard with her friends in tow.

'That's Bridget Mason. She's the school bully, and everyone avoids her. She tripped me up yesterday,' Lizzie said and looked down at her scraped knees that were covered with gravel rash. 'I'd keep out of her way and not get on the wrong side of her.'

'I'm not frightened of her and neither should you be. There are girls like that at our school and they never bother us. It's only because we're new here; she'll soon get used to us,' Maggie said and put her arm through Lizzie's. 'Let's make plans for the weekend. On Saturday, there will be no school so I'll come down to where you live and we'll go and explore. I'll bring Archie with me if you want; he seems all right. He came on the train with us and he lives in the hall with me. It's a good job bullying Bridget didn't meet him yesterday because he did have nits and he stank. It's a pity he can't pass them on to her.' Maggie laughed.

'Oh, Maggie, I have missed you. Perhaps things are going to get better now if we have one another,' Lizzie said, smiling at her life-long friend.

'Of course they will. We're in the country and up at the hall I've never been so well fed. And they have a Rolls-Royce car and a butler and maids . . . It's like living in a palace. I have everything I need and Alice, the girl who looks after me and Archie, is nice and kind.' Maggie tried to sound positive.

'Unlike the vicarage where I'm staying. The saying "as poor as a church mouse" is right. He watches everything and shares out the bread nearly crumb by crumb.' Lizzie sighed.

'Never mind, Liz, you can share my dinner with me. Mrs Perceval has packed enough sandwiches for the two of us. We have one another now, we'll be all right. Didn't you say you'd enjoy the country? That there were fields, sheep and rivers to play in? Well, that's what we'll do together and try to forget how homesick we are,' Maggie said as the school bell rang, putting an end to playtime.

'I can never stop feeling homesick, Maggie,' Lizzie whispered.

'No, I can't either, but we'll not be here for ever,' Maggie replied, hoping that what she said would turn out to be right.

Chapter 7

Nancy Shaunessy nearly jumped out of her chair as she heard the letterbox's flap snap shut. Even a few days had seemed like an age while she waited for a letter to arrive from those that were looking after her Maggie, or for Maggie to even write a letter home herself, since she had begrudgingly placed her beloved daughter on a train to who knew where. She bent down and picked up the envelope and felt her heart beating fast. It was Maggie's handwriting; it was a letter from her lass, one that she would take time to read so she could listen to everything that she said. She looked at the envelope. It was of good quality, even having a faint watermark on the paper, so she had been placed somewhere decent, she thought as she sat down at the table and poured a mug of tea out from the teapot before opening the letter and drowning herself in the words that Maggie had written. The paper was headed with the address of Hawith Hall, Gargrave, near Skipton, North Yorkshire, confirming that Maggie was in Yorkshire, miles away in the country, safely away from any threat of bombing or invasion – not that there had been any of either yet. Nancy sighed, took a sip of her tea, and then read every precious word:

Dear Mam, Da and Raymond,

I hope that you are all well and that no bombs have fallen anywhere near you. I had a good journey on the train here to Yorkshire. I am living in a place called Hawith Hall, which is a really big house with cooks and maids, and the people that own it are ever so posh. So posh that I hardly ever see them. Archie and I stay in our rooms or live in the big kitchen, although Archie tends to be outside all the time. He likes the horses that are here.

You don't know Archie but he came on the train with me and is from Wallasey. Lizzie was supposed to stay with me but she's living with a vicar and his wife in Gargrave just down the road. I hope to see her at school tomorrow. We have plenty of food to eat and Alice, the maid, looks after us well. She took us to Skipton today for some new school clothes, although I thought mine were good enough anyway. Archie's weren't. He had holes in everything and he's had to be treated for nits.

Don't worry about me, I am all right, although I miss you all and wish I was home. It is the worst at night when I think of you all when I am going

to sleep. Alice doesn't tuck me in as you used to,
Mam.

    Lots of Love,
    Maggie

    PS Can you send me Ted, now that you know
my address, and maybe come to see me soon? XXXX

Nancy looked at the blotched last line where a tear had fallen onto the ink and held the letter close to her chest. How she missed her Maggie but at least she knew where she was and, by the sounds of it, she was safe and in a good home and that was all that mattered. She had no sooner read the letter than she heard a knock on the front door and the cheery voice of Annie shout down the hall, 'Are ya in, yuse?'

'I'm here, Annie. Have you had a letter like me?' Nancy said as Annie walked into the kitchen with Nancy giving her feet a quick glance to make sure that she hadn't any of her high heels on as she crossed her new oilcloth-covered kitchen floor. The last thing she wanted was a track of holes where Annie had walked. Dan had moaned enough about the cost of it as it was. Nancy loved her kitchen and although sparse with just a cooker, kitchen table and shelves made by Dan and Raymond from wooden crates from the docks, it was kept absolutely spotless. 'I have. They're in Yorkshire and safe.' Nancy sighed and poured her best friend a cuppa as she sat across the table from her.

'Oh, eh, I cried this morning when it came through the letterbox. I've looked out for postie, not that they've had time to write and get it to us,' Annie said. 'Go on, I'll show you mine if you show me yours. We sound as bad as them two, don't we?' Annie said and smiled. 'They're not together but in the same village by the sound of it,' she said as she passed Lizzie's letter to Nancy and Nancy gave hers to Annie.

'Oh, Lord, Annie, she's staying at a vicarage with a vicar and his wife! How do you feel about that? After all, you practise more than I do. She's living under the other side's roof, as my mother would say.' Nancy read more of Lizzie's letter. 'She doesn't sound as settled as my Maggie. Perhaps she'll settle better once she's at school and back seeing Maggie. They're both as thick as thieves and will always stick up for one another.'

'It sounds as if your Maggie has landed on her feet, which is good to know. At least she sounds fed. I don't know about our Lizzie. I can't say I'm happy that she's staying with a vicar but at least I know that she's safe with a man of the cloth and his wife. I'll see what my Jack says, and Father Briggs at confession. You'd think they'd check what religion they were . . . Everything has happened so fast.' Annie wrapped her hands around her mug and seemed broken-hearted as she looked across at her friend.

'I know. I miss my Maggie so much. I curse her many a time but now she's not here, all I do is worry about her. Raymond's as bad. When she's at home they argue like cat and dog but now he's lost without his sister. I'm just so glad that they've both written. At least we know where they are and that they're safe.'

'We've maybe sent them away for no reason as not a

bomb has fallen yet, and all the fighting is in Europe. I hope I haven't talked you into something just because I was worrying that we were going to get blown to Kingdom Come at any time. I worry too much, my Jack says, but I can't help it.'

'They'll come, though. I bet your Jack keeps telling you of ships lost because of U-boat hits and the number of troops along the dockside was nobody's business. Poor buggers. I looked at them; some were only my Raymond's age. I'm just thankful he'll not be enlisting, because of his hearing. Hitler could be yelling as loud as he could in his left ear and he wouldn't hear him. Although he puts it on sometimes if he wants to ignore me when I tell him I want something doing. But, just for once, I'm glad he did go part deaf after having mumps.' Nancy shook her head. 'I don't know why we bother having families, they're only a worry.'

'Maybe because we have no choice. I think myself lucky that we've just been blessed with our Lizzie. I was broken-hearted when I found out I couldn't have any more after she was born. I always wanted at least two but it wasn't to be. Perhaps it was a good thing because some folk struggle with the size of their families; you've only to look at the Catholic families all around us. Perhaps we should both be thankful,' Annie said, drinking deeply as she thought about her only child in a home that was not of her liking.

The first week of life at a village school in the Dales had been an eye-opener to all the evacuees that had been placed there. Maggie, Lizzie and Archie stood at the school gates at three thirty on the Friday afternoon and felt exhausted. Not only were they miles away from their homes, they were also miles apart from the regular school-children that attended the small village school.

'I suppose I'll have to go home to the vicarage. Reverend Brown said that I had to come straight home and was not to wander.' Lizzie looked with sadness at Maggie and Archie.

'Well, I'll come and pick you up in the morning now I know where you live. We can have a look around Gargrave, and we can look in the shop windows even though we have no money,' Maggie said and grinned.

'I'm not coming with you two girls, you can forget that. I've better things to do with my time. Tom's going to show me how to groom his horses and he's going to let me go near Lord Bradley's hunter. He's not let me into the stables until now, but he's promised me that I can in the morning,' Archie said excitedly. He'd followed Tom around every evening after school and begged him to show him how to groom the gentle giants that were worshipped by the old man.

'That's fine by us; we never said we wanted you anyway,' Lizzie said sharply and stuck her nose up in the air.

'No wonder you keep getting picked upon, Lizzie Taylor. You can really be nasty sometimes,' Archie said and wandered off across the main road in the direction of home, leaving the girls standing alone.

'You've gone and upset him now. He gets a bit tetchy, but you were nasty with the wrong one there. He's all right is Archie. You should be like that with Bridget Mason and then she wouldn't give you so much grief. She's all gob, that's all. If you stuck up to her, she'd say and do nothing. She always picks on you when I'm not about, I've noticed. Next week we sort her out. We never got picked on at All Saints and that was a lot rougher than here.'

'But Bootle was our home! We knew everybody there and everybody knew us.' Lizzie sighed. 'If it wasn't somebody's cousin, it was somebody's brother or sister that you could upset. Everybody was related back home and you knew it, so you knew who not to pick an argument with. Besides, I'm frightened, Maggie. I'm on my own.'

'No, you're not. We've got one another and Archie, even though he's a lad and a grubby one at that. Everybody here is just the same as at home, we just have to learn to fit in and find our way. It'll get better. I know it will,' Maggie said, hugging her best friend. 'I'll come and knock for you around ten and we'll have a wander. I bet both houses will want us out from under their feet anyway. I know Mrs Perceval doesn't want me in her kitchen and the other posh lot has nothing to do with us. There's only Alice and she will want time to flutter her eyelashes at the chauffeur, Jeff. I'll just be in the way.' She let go of her best friend and stood back. 'It'll get better and turn into the countryside that you told me all about on the train. Remember fields, lambs and streams?'

'It's the wrong time of year for lambs, so Bridget Mason

told me when I asked, and all the class then laughed at me. We'll never fit in, Maggie.'

'Oh, yes, we will. Give us a few weeks and we'll even talk like them around here, although sometimes I look at them and wonder what they're on about with thee and thou! They think we talk differently? They want to hear themselves! I'll have to go; I'll see you in the morning. Alice will be wondering where I'm at because Archie won't have told her I'm with you.' Maggie looked up and down the road. There was hardly any traffic on it, unlike at home. Here it was the odd motorcar and wagon and there were still a lot of horses and carts being used as she crossed to the other side of the road and watched a dejected Lizzie walk home in the opposite direction with her head drooped.

'See you tomorrow,' she shouted but Lizzie could not hear as a wagon full of wooden crates went past. Poor Lizzie, she had it bad both in her placement and at school, but things would hopefully get better soon.

Maggie lay in her bed and looked at the clock on her bedside table. It showed her that it was nine in the morning, and she surmised that Alice must have been told not to disturb her on a weekend. She was late up and she quickly went along the empty corridor still in her nightdress to the bathroom. There was nobody about in the servants' quarters; they were all downstairs doing their various tasks as Maggie ran quickly back and changed into her clothes that her mother had sent with her. She was going to leave the pinafore and jumpers just for school; the clothes that she had come with were a bit different to what everyone was wearing at school. The patterns were brighter and the skirts fuller, so she would play it safe and try and fit in with her new surroundings, but now it was the weekend and she was going to wear what she wanted.

She pulled back her bedroom curtains and looked out. Archie was already outside, carrying a bucket of water following Tom across the yard. He never left the old man alone, she thought as she quickly brushed her hair and looked at herself in the mirror. Last week at this time, she thought, they were travelling on a train bound to who knew where, and now she was in her own room in a fancy hall in Yorkshire with nothing to do but entertain herself all day. Her mam would have been up for hours. Saturday was the day she cleaned the front step with a donkey stone, scrubbing brush and bucket of water, her apron tied around her and a scarf wrapped around her head keeping her hair out of the way while she was on her knees and working hard. Lizzie's mam would be cleaning hers at the same time and then both would finish and go into one another's kitchens for their weekend gossip over tea. She could hear their accents now, as they laughed about who had been drunk on the corner of the street and who had run off with whose wife. There was none of that at the hall. The nearest that she had got to it was the woman in the milliner's shop discussing Jeff the chauffeur with Alice and that had been all one-sided. Even though Archie had shown interest in Jeff's wife's accident, Alice had not commented upon it. Maggie sighed. She loved home and family but no matter how much she missed them, there was no way she could get home, so she had better make the most of where she was.

'Well, young lady, what time do you call this? We thought you were going to sleep until dinnertime,' Mrs Perceval said as she placed a cup of tea and a slice of cold toast in front of Maggie. 'I'm not making you a fresh slice. It might be cold but I'm not pandering to you as Alice does.' She scowled and went back to her sink.

'Is Alice not here today?' Maggie asked as she bit into her toast and looked around the kitchen that was empty apart from her and the cook.

'She's walked into Gargrave. The Bradleys are having visitors tonight, just drinks and canapés, but we were short some cheese, and Lady Bradley likes her olives, not that I think she'll be able to get them in the village. She'll have to make do. It's her own fault, she should have told me earlier and then she would have had some proper things to eat.' Mrs Perceval scowled. 'Besides, I reckon nowt to this foreign muck. "What's wrong with cheese and pickle on a water biscuit?" I asked Alice. Now, what are you going to be doing today? The weather is fine, so you can go out, get from under my feet, and don't go bothering Millie; she's enough on with twenty guests arriving tonight.'

'I'm going to have a walk into Gargrave to meet my friend Lizzie at the vicarage; she's staying with the vicar and his wife,' Maggie said and cleaned her plate of every crumb and drank her tea before taking it over to the sink next to Mrs Perceval.

'Now, wash it up. I might be cook and pot washer for them upstairs but I'm not washing your pots when I'm rushed off my feet. The dishcloth is there, the tea-towel is over the rail on the oven and the pot cupboard is the big wooden one on the far wall. It's no good having a dog and barking yourself,' Mrs Perceval growled as she watched Maggie wash her cup and plate without argument. 'So your friend is with the vicar and his wife. That'll not be a fun place to stay; there'll be no parties and cake there. He might be a good vicar but he's a miserable devil and his wife is worse. I don't think I've ever seen her smile once.'

'Lizzie isn't liking it there. She's homesick and she's being bullied at school,' Maggie said, looking at the old cook who always said what she thought but who everyone knew to be caring.

'Who's bullying her? We cannot be having that.' Ada wiped her hands and walked over to the cake tins on the kitchen shelves and opened them up as she listened to Maggie.

'A girl called Bridget Mason. She and two other girls that seem to think it's fun to mock our accents,' Maggie said as she watched the cook place two buns in a paper bag along with two apples from the fruit dish.

'Well, she needn't say anything. Her father keeps the piggery in between here and Broughton. He's as ignorant as his pigs and he stinks. Just tell her there's a whiff of pig muck around her, she'll shut up then. Play her at her own game.' Ada Perceval winked and passed Maggie the two paper bags with edibles within them. 'There you go,

94

dinner for two. Now, no later than five back home. The guests will start coming at eight and I want my kitchen clear of children by then.'

'Thank you.' Maggie grinned. Mrs Perceval was all right, you just had to take her with a pinch of salt.

Maggie opened the iron gates that led up to the large Victorian vicarage that stood just proud of the main road and rang the brass polished bell. She held her breath and hoped that she wouldn't have to ring it again as what seemed like ages passed before she heard a voice from behind her.

'Yes, what can we do for you?' Reverend Brown said and looked down at the young girl standing in front of him.

'I've just come to see if Lizzie can come out and play. We came on the same train together; I remember you from last weekend,' Maggie said and looked at the vicar who was dressed in trousers, shirt and pullover with his dog collar visible around his neck.

'She's busy in the kitchen with my wife; she's peeling apples to be made into chutney and apple jelly for the produce sale next weekend. I don't think she will want to come with you.' The vicar looked down at the girl he recognized from the hall at Skipton station. 'Where are you billeted at? Somewhere near or have you walked all the way from Skipton?'

'I'm with Lord and Lady Bradley at Hawith Hall. It's lovely there but I'm like Lizzie, I do miss my family. That's why I thought I'd call for my best friend from

95

home. We can cheer one another up and I've been given some dinner to share by the cook at Hawith,' Maggie said and showed him her two bags of food.

'Ah, Hawith Hall. They are a good family the Bradleys, support the church well, good Christian folk. You will be looked after in their care.' The vicar considered things for a minute, not wanting Maggie to go back to Hawith and tell a tale of him not allowing Lizzie to be with her best friend on a Saturday. The Bradleys gave well to the church and he didn't want to damage his reputation. 'I don't suppose it will hurt for her to be with you for a short while, a stroll down by the river or suchlike.' Reverend Brown beckoned her to follow him to the back of the house, where the kitchen door was open, letting the smell of pickling vinegar and spices out into the morning air.

'Lizzie, you have a visitor and she brings lunch with her for you both to share,' the vicar said and then turned to his wife. 'Maggie here is staying with Lord and Lady Bradley and is friends with Lizzie; she came on the same train.'

'I needed Lizzie to help me fill the jars,' Dorothy Brown said, looking at her husband.

'I'm sure you'll manage on your own, Dot. It will do Maggie and Lizzie good to catch up with one another, my dear.' The vicar scowled at his wife and hoped that she would say no more.

Lizzie looked up at Maggie and smiled. She was her saviour from filling another jar with the chutneys and pickles that she had been railroaded into making with the vicar's wife.

'Oh, very well, if you say so. I specifically asked for a girl so that she could help around the kitchen, as some days I feel so unwell,' Dorothy Brown said and glared at Lizzie. 'You'd better take my apron off and go with your friend, but don't be long.'

'Thank you,' Lizzie said and grinned across at Maggie as she took off the apron and crossed to the doorway as fast as she could.

'Don't be too long, though, we'll only worry where you are,' Dorothy Brown said and stood with her husband at the kitchen door as they watched the two girls disappear around the side of the house.

'She's not your maid, dear, remember that,' Reverend Brown said to his wife. 'You should give her some of her own time. One day she'll go home to her parents and we don't want our care of her reflecting badly upon us or the Church.'

'Yes, but she should earn her keep and you do realize that she's Catholic, don't you? I found a rosary in her suitcase the day she came and wondered if she should be staying with us.' Dorothy looked expectantly at her husband.

'I didn't! Perhaps I should enquire if she should be with us? Or do I try to save her soul and bring her into our Church?' Reverend Brown replied and shook his head. 'Oh dear, and she is under our roof.'

'You don't know how grateful I am to see you; she'd have me doing everything in that house. I hate the smell of onions and vinegar and her forever saying that the jam jars have to be warm and clean,' Lizzie moaned as Maggie put her arm through hers and they walked along the pavement towards the centre of the small village. 'Look at it! There would be more people in our houses chatting and gossiping than there are on the streets on a Saturday morning here. There's no shop windows to look in and all the children do jobs on the farms. I hate this place, I hate it.'

'Come on, we'll go down by the river. There's a nice open space and some seats there; we can have this cake and apples that the cook has sent with me. Then I noticed that there was a swing hanging from a tree at the bottom of our drive. I can show you where I live and we can play on the swing if you dare stay that long.' Maggie looked across the road at a small sweet shop and wished that she had some money to go in and treat herself and her friend.

'I'm going to stay out as long as I can, any time I can get away from the vicar and *her*. She's only ill because she likes a tipple of sherry. I've seen her hide her glass and bottle from the night before as she's making break-fast the following morning. Mam would be fuming if I told her everything in my letter but I've told her that I'm living at a vicarage with a vicar so she'll have something to say about that, I'm sure.' Lizzie leaned over the bridge that led to the park area. 'It's quite nice here, isn't it? Look at all the ducks and swans and people always say hello to you as if they know you,' Lizzie commented as a woman passed them and said, 'Hello, dears.'

'Yes, it's not like Liverpool but it's all right. You've

just been put in a bad place, albeit with a vicar and his wife. Things will get better once they get to know you. I take it they have no children of their own?' Maggie enquired and watched as some moss that they had torn from the bridge floated down the stream after being thrown into the fast-flowing waters.

'No, they haven't. I think that's why they don't know what to do with me.' Lizzie sighed.

'It could be worse. You could be staying with Bridget Mason at her father's pig farm,' Maggie quickly said and waited for Lizzie to react.

'What? Bridget Mason's father is a pig farmer? That is just what I wanted to hear! Oh, I can get her back now.' Lizzie was delighted.

'That's just what Mrs Perceval, the cook, said; I don't think she likes the family either. Therefore, you're not on your own. Come on, let's go and sit on that seat and have a natter then we'll go and play on that swing. It'll be grand as long as it doesn't rain.' Maggie glanced up at the skies and hoped that it would keep fine long enough for them to spend an hour or two together.

'Yes, that will be just grand. Sometime next week we'll try and pick up a piece of chalk from school and then we can play hopscotch like we used to at home. Mrs Sanderson often throws hers at the boys at the back of the room and it rolls on the floor; we'll keep our eyes open for a piece.' Lizzie grinned.

'See, that's better, Lizzie. We've just got to make the most of what's here and dodge and dive just like we used to back home on Marsh Lane. Our mams should be writing back this next week and it'll be good to hear from them. I haven't heard of any bombings or anything so they must be all right.'

'No, the vicar keeps talking about an expeditionary force, whatever that is, going to France but he's not mentioned bombs being dropped anywhere.' Lizzie sighed and smiled as they reached the bench and sat down.

'Then we're all safe and the Holy Mother is looking after us even though we're both in Proddie homes. A Proddie home with good food in my case,' Maggie said and grinned as she passed Lizzie her cake and apple.

'I'll have the cake but not the apple; I've been peeling those all morning. Ta very much for being my friend, Maggie Shaunessy. I might just survive in this place.'

'Of course you will. Just wait until Monday and school,' snorted Maggie and laughed as both of them ate their cakes.

Chapter 8

Rain was dripping down Maggie's face as she ran quickly up the drive and around the back of the hall. The heavens had opened as she had walked back from spending time with Lizzie on the swing and now she was soaked and shivering as she entered the warmth of the kitchen.

'Just look at you! Did you not realize that there was going to be a downpour? It's been building up to it all day,' Alice said as she looked around at Maggie as she came through the door. 'I haven't time to see to you tonight. I'm busy helping out in the kitchen as we have guests and it's all hands on deck. His lord and her ladyship might still like to entertain but they seem to forget that there's only half the amount of servants that they used to have. Go upstairs and change, although another hour or two and you'll be changing into your nightclothes,' Alice continued, just for once sounding flustered.

'The weather caught me out. I'd have been all right if

I hadn't walked Lizzie home. It just started raining at the bottom of the drive,' Maggie said and made her way across the kitchen. 'I'll go up to my room and dry myself and change. Do you want me to help with anything here? I'm sure I could do something. You all look so busy.' Maggie glanced around the kitchen, whose every flat surface was covered with small delectable pieces to eat. 'I thought it was just crackers and cheese?'

'That's what Mrs Perceval always says and then she does all this because Lady Bradley decides it's not enough and that she has to do one better than some of her guests that are coming. She's going to be in for a shock when or if food rationing comes in. She's also told Baxter not to close the blackout blinds tonight. Let's hope that no stray German Luftwaffe bombers are going over our heads as we'll be lit up like a giant candelabra.' Alice placed her hands on her hips. 'Go on, go and get changed and then you can perhaps help make some sandwiches for our suppers down here. That is, if we get a chance to eat. There's a pan of chicken broth simmering for all of us too. It's an easy supper for us tonight.' Alice sighed and added an olive on the top of a cream cheese canapé. She thought with war being declared parties would have come to a stop, but no such luck. Not yet anyway.

'Have you not got those finished yet, Alice? There's more to do when they're ready. Oh, my Lord, I don't know how we're going to get this all done.' Ada Perceval came bustling in from the pantry. 'Four hours before her guests arrive and she expects me to change the menu. She always does it and I'm never prepared,' she said, flummoxed, as she tested small blancmanges in moulds to see if they were set.

'I've asked Maggie to make our sandwiches for later. Is that all right?' Alice said and turned to the flustered red-faced cook.

'As long as she keeps out of my way and you see to what she wants. Now, where's my piping set?' Ada searched through various kitchenalia that was around her.

'It's there, Mrs Perceval, next to the bread bin,' Maggie said, smiling at Alice before getting out of the madness of the kitchen and up to the peace of her bedroom. Halfway up the stairs, she met Archie; he was just sitting there kicking his boot against the stairs. 'What are you doing here? I thought that you'd be with Tom.'

'No, he's finished in the stable for the day and the horses are all fed and bedded. He wanted to get out of the way of the nobs that are coming, he said. And now it's raining so there's nothing I can do and I daren't show my face in that kitchen – it's full of mad women all yelling and shouting.'

'I know and I've just volunteered to make the sandwiches for supper for us all. I tell you what, once I've changed and made them, I'll come back up to you and we'll have a game of eye-spy or hangman before it's our bedtime,' Maggie said and shivered as the rain and the cold of the servants' back stairs clung to her.

'Go on then. Do you think you could bring our supper up with you to our bedrooms? I don't fancy sitting among them lot in the kitchen tonight. There's too much fuss and flapping for my liking. Even Jeff told me to keep out of the way, and said that when there are do's like this, it's a madhouse. He was moaning, saying he'd been told at the last minute that he was to pick up the Lord Mayor from Skipton and he doesn't like him, he said.'

'Oh, well, it will all be over and done with soon enough. I'd like to watch who comes and goes, just to see what everyone looks like. I bet the women are beautifully dressed and the gentlemen will be so handsome,' Maggie said as she started to climb the stairs to her room with Archie following her. 'I'm frozen, Archie. Let me get changed and then I won't be long. I'll knock on your bedroom door when I come back up from the kitchen.'

'I'm going to have a nosy in some of the empty servants' rooms; you do know that hardly any are used? Tom says there used to be tons of staff but over the past few years, they have all been made to leave now that the Bradleys aren't that wealthy. All fur coat and no knickers is what he said and then told me not to repeat it.'

'Well, you didn't listen to him, did you? Don't you be going into anybody's bedroom that you shouldn't, else you'll be in bother,' Maggie said as she reached her own door and opened it.

'I won't. I'll see you in a bit. Bring supper up if you can, Maggie. It'll be nice just you and me eating together and I've got a table in my room that we can sit around.'

'I'll try.' Maggie closed her bedroom door behind her and started to change into her red jumper and pinafore.

They were warmer than her clothes she had brought from home and she was glad that Alice had bought her them as she felt the warmth of the jumper on her skin.

Opening the door to the kitchen, Maggie realized that order had been restored. Everything was ready to be served on platters and now just the food that needed to be warm was in the oven. It looked like nothing she had ever seen, with serving plates of sliced ham, sausage rolls, quiche and various mysterious concoctions.

'Ah, Maggie, all's in hand now. There's no need for your help we were all just flapping a bit because of the short notice. Now, have you seen Archie? He came in here and then disappeared up the stairs,' Alice asked as she stood with her cheeks glowing from the warmth of the kitchen.

'Yes, he's in his room. He wondered if we could have our supper together up there and then we are out of the way of you all because we know you're busy,' Maggie enquired and rather hoped that he would get his way as she looked at the filled table and couldn't see Archie and herself sitting amongst everything.

'That sounds like a very good idea. I'll get you both a tray and will put your supper on it. Perhaps when the guests have been served I could take you to the top of the main staircase and you can watch some of them from there. I bet once they've eaten and played the odd card game or two, they'll wind the gramophone up and dance in the main hallway. They usually do. I often sit quietly and watch. It's so romantic with the ladies in their dresses and the gents in their penguin suits. I used to love helping Lady Bradley dress but now she insists she can manage herself. I'm afraid things have changed at the hall of late.' Alice sighed sadly as she reached for a silver-plated tray to place the supper upon.

'Were there a lot more servants here at one time?' Maggie asked.

'Yes, there were – gardeners, under housemaids, ladies' maids and grooms – but the family has had to cut back as all the grand halls are struggling to survive. Besides, since Master Michael and Miss Charlotte have left there's no need for more of us. Now, take this and I'll come up and see that you and Archie are all right once our guests have been served.' Alice passed Maggie the laden tray and checked that she could manage it as she opened the door up to the stairs.

Maggie balanced the tray, struggling as she climbed the steep stairs, and imagined how busy the servants' stairs would have been in years past. Even now it was a whole new world to her; she had never been waited upon or had any meal made for her other than her mother's making. As for Archie, she knew that he thought he was in heaven as he was lucky if there was a loaf of bread on his table at home.

'Open the door, Archie, before I drop the lot!' Maggie shouted as she got to Archie's bedroom, only to see him open a door at the opposite side of the landing and call for her.

'I'm here, in this room. You can see who's coming and going because it's at the front of the house, all be it all the way up here. You should see all the posh nobs and their cars and they haven't got their headlights covered; the coppers would do them if they were driving like that at home in Liverpool. Just listen to the music that's being played somewhere down below, it sounds absolute rubbish.'

Maggie placed her tray down on a dressing table and looked around. The iron bedstead had a mattress rolled up and tied upon it. Nobody was living in the room but she still felt as if she shouldn't be in it. She listened to the faint sound of music drifting up from downstairs. 'It's Noël Coward singing "Mad Dogs and Englishmen" but just listen to them all talking and making their racket. You wouldn't think there was a war raging. They're laughing and carrying on when our parents will be listening and dreading the sirens.' Maggie couldn't believe the difference between city and country and felt quite annoyed.

'Come on, come and look out of this window. You wouldn't think that petrol was about to be rationed either. Just look at all these posh cars. Even Jeff has been out in the Rolls-Royce and chauffeured somebody here – the Lord Mayor, I think he said – but he thought that he'd not be using it again for a while when he was talking to Tom.' Archie pushed his nose up to the window trying to see as much as he could of the visitors and their modes of transport.

'Never mind them out there. Come on, let's have our supper. There's hot chicken soup and guess what? Egg sandwiches and a drink of cocoa! You can't complain about not getting enough eggs here, it's all we seem to be fed on.'

Maggie put the tray down between them as they sat on the windowsill and looked out of the window as they ate their supper. There was no sign of blackout rules being followed, the lights blazing across the tended lawns and down the granite step, lighting up the drive and gardens. They wouldn't get away with it back home – the ARP warden would be knocking on their door. They were even doing that before we were at war with Germany, thought Maggie.

'We get fed eggs because Tom has hens. He's got twenty of them in a hut behind his house and he's got a sty with two pigs in it. Although he says they're going to be killed and butchered next week and then he'll be supplying the hall with bacon and whatever else you get from a pig,' Archie said while slurping his soup and cocking his head to one side to listen for the music that seemed to have stopped for the time being.

'Have you been to his house? I know he lives here on the estate but I didn't think he'd ask you to his home?'

'Yes, I was there for an hour or two this afternoon. His wife made a right fuss of me. She said that you had to visit her the next time I went. She makes good ginger biscuits; I ate six of them, and she just kept giving me them on a big plate.' Archie started tucking into the sandwiches. 'I love it here. I've never been so full and happy.'

'Do you not miss home, Archie? I miss it so much, I sometimes cry myself to sleep thinking of my mam and da and home. Even our Raymond, who does nothing but tease me most of the time.' A big sigh came from Maggie and she felt a lump come to her throat.

'Nah, I don't miss home. My mam was too busy trying to make enough to live on and there was always one of the babies crying with hunger.' Archie had begun to realize that life was good with the Bradleys. 'We had nothing like this, I think I've landed on my feet here; I never want to go home. I hope my mam never finds out where I'm at. I even pinched the letter I wrote to her out of the posting box in the hall so that she didn't get to know where I was. She wouldn't come to see me, and she wouldn't waste her money on me even if she could write.'

Maggie looked at Archie. He had no home as she had and she felt sorry for him but, at the same time, he was lucky his heart didn't ache like hers. 'I've been with Lizzie all day today. She's worried about what her mam will say about her staying with a vicar when they're Catholic.'

'Never been in a church or cathedral. I don't think I'm even baptized, not that I'd remember it.' Archie chuckled. 'It's all about nothing if you ask me. You live and you die and that's it, as far as I can see.' He bit into his last sandwich and looked longingly at Maggie's remaining one.

'Go on, you can have it. I'm full.' Maggie pushed the sandwich towards him and grinned. If he carried on eating like he was, his mother wouldn't recognize him by the time he returned home. Both heads turned as they heard the door handle being tried and Alice walked in with a scowl on her face.

'So this is where you both are. I was starting to worry where you'd got to when neither of you was in your bedrooms. Nobody's been in this room since Annie the downstairs maid lived in here. Ironically, she had the best view out of all the servants' quarters and yet the worst job. She looks right over the lawns. Have you been watching the comings and goings of the night? They're all eating in the dining room at the moment but Baxter has been told to take the gramophone into the main hall so I thought that you'd like a sneak look at them all in their finest as they dance around.'

'Do you think we could watch? I'd like to see everybody, especially the ladies in their dresses and jewellery, but I don't want them to see us,' Maggie said coyly.

'No, they won't see us. We can peer down at them from the top staircase. We'll be in the shadows there, and anyway, if they do, it would be of no consequence as you are guests to the hall. What do you think, Archie? Bedtime or an extra half hour watching the great and the good of the district?' Alice grinned, knowing the answer before she had even asked the question.

'I don't know why I'd want to watch a lot of snobs making fools of themselves dancing but if it means an extra half hour up, then yes, let's go and gawp at them,' Archie said and led the way. He was more interested in seeing another part of the hall, which he had so far been denied access to.

As Alice led them down the first set of servants' stairs and opened the side door on to the landing of the guest bedrooms that ran around the top of the hallway, both children gazed around them. Everything was richly carpeted, not like the servants' quarters with bare floorboards and spartan furniture. This part of the house was plush and had paintings of previous owners of the hall looking down upon them as they kneeled next to the mahogany hand railings and peered down into the hall's main entrance. They could see Baxter placing a selection of records in a pile next to the record player and watched as he moved a large palm plant in fear of it being knocked over by the night's frivolities. All sat in silence and hoped that they would not be noticed as Lady Bradley came out of the dining room.

'Ah, Baxter, put on something lively to dance to and then leave us. Maurice will see to what we listen to after that and, Baxter, make sure that there is a sufficient amount of brandy and whisky available in the drawing room. Some of the drearier of our party would rather discuss politics than enjoy themselves. It's their loss. Live for the day, that's what I say.' Rebecca Bradley was dressed in a long green shimmering ball gown and took a long draw from her cheroot that she held in her hand and then turned around and looked at the man dressed in a police officer's uniform that had come into the hall to join her. 'Richard, what would you like to hear? That is, if we have it. Maurice can be a little bit mean when it comes to buying records. He thinks they're frivolous.'

'I'm not bothered, Rebecca. Whatever is played will be fine by me. I just wanted to catch you on your own before everyone else pounces on you. To ask if everything is all right? Nobody . . .' The rest of the officer's question couldn't be heard as he whispered into Rebecca's ear. Rebecca responded by nodding and then took his hand.

'Good choice, Baxter, you know me well,' Rebecca said as she took the police officer's hand and smiled up at him as Gershwin filled the hall and people started to wander in at the sound of the night's entertainment.

'He's a copper; what's he doing here?' Archie said and looked at the couple dancing.

'He's not just any copper, Archie. That's the Chief Constable from Harrogate and North Yorkshire, a good friend of the family. Jeff had to go and pick him up, along with the Lord Mayor, tonight in the Rolls-Royce. He's always given special care by the family, although Jeff hates driving him here. He's always aware that he's a policeman and is frightened in case he does anything wrong. He also was called in by the family when Jeff's wife was found dead at the bottom of the stairs, so it will bring back bad memories for him.' Alice sighed and went quiet.

'Why did they get the police, if it was only an accident?' Archie asked and thought about what the woman in the draper's had said when they had been given new clothes.

'There's always police involved after an unexplained accident. Just in case there's been foul play. However, in the case of Maureen it was an accident; everyone agreed that she'd fallen on a loose runner on the stairs. Poor Jeff was heartbroken; he's never been the same since,' Alice said and gazed back down into the hall. 'Look, there's the Lord Mayor for Skipton and his wife, and that couple that have just come in are Lord and Lady Benson from Carleton. How beautiful the ladies look. I'd love a dress like they're wearing.' Alice sighed again

112

and watched with eyes twinkling as the gents took their ladies' arms and guided them around the hall.

Maggie glanced at Archie, who wasn't interested in the dancers below but she could tell would like to have asked more about the death of Jeff's wife only because he was nosy. She couldn't help but think that Jeff was not that heartbroken. After all, it was quite obvious to her if none of the adults that Jeff and Alice were more than friends. Perhaps the woman in the clothing shop was right and Jeff was just a ladies' man, as her mam would have said if she was back home.

After a short time, Archie lost interest in the night's entertainment. 'All right, I've seen enough now. Tom has given me this and I'm going to play with it in my bedroom rather than watch these swanky lot dance all night.' He stood up and pulled a home-made wooden cotton reel tank out of his pocket but at the same time, a tin whistle made from the top of a tin can fell out from his pocket by accident and fell in between the bannisters, dropping as if in slow motion to the horror of the three secret viewers as it landed on the dance floor. It narrowly missed the Lord Mayor and his wife as they gracefully foxtrotted around the room and the piece of metal finally came to a halt on the tiled floor. The entire dance floor stopped and looked up at the three faces set back in the shadows.

Alice stepped forward and peered down over the bannister as Lord and Lady Bradley looked in dismay at their maid.

'Alice, what is the meaning of this? Why are those

children not in their beds?' Lady Bradley shouted up to the group and looked sternly at her disobedient servant.

'I apologize. I thought that they would love to watch the dance, especially Maggie, as I knew that she would enjoy seeing the wonderful dresses. Neither are used to such evenings. However, I was about to take them to their beds when Archie accidentally dropped his . . .' Alice stopped, not knowing exactly what Archie had dropped.

'It's mi whistle, Alice; Tom made it for me this morning from a tin lid,' Archie said and everyone smiled as they heard his voice.

'And a very fine whistle it is, young man.' The Lord Mayor bent down and picked up the circle of tin bent in two with a hole in the centre from the floor and smiled, holding it up. 'Why don't you and Maggie come down and say hello to us all? I'm sure we would all like to meet you before you are put to your beds.'

There was a buzz around the hall as the guests all smiled and whispered, 'Evacuees and from Liverpool, poor things.' Alice hesitantly nodded to both Maggie and Archie to follow her down the stairs to the main hall.

'Well now, what do you think of our little shindig? It's rather grand, isn't it?' the Lord Mayor said as the guests gathered around the trio.

'It is, mister. I've never seen anything like it ever before,' Archie said and put his hands in his pockets as the whistle was swiftly tucked away.

'And you, my dear, what do you think?' the mayor's wife asked Maggie. 'Are you missing your homes?'

Maggie nodded her head and felt the tears welling up in her eyes. Everyone was looking at her and she felt alien to the people and world around her.

'There now, dear, there's no need to cry. I'm sure you will be home shortly. Now here, let me give you a few pennies, just enough to buy you some sweets from the toffee shop down in Gargrave. That will help, I'm sure.' The mayor's wife prodded her husband to put his hand in his pocket and empty what change he had into Archie and Maggie's hands and he smiled as he did so.

'There now, that will sweeten the stay,' the Lord Mayor's wife said and looked around her for recognition of the good deed as the crowd sighed at the sight of the two children a long way from home. 'There will be a lot worse off than you two, I think I can safely say. You will be looked after well by our good friends.'

'They will indeed, Mary. Now, Alice, leave us to our dance and take the children back to their rooms. I think they've had enough excitement for one day,' Lady Rebecca said and watched as Alice ushered them back upstairs.

'I've got three-pence ha'penny! How much have you got, Maggie?' Archie said excitedly, grinning at Alice.

Maggie unclenched her hand and looked at the silver sixpence in hers. 'I've got the same,' she whispered thinking she should share the extra with Archie but already deciding that it would only be fair to share with her best friend Lizzie.

'It was your tears that made them feel sorry for us; you played a cracker there, Maggie. They all felt sorry for us then.' Archie giggled.

'I wasn't playing. I wanted to cry my heart out, all those people enjoying themselves when all I can think about is my old home and my mam and da. How can they?' Maggie said and looked up at Alice.

'They are just coping with what's going on in the world their way. The Lord Mayor has a son in the navy and as you know, Michael, Lord and Lady Bradley's son is in the air force, and I heard that Charlotte, their daughter, has signed up to become a Land Girl. That will not be going down well with her parents but she always was free-willed was that one. Don't be hard on those that are partying because they're just enjoying themselves while they can. Times will soon be hard enough for everyone in this country if the war turns out to be a long one,' Alice said as she opened the door on to the servants' landing. 'Now, let's get you both to bed. At least this high up in the house, you can hardly hear the frivolities.'

Archie stood in his doorway. 'I don't mind them partying every night if they give me money as they have. I've never had as much.' He grinned as he felt the change and his precious whistle and cotton reel tank. 'Night, Alice. Night, Maggie. I'll see you in the morning,' he said, happy as Larry as he went to his room to plan on how he was going to spend the precious money. Would it be on a comic or some gobstoppers? The world was his oyster when it came to the sweet shop.

'Now, Miss Maggie, no more tears. Everything will work out well in the end and no good comes of worrying,' Alice said quietly and hugged the heartbroken little girl.

'I just miss home,' Maggie said, hanging her head.

'I know you do, pet, but unfortunately we can't do anything about it at the moment. Now, come on, pop into bed while I go and get the tray and plates from the other bedroom that we left behind. Then I'll come and make sure that you're all right before turning the light out.' Alice watched as Maggie went into her bedroom. She felt for Maggie. When she had come to Hawith Hall at the age of fourteen she had been homesick, longing for her mother's kind words that she had left behind her. Maggie was a lot younger and a lot further away from her home than the five miles that Alice had been from her family. Plus, there had been no war raging with the threat of bombing raids on her home. She had every sympathy for her two wards and would keep them in her care as well as she could. Just as long as Hitler and his army kept their distance from their homes.

Maggie lay in her bed. She'd heard Alice open her bedroom door and peer in at her but she had pretended to be asleep. Downstairs she could just hear the music still playing and the sound of laughter in the air. If it had been a party night at home, she would have gone to bed smiling. But her pillow was wet with tears and her heart ached, and she was alone with nobody to share her worries. Sixpence was lovely but going home would be better.

'Oh, Lord, no! That terrible little man that thinks he runs the world at the moment is walking up the drive, dear. He'll be coming to complain about last night, I know he will,' Rebecca Bradley said as she looked out of the French windows and saw the figure of the ARP warden from Gargrave approaching the hall.

'Leave him to me, Rebecca, darling. I'll go out and meet him, there's no need for him to enter the house,' Maurice Bradley said, laying his paper down on the table and placing his pipe in the ashtray. 'He can't say anything. After all, Cyril was at the party and surely he can't pull rank on the Chief Constable of North Yorkshire?'

'I don't know, dear. He's a law unto himself and we were a bit uncaring, but there's not been a bomb dropped anywhere since this terrible war was declared and I don't think Jerry would go out of his way to bomb our home.' Rebecca sighed. 'That, I suppose, will have to be one of our last events. Life is going to be so boring. You heard what Cyril said about food and clothes rationing, the next few months, or even years, are not going to be that pleasant for any of us.'

'Don't worry your head over suchlike.' Maurice paused. 'I meant to ask, did Cyril mention the incident? He never said anything to me.'

'No, apart from asking if we were all right and saying that he was surprised that Jeff Robinson was still in our employment. It wasn't the time or place for an intimate conversation, dear. I do think he would rather see him gone from the hall.'

'Right, we might need to talk about that. But for now, let me deal with the irritant that is knocking on the door.' Maurice yelled at Baxter as he heard his footsteps go across the hallway to answer the door. 'I'll see to him,

118

Baxter. It's the upstart from the post office with his ARP uniform on. How he thinks he can lecture someone who served His Majesty in the last war and whose son is doing so now I just can't imagine,' Maurice said while Baxter held back and watched as his employer opened the main door.

'Trades and business to the back door if you please,' Maurice Bradley said before Steven Lawson, dressed in his khaki uniform with ARP bands on his arms, had time to introduce himself.

'You know I'm neither and you know exactly what I'm here for this morning. So don't give me that. You might be Lord Bradley but when you are putting Gargrave and the surrounding area in danger then it's my job to stop you.' Steven Lawson stood his ground. Lord Bradley might be a big name in the area and was rumoured to have his fingers in various banks and investments but he wasn't going to be frightened of him when he was definitely in the wrong. 'You were lit up like a blooming big birthday cake; you could see the lights down into Gargrave and hear the noise. I'll not be having that again, not on my patch.'

'We had the Chief Constable of Yorkshire here last night and he said nothing, didn't even comment. Now, you've done your job, you've been here, slapped my hands and told me, thank you. We will take note and be more careful in the future.' Maurice Bradley started closing the door.

'I don't care if you had Hitler himself partying with you last night. If there's so much as a hint of a light

119

tonight, I'll make you pay. And don't think mentioning the Chief Constable will put the frighteners on me. Everybody knows he's as bent as a ten-bob bit,' Steven Lawson said with his face going purple and blue with stress. 'And another thing, put some blast tape on your windows. If you did get bombed, there would be glass all over the place.'

'Just be careful what you are insinuating about my good friend. Now, go home, my good man, sit in front of the fire with your wife, and stop telling people how to run their lives. If you think I'll be worried about the fine of two pounds, then you can think again. Besides, we're nowhere near any industries or the coast so we were not putting anyone but ourselves at risk,' Maurice Bradley said as he cursed under his breath and closed the door as he heard Steven Lawson yell.

'I want a complete blackout, no lights at all, and get some bloody tape on the windows.' He would have the last word on the matter.

'He's just like a strutting cock. Give some people an inch of power and it goes to their heads,' Maurice said as he re-joined his wife in the morning room. 'I'd like to see him make me pay the measly fine; it would get thrown out of the court.' He sat down and scowled, and picked his paper up again, shaking it as he did so.

'Keep him sweet, my dear. We don't want to be attracting the attention of the courts or the police. Not everyone is to be relied upon like our friend Cyril. It is as I feared, that we will have to curtail our parties in the future. It'll be our way of showing the locals that along with housing the evacuees, we are doing our bit for the war,' Rebecca said, picking up her compact from the side table to scrutinize herself. 'I also think that perhaps now is the ideal time to tell Jeff that his services are no longer needed. After all, petrol is being rationed and we will not be making as much use of him. Every time I see him, he reminds me of the terrible time we went through when his wife died.'

'I'll think about it. He is useful and at the moment he's just grateful that we still employ him. We don't want him talking to anybody about his wife's misfortune when things are just settling down.'

'Whatever you think, dear, but I personally would be glad to see the back of him.' Rebecca snapped shut her compact and pretended that she didn't care.

Chapter 9

'I hate school. I always have. It's a waste of time, and they don't teach me anything that's of any use,' Archie complained as he wandered down the driveway from Hawith Hall. 'I'd be better staying at the hall with Tom and looking after his horses. Did I tell you that he let me water Saxon, Lord Bradley's hunter, yesterday morning? I don't think I've ever seen a horse like it, really sleek and tetchy when you go near it. Tom says he's part Arab.'

'Lord, Archie, if you've told me once, you've told me a hundred times. Not everything revolves around horses. You've got to learn to read and write and be able to add up, else you'll never be able to get a job or do anything.' Maggie stopped for a minute to pull her stockings up and replace her backpack, which held her and Archie's lunch within. 'If your mam could read and write, she could let you know how things are at home, although saying that, I've not heard from my mam and it's been well over a week since I wrote to her,' Maggie said and ran to catch up with Archie.

'My mam makes her own way in the world without reading and writing, and she doesn't do too badly. It's just when something comes from my school that she has to get our next-door neighbour to read it for her. But most of the time I don't let on there's a letter for her. They only send something when I'm in bother anyway and she would only clout me around the ear.'

Maggie shook her head. Archie's mother was not setting a good example to her son but at least she didn't know that Archie had been told to write home. Every day she had been hoping that her mam would have replied to her and that Alice would have a letter or even a parcel for her with her favourite Ted inside it.

'Hang on! For someone who doesn't want to go to school, you're walking fast,' Maggie said as she marched alongside Archie.

'That's because I want to get a game of Jacks in before the morning's bell. Graham Iveson from the garage has bet me his ham sandwich for my egg one if I beat him and I want to show him my tin whistle,' Archie said. 'Anyway, you're dragging your feet. Lizzie will wonder where you're at and not want to be on her own with them lasses from Broughton.'

'Oh, they're going to be no problem today, believe me, especially that Bridget. Even Alice and the cook have helped me with her this morning.' Maggie chuckled and felt for a small bottle that contained a precious amount of eau de violette – which Alice had lent her for extra

123

effect when putting Bridget in her place – and the item that the cook had given her with a smile on her face.

'What are you going to do?' Archie asked, intrigued.

'You'll see. She usually comes and tries to bully us in the mid-morning break but she'll not do it again after today. I have a plan,' Maggie said with confidence. 'Are you calling in at the sweet shop on your way back from school with the money we were given on Saturday night?'

'Nah, I'm keeping it until Saturday. I can wander down and then go to Tom's, but I'm not going to spend it all on toffees. I want to buy my own copy of *Triumph*, which is tuppence, and then I'll still have a penny left for some toffees. I can share my comic then and win some of the older boys onto my side. They're always bragging and sharing comics,' Archie said and grinned. 'Neither of us is as daft as they all make us out to be, even though we do sound Scouse. They'll soon find that out.'

'Well, Bridget Mason will soon find out, that's for sure. I'll not be bullied and neither will Lizzie. Can I ask you for help, Archie, if you dare?'

'You bet you can. Nobody likes Bridget Mason, not even the lads,' Archie declared.

'We can't do that!' Lizzie said as Maggie whispered in her ear while Bridget walked towards them with her two henchmen.

'Yes, we can. Here, you hold Alice's perfume and spray it and Archie and I'll do the rest.' Maggie leaned with her foot against the school wall and purposely looked at Bridget and her friends.

Lizzie felt her stomach churn as she opened the bottle of perfume and dabbed it on herself like Maggie had told her to do.

'You are right, Lizzie; there's an awful smell around here. No wonder you're needing to wear perfume. It's just come over me right now.' Maggie turned to a group of girls that were standing a little away from them and then she turned to Archie who had hung around them with his group of friends. 'Can you not smell it? Pooh, just like pig muck!' she said to Archie and grinned. 'Here, Lizzie, put some of your perfume on me; I don't want to smell of it. You know, it's getting worse. Oh, Bridget, can you not smell it, or have you not washed this morning? It's coming from you! I think it's on your feet. Perhaps you trod in it when feeding all those pigs before school?' Maggie said as Bridget came and leaned threateningly on the wall next to her.

'You shut your mouth, you bloody Scouser! Nobody wants you here. Go back home,' Bridget said as her friends stood back and realized that she had perhaps met her match or that she was asking for a good beating.

'What's that? Grunt, grunt, grunt! I'm not one of your pigs. I didn't quite hear that.' Maggie tried to hold her nerve as Bridget looked at Lizzie and her with hatred in her eyes.

'I'll give you bloody grunt!' Bridget pulled on Lizzie's hair knowing she was the weaker one. She took the bottle of perfume out of Lizzie's hand and threw it across the yard before leaning so close to Maggie that she daren't breathe, allowing Archie to help them out by attaching the cook's gift to Bridget's skirts with the aid of a safety pin.

Archie's newfound friends started laughing and shouting, 'She's got a tail! Bridget the pig farmer has grown a tail! Look at her, oink, oink oink!' they snorted. The whole playground of children ran to see what the noise was and gathered around the group before starting to laugh. Only Bridget's friends didn't laugh as they slipped to the back of the group.

'Piggy Mason has a tail!' Everyone whispered and grinned as Bridget turned around and looked at them all. 'You've got a tail, Piggy Wig! Oink, oink!' everyone chanted, laughing at the school's bully.

'Shut up, shut up! I haven't got a tail and I don't smell!' Bridget yelled, staring wild-eyed at the group that were all getting their own back at the lass that had bullied nearly everyone she went to school with.

'You have! You have got a tail and you do sometimes smell,' a voice shouted from the back as Bridget looked for support from her friends, who just urged her to feel around to the back of her skirts towards the pig's tail that had arrived from the butcher's to the hall's kitchens.

'How could you? How could you? You're all rotten!' Bridget screamed as she grabbed the tail to pull it off her skirt and threw it to one side.

'Piggy Mason! Piggy Mason!' the crowd jeered. They were going to have their pound of flesh while they could. Bridget's eyes started filling with tears as she made her way through them and into the sanctuary of the school, still hearing the crowd of children that was grunting and laughing at her.

'Now you know what it feels like to be picked on!'

Maggie yelled. 'If you can't take it, don't dish it out!' She put her arm around Lizzie and grinned at Archie. They'd not be bothered by Bridget Mason again, not if the girl had any sense.

The day flew so quickly, everyone saying hello and wanting to know the three from Liverpool. Nobody had dared stand up to Bridget and her hangers-on and now they all wondered why not. She was as soft as the rest of them, if they had only realized. Bridget herself had been very quiet, but to give her her dues, she had not snitched to the teachers about the playground ribbing, even when one of the teachers asked who was responsible for putting a pig's tail in the playground when she found one of the smaller children running around with it in his hand frightening the others.

'Well, that sorted her out,' Maggie said as she and Lizzie made their way through the school gates to go home.

'It did. I don't think she'll give us any more bother, do you? Archie was the bravest, pinning the tail to her,' Lizzie said and grinned.

'He was so deft with the pinning of it, she never felt a thing. I think he might have felt a pocket or two in his time, although he's never said as much. I know his family have nothing. Ours haven't much but he's only got a mother and other brothers and sisters, he's not got a father,' Maggie said and put her arm through Lizzie's. 'How are you doing? Have you got time to visit the sweet shop across the street before you go home?'

'You think Archie steals? I hope not.' Lizzie was horrified.

'Only because he's had to and I'm sure that he has no need to now he's fed and looked after. I don't think he would now. The sweet shop then, is it?' Maggie asked.

'I haven't any money, but I can say that things are improving at the vicarage. I think that they're getting used to me around the place. I suppose it must be strange when they've been on their own for so long and then I come along.' Lizzie put her head down and tried not to seem so dejected.

'You might not have any money, but I have! There was a party up at the hall and this posh-looking fella who was the Lord Mayor of Skipton gave Archie and me some money. So, come on, cheer up, I'll treat you.' Maggie pulled on Lizzie's arm as she made her way across the main road to where the sweet shop stood. She smiled as she pushed the old wooden door open and heard the bell tinkle above their heads.

The two of them breathed in deeply and took in the smell of sugar and spice mixed with the aroma of tobacco for the adults. Both girls gazed around at the shelves as the woman behind the counter noticed them.

'Hello, I haven't seen you two before. Are you among the evacuees that I hear our villages have been allocated?' the lady asked as both children stared at the goods that were for sale.

'Yes, we are. Lizzie is staying at the vicarage and I'm staying at Hawith Hall.' Maggie didn't want to talk to the shopkeeper; she just wanted to see what she and Lizzie could get with their sixpence and there were so many sweet jars and ha'penny dips to be tempted by.

'How much money have you girls got between you? I take it you do have money and are not just here to browse and waste my time or to pinch something from under my nose?' the shopkeeper asked with a questioning look as Maggie picked up a penny twist of barley sugar and Lizzie did the same, putting them onto the glass-topped counter.

Neither girl replied, knowing full well that just because they were not local they were not to be trusted in the shopkeeper's eyes. Maggie pointed to a jar of Barrett's Paradise Fruits and whispered to Lizzie that they could afford four ounces as well as the barley sugar if she liked them. Lizzie nodded and then Maggie replied.

'Please could we have four ounces of Paradise Fruits and I think that you will find my sixpence will pay for all of it. Could I ask for two ounces in two bags and then we don't have to share?' She placed her sixpence on the counter and smiled as the woman carefully weighed the sweets out on the large white weighing scales, not giving an extra sweet either way to one or other of the bags.

Passing them over once she had twisted the white bags closed, she said, 'Thank you, girls. Call again when you can.'

'I don't think we'll be calling back for a while. She didn't exactly make us welcome and we're not likely to have any money for a while now,' Maggie said as she closed the shop door behind her, putting her bag of sweets in her coat pocket before linking arms with Lizzie as they both sucked on their sticks of barley sugar and thought them to be the best they had ever tasted.

129

'I'll have to eat it quick or wrap it up with my other sweets. I don't think that they agree with sweets at the vicarage, or puddings or cake or biscuits, unless someone else brings them as a gift,' Lizzie said and tried to smile. 'But at least we're safe, I suppose.'

'Yes, we are safe and we have one another. We'll manage, won't we, kiddo?' Maggie replied and squeezed her friend's hand tightly.

'Yes, we'll be all right, especially now we've sorted bully Bridget out. These sweets can be our payment for being victorious in our battle with her.' Lizzie grinned. 'I'll have to go now though, Mrs Brown will be waiting for me. She worries that I'll get lost! As if I can get lost in this small village after wandering the streets of Bootle, Wallasey and the Pool?' Lizzie stood on the edge of the pavement and waited as two camouflaged army trucks went past filled with soldiers on the way to the nearest army camp. The reminder that the country was at war was never far away, she thought as she waved goodbye to Maggie until the following morning.

'I'll see you in the morning, Lizzie.' Maggie popped a jellied fruit into her mouth and put her hands in her pockets before making her way back to Hawith Hall. She felt happy for the first time since arriving in the Dales. Lizzie and she were still friends, she had sweets in her pocket and the bully Bridget had been given a taste of her own medicine. If she was back home, it would be a perfect day, she thought as she turned the corner onto Hawith Hall's drive. In front of her, she could see Alice carrying a bunch of flowers and heard the front door of the gatehouse being closed as she passed the garden gate, and noticed the same colour flowers growing in the garden there. Alice must have been visiting Jeff, she thought.

'Alice, wait a minute, I'll walk with you!' Maggie yelled and started running to catch her up.

Alice stopped in her tracks and waited for her. 'Is it that time already? I didn't realize it was that late in the day,' she said, blushing. 'Is Archie not with you?' She dropped the flowers down by her side as if ashamed of them.

'No, he wouldn't walk home with me. He couldn't wait to get back to see Tom and the horses and Tom's wife Ethel – it's all he talks about. I think he gets fed there as well; he's always talking about lemon curd sand-wiches and cake. All he thinks about is his belly.' Maggie grinned.

'He's a growing lad and he's helping Tom so he needs his food. The weather is turning and it will soon be too cold to wander outside with Tom, and we get a lot of snow here. The leaves are starting to change colour already,' Alice commented. 'You'll have to go sledging in the high field; there will be a sledge in the barn, I think. Archie will have to ask Tom or Jeff to hunt it out for you both.'

'Are those flowers from Jeff? I noticed them in his garden as I passed,' Maggie asked with an innocent look on her face.

'Yes, they are. He picked a bunch and said they were especially for me. They're chrysanthemums – a sure sign that autumn is upon us. I love the smell of them.' Alice smiled, lifting them from her side and smelling them.

'I think that you might be a little sweet on Jeff as well, just like Archie said. I can't help but notice how you look at one another,' Maggie said quietly and hoped that Alice would not be cross at her. Although she was only nearly twelve Maggie knew the signs of a girl in love and Alice was only at the most six or seven years older than her. However, Jeff was a grown man and had only just lost his wife.

'It doesn't show, does it? It isn't that obvious, I hope. I think he's so handsome and I know I shouldn't but I do.' Alice blushed. 'Everyone is forever saying that he's nothing but a flirt and that he might even be responsible for his wife's death. But he isn't like that once you get to know him. He was heartbroken when he found his wife dead at the bottom of the stairs and especially when the gossip wouldn't leave him alone. He's a good man once you know him,' Alice said quickly, unburdening her feelings, hardly taking a breath as she did.

'I hardly know him but he seems all right. You can't help your feelings sometimes, that's what my mam always says. She used to say that to my gran when she was complaining about my da. According to my gran, no matter what my da did, it was never right. My mam said it was because he was only a docker and he liked a pint on a Saturday night. But my mam loves him despite what Gran says.' Maggie thought about the times that she had heard her gran say, 'You could have done so much better, Nancy Donaghue, if you had only listened to your father

132

and me and not married a penniless docker.' Usually, after her mother had asked for a few slices of bread for their supper or run out of milk. However, that was not in the same league as finding your wife dead at the bottom of the stairs and everyone blaming you for it.

'You'll not say anything to anyone, will you, Maggie? It'll be our secret,' Alice said as she touched her arm before they walked around to the back of the hall.

'No, I'll not say anything. It's nothing to do with me,' Maggie said, wondering why it was so bad if she did let it out.

'Good. Now, I'm going up to my room with these, but if you see Baxter, ask him for the package that came for you this morning. It looks like a parcel from home, the one that you've been waiting for. It'll be nice for you to hear from your family.' Alice hesitated for a moment before she opened the door to the back stairs. 'Remember, not a word.' And then she ran up the stairs out of sight.

Maggie couldn't enter the kitchen fast enough, asking where Baxter was as she flung her coat off without hanging it up.

'Hey, lady, pick that up! I'm not your servant,' Mrs Perceval shouted as Maggie, looking flustered, ran up to her.

'I will in a minute. Where's Baxter? Has he got a parcel for me? Alice says a package came for me this morning.' Maggie couldn't wait another minute longer to hear from her family.

'It's over there. Look, by his newspaper on the table. He's just talking to Lord Bradley in the drawing room.

It came with the post this morning.' Mrs Perceval smiled and watched as Maggie pounced on her package and held it tight to her before going up the servants' stairs to read her letter in private.

'Coat!' Mrs Perceval said and then shook her head as she picked it up where Maggie had left it. A letter and parcel from home was far more important than the care of a school coat and she knew it as she hung it up on the coat rack.

Maggie sat on the edge of her bed and looked at the package wrapped in brown paper and tied with string, smiling as she recognized her mother's writing. She couldn't wait to hear the latest news from home as she unwrapped her parcel, her hand-knitted teddy that she loved so much tumbling to the floor with two extra pairs of knickers that her mother must have thought she might need. She picked him up and squeezed him tightly. Even though she was nearly twelve Ted and her had never been parted and she was glad to have him back in her life as she propped him up on her pillow. She then unfolded the writing paper, recognizing it as her mother's shopping list paper that hung up on a hook next to the kitchen cupboard, and memories of home came flooding back as she unfolded it and read the contents:

Dear Maggie,

It was so good to hear from you and to know that you are safe and living at Gargrave in the Yorkshire Dales. There isn't a minute in the day that goes by without us thinking about you and praying that you are all right. It broke my heart to have to send you away, but I hope that you understand that it was for your own safety.

Raymond sends his love and so does your da. They are both busy building an Anderson shelter in the backyard for us and Lizzie's family to share if it comes to the worst and Liverpool does get bombed. Don't worry about that, though, there's been no sight of any bombers in the skies. Perhaps everyone has been too cautious, but we will see.

There are not many at your school. I walked past the other day on the way to the market and the playground was nearly empty, so you are not on your own living a new life.

Annie said Lizzie wrote and said that she's living at a vicarage with a vicar which is not going down well with her mother, although I don't think she can do much about it. I hope that you are looking after one another at school at least. I know you will be. You two have always been thick as thieves since the day you were born, so at least she has you.

Mrs Ackroyd down the street gave birth to twins yesterday. All are doing well as far as I know. Annie says they weighed nearly six pounds each, so no wonder she could hardly walk, the poor woman.

I've sent you Ted and two extra pairs of knickers. You never know when you might need a clean pair if you get to go anywhere.

Hopefully you will not be long at Hawith Hall and will soon be back home. No matter how far

away you are, Maggie, you are always in our hearts. Make sure you keep yourself clean and well fed and do your best at school. Hopefully it will not be too long before you can come home.
    With all my love,
    Mam xxx

Maggie read the letter over and over again and brought it to her nose. The smell of the kitchen she loved lingered upon it, as did the smell of her mother's soap on the bear as she lay down with her letter in her hand and wiped a tear away from her eye. She sat up quickly on the edge of her bed as she heard a knock and Archie put his head around the door.

'It's only me. Tom's wife, Ethel, has sent you this, and do you want to go to tea with Lizzie on Sunday?' Archie passed her a knitted doll made out of scraps of cast-offs of wool. He noticed the letter on the bed as he passed Maggie the doll. 'A letter from home? Is everything all right?' he asked quietly and felt the pain of her homesickness as he looked at the tears running down Maggie's face.

Maggie nodded her head. 'Yes, thank you. I just miss my mam.' She smiled at the knitted doll. 'Ted's got a friend; they're like us two, becoming friends.'

'Just like us, Maggie. We'll be all right as long as we stick together.'

Chapter 10

Maurice Bradley sat back with his pipe of best Golden Virginia; he was enjoying the silence and lack of visitors in his home. Even his wife Rebecca was quiet for once. She was usually planning the next party or telling him their busy diary of events but instead, she was at the desk writing to their daughter Charlotte with her head down, trying to find the correct words to say to their wayward one. The silence was broken by the ringing of the house telephone and both stopped and looked towards the hallway as Baxter answered it and then knocked on the morning room's door.

'It's Mr Michael, sir and madam. He would like to talk to either of you.' Baxter held the receiver and waited for one of the Bradleys to come and relieve him, both seeming hesitant and not wanting to do so.

'I suppose I'll go,' Rebecca said, breaking away from her letter writing as Maurice did not attempt to move from the comfort of his chair. 'It's only your son and heir that's on the telephone.' Rebecca walked over to take the call, thanking Baxter as she placed the phone next to her ear.

'Michael, my love, how lovely to hear from you,' she said as she listened to her son and nodded her head in response to his conversation. 'Of course, that will be lovely and, no, you know of course that you and your friends will be welcome. Your bedroom is always ready for you at any time.' Rebecca smiled and looked at her husband as she heard the voice at the end of the line reply to her. 'Yes, of course, darling, this weekend and there will be three of you. I'll tell the staff. Now, you take care of yourself and we will see you then.'

Maurice looked up at his wife as she came back and sat down in her chair.

'I take it Michael is honouring us with his presence this weekend?' Maurice breathed in deeply, seeming concerned.

'Yes, he was telephoning from an inn where they were having a drink. They stood down from ops today and he says that he has a few days' leave so he is going to come home just for the weekend. He sounded quite excited.'

'I worry about him, Rebecca. He's going to be at risk every day when this war gets going. He's so young to be giving his life for this country.' Maurice put his pipe down.

'Oh, Lord, Maurice, don't say that. It hasn't come to that. He's only based at Linton on Ouse. Thankfully he's not down on the southern coast; then I would be worried,' Rebecca said, knowing that the squadrons of the RAF would be more at risk the further down south they were based.

'It won't matter where he is once this war starts. Nobody will be safe. Including our son. After all, he is paid to defend our country.' Maurice hesitated for a moment. 'I've been thinking of giving my services to the effort. I can't just sit here and do my duty as a local magistrate on the board once a month. I know they want people to help on the War Ag Board in Skipton, so I think I must apply. I'm too old to serve on the front line but I can help in other ways.' Maurice held his pipe in his hand and looked at his wife.

'The War Ag, my dear? Now, I'd not have thought that would have been something you would turn your hand to. After all, you might own several acres but farming has never been your strong point.'

'Only in the office, dear – administration if they have a place for me. I'll enquire next week. After all, we must all do our bit. I need to talk to Old Tom. I think we should plough the bottom field and plant it with root crops. If nothing else, it will keep his two Clydesdales busy and we will be doing as the government is asking by growing more food. I'll see to both. We must be seen to be doing our bit.'

'I think this family is doing its bit already. We have the two evacuees staying, our son is in the RAF and now our wayward daughter is to start in the Land Army. She's got a posting down in Norfolk on an arable farm; did I tell you? I'm just replying to her now.'

'You told me she was joining the Land Army, which I find quite amusing. She will moan as soon as she breaks the first nail. However, my dear, at least she's safe out of London and she is far enough away from us and out of the temptation of Robinson. It was all her own doing, you know, whether you like it or not.'

'You're still so quick to judge your daughter and to take the side of Robinson, just because you don't want to lose him as a chauffeur. Anyway, if this war continues, he will be enlisted and then the problem will be resolved.' Rebecca scowled at her husband, who always seemed to get his way.

'That's because I know Charlotte is a flirt, and besides, you wanted the scandal kept quiet. He could still cause problems if he wanted to. Now, my perfect morning has been spoiled! I'll leave you to your letter writing. I'll go and have a ride on Saxon as a bit of exercise will do us both good; it'll clear the cobwebs away and clear the mind.' Maurice stood up and gazed around him. 'I love my home, Rebecca, but I don't doubt things will have to change shortly. All I ask is for you to humour me with keeping Robinson on for a little while longer, just until people forget the incident. It won't be long before we are running with hardly any staff the way things are going.'

Rebecca watched as Maurice walked across the room and heard him close the front door behind him. She knew he was worried about finances as well as his two children; things at Hawith Hall were not as they seemed to the outside world and the war was just adding to his anxieties. The return of Michael and Charlotte would only raise the tension in the family home. Especially the appearance of Charlotte. She always turned everybody's heads – especially that of Jeff Robinson, to Rebecca's dismay.

'He's in wonderful shape, Tom, thanks to you.' Maurice patted his beloved hunter and then mounted him.

'Nay, he takes no looking after, sir. He's a real gentleman, a bit like yourself,' Tom said and touched his cap. He knew his place, unlike some he could mention.

'No, he's fit because you take care of him and I appreciate that. Now, how are you and your wife coping with everything going on in the world? I notice that you have taken one of the evacuees under your wing. He looks as proud as punch walking by your side with the horses.'

'Aye, we are all right, sir. Seen it all before. What will be will be. It's to be hoped Hitler won't invade. We stopped them last time and hopefully we will again. As for the lad, he's no bother; he's a grand soul once you get to know him. Eager to get to know about the horses.' Tom looked up at his employer and master and held his horse steady as he mounted the seventeen-hands-high hunter.

'He'll be in good hands with you and your wife, I'm sure,' Maurice said and looked down at his faithful groom that he had inherited from his father. 'Things all right at the cottage? Anything that you need doing?' he asked out of habit and hoped that there was nothing required that would hit his bank balance.

'Nay, we are all right, sir. Me and my old lass don't need much. We are grateful for a roof over our heads and food on the table and anything else is a bonus,' Tom said and considered the middle-aged man he had known from a lad. He had aged of late and the scandal at the gatehouse that the Bradleys had tried to keep quiet had not helped.

'Very well, Tom. I'll be about an hour. Just going for a bit of exercise to keep body and soul together,' Lord Bradley said, smiling at the old man who knew everything that went on at Hawith.

'Aye, you do that, sir. Sometimes you need time to yourself. That's why I'm here with my horses that never answer back no matter what I tell them.' Tom watched as Maurice gently ambled out of the yard astride his favourite horse. He was not a happy man, he could tell that just by the look on his face; his father had been just the same.

Maurice sat on the top of his horse and gazed across the still waters of Winterburn Reservoir. The reservoir acted as the backup for the Leeds to Liverpool canal three miles further down in the valley near Gargrave and it was deep, dark and desolate, with nobody else in sight. The smell of the peaty fellside and the cooling September wind hit his senses as he looked around and a sense of desperation swept over him as he thought about the mess his life was in. For two pins, he would wade into the reservoir and leave his cares behind him but he loved his wife and family too much to give them that heartache. The bank was after his family home, mortgaged to the hilt he could not borrow any more, his wife was having an affair with his good friend the Chief Constable and his daughter was taking after her mother and had decided to have an affair with the chauffeur of all people, which had ended in tragedy. What a mess, he thought as he hung his head and seriously wondered if life was worth living. His father had entrusted him with the Hawith estate at an early age after his unfortunate death out hunting but things were better then. Now the big estates were struggling with their upkeep and servants were a luxury. A luxury his wife still expected. He had hardly been able to look at Tom when he had spoken to him in the yard, knowing full well that he had just put his whole life in jeopardy with the latest round of loans from the bank. Things were going to have to alter; he was going to have to find work as well as keeping his job as a local magistrate. He would find employment with the Department of Agriculture. He knew the locals and he had contacts who would see him right, and hopefully that would keep the wolf from the door and still keep him looking respectable. After all, respectability was everything in his world. The war had come along at just the right time for him. Everything was focused on that; people wouldn't be too worried about what was going on at the big house if they were too busy worrying about Hitler invading. He breathed in deeply, stroked his horse, and whispered under his breath, 'You don't win today, black dog. The waters look too cold and things are not that bad yet!'

He turned his faithful Saxon home, kicked his sides and let his spirits rise as he galloped along the fellside towards home.

It was the following weekend and the servants, with orders from Maurice and Rebecca, were waiting eagerly for their visitors. Michael's bedroom had been made ready for his visit, along with two other guest rooms, with fires being lit within them and fresh flowers being cut from out of the garden of the hall and displayed in vases in each bedroom.

'He's a right case is Mr Michael, a right good soul. You wouldn't think that he was so well bred. He never acts like he is, not like his sister. Now, she's a different kettle of fish,' Mrs Perceval said to Maggie as she plucked the two chickens that were going to be served for dinner that evening. 'A right snooty one that one is, but she needn't act that way. She's been a devil with some of the young men in the village, leading them on and the like.'

Maggie listened to whatever Mrs Perceval was only too willing to divulge as she busied herself around the kitchen.

'Are you telling Maggie the hall's gossip, Mrs Perceval? There's plenty of that to be had. They're always up to something.' Alice smiled and looked at Maggie as she sat on the usual kitchen chair that she seemed to have called her own. 'Are you not going down into the village today? I think I saw there was a tabletop sale in the village hall on behalf of the church. I thought that you and your friend would be helping.'

'Lizzie is but they said they didn't want me when she asked them, and besides, I haven't any money anyway,' Maggie said and blushed.

'You shouldn't have spent all that you were given on toffees; they'll only rot your teeth.' Mrs Perceval shook her head.

'I shared it with Lizzie, so there wasn't so much. Besides, I don't want to go. I'm meeting Lizzie after the sale's finished at one if it keeps fine.' Maggie sighed.

'The weather is beginning to change. It feels more like autumn now. The leaves on the conker trees in the church-yard are on the turn – sure sign autumn is nearly upon us,' Alice said as she set two trays ready for the day's visitors. 'Then it will be like working in an ice box in this hall. I don't know why the Bradleys haven't invested in central heating over the years as it would make every-body's lives easier.'

'I tell you why, missy, it's because it costs. It would cost hundreds to pipe all this place out and from what the butcher was telling me, them upstairs have had to be sent red reminders for their bills of late. I don't think things are so good money-wise upstairs so you'll have to whistle for your central heating and just hope that they can afford to keep us all on,' Mrs Perceval said as she singed the feather pens that she could not manage to pluck out, sending a stench into the kitchen air as the feathers burned.

'No, they have money, don't talk daft. There's always parties and goings-on,' Alice said to Mrs Perceval with disdain.

'I'm only saying what I was told. You cannot live on your family's inheritance for ever and her ladyship up there likes the good life.' Mrs Perceval shrugged her shoulders and looked at Maggie. 'I'm going to clean these birds now so if you can't do with the stench, go up to your room or get yourself outside.' She picked up her carving knife.

'I'll go outside; the smell of burning feathers was bad enough,' Maggie said and grabbed her coat from behind the kitchen door. She'd go and have a look for Archie and see what he was up to. The kitchen was busy and she wasn't wanted, so best to find something to do, she thought, as she wandered across the yard and made her way to the stables. The doors stood open and there was no sign of Tom or Archie as she looked inside. The two pens that the Clydesdales were usually in stood empty and the only horse to be seen was the majestic hunter that Maggie went up to. Saxon bowed his head to look at the new visitor and snorted as he took in her scent.

'You are a bonny one, aren't you? A bit posher than your stable mates.' Maggie reached her hand out and stroked the face of the horse.

'He's a temperamental devil,' a voice said from the back of the stable. 'With a mind of his own if you don't curtail his will.' Lord Maurice came out of the shadows and took Maggie by surprise. 'I'm sorry, did I frighten you? I was just having five minutes of peace before the rabble arrive and take over the house. Michael is such a noisy chap and if he's bringing two friends with him, there will be no peace this weekend.'

'No, I'm all right, just didn't realize that I wasn't on my own, sir,' Maggie said politely.

'Are you looking for Tom and his little friend? They're both down in the bottom field, ploughing an acre or two to plant in the spring with vegetables for the hall. We all have to do our bit now.'

'Yes, I was, but it's all right. I'll just go for a walk until my friend Lizzie is able to meet me. She's busy helping the vicar and his wife at the tabletop sale.'

'Did you not want to attend?' Maurice asked and looked at the young girl who must be missing her home and surroundings.

'I'm not that bothered, and anyway, it'll nearly be over now. I'll go and have a look at the swans on the canal and watch the one or two barges that sail up it. They remind me of home,' Maggie said wistfully and thought of the hours that she had spent down by the docks.

'Of course they will, that's where they're going. The canal comes to the end of its journey at Stanley Dock in Liverpool and starts at Leeds, so you're not that far away from home if you think about it.' Maurice smiled as he saw Maggie take in what he said.

'My da sometimes works at Stanley Dock; he'll probably see the canal when he works there. I'll have to tell him that I live near it.' Maggie's face lit up thinking of the meandering canal connecting her and her da together.

'You do that the next time you write to him. Now, excuse me. Lady Bradley will be sending Baxter out to look for me. I'm supposed to be changing ready for our

147

guests.' Maurice made for the hall but then hesitated. 'Why don't you write your father a letter in a bottle and see if he gets it when it arrives down the canal at Liverpool? It will be something to talk about in your letters to one another.'

Maggie smiled and waved as she watched Lord Maurice run up the front steps of the hall. A letter in a bottle in a canal that went direct to her da! Now, that's what she would do and she'd beg a bottle from the cook for Lizzie as well. Neither of them had realized that the canal they crossed each day to go to school went to Liverpool. They perhaps weren't that far away after all.

Maggie and Lizzie stood on the bank of the canal, Maggie with an empty Camp coffee jar in her hand which she had begged for from Mrs Perceval and in her other an empty bottle of HP sauce which Alice had found outside in one of the rubbish bins for her. She reached into her pocket for a pencil and the two pieces of paper on which both were going to write to their parents. She looked around her at the canal. It was deep and murky and, unlike a river, there was very little tide. The bank was well trodden where horses had guided the barges but now flowers and plants were starting to grow with the advances in power-driven barges.

'Here, Lizzie, write what you want to your mam and then put it in the bottle and throw it into the canal. Lord Bradley says this canal comes out at Stanley Dock, where our das work. Let's see how long it takes for them to find them and if they make it all the way.'

148

Maggie scribbled a loving message upon her piece of paper and rolled it up tight before screwing the lid back on the bottle. 'I didn't know this canal goes to Liverpool. We can't be that far from home,' Maggie exclaimed with a big grin on her face as Lizzie sat down on the bank and wrote her message.

'It's far enough. These bottles may never make it through the locks; they'll get smashed as the barges crush against the side,' she said and wiped back a tear as she finished her simple message of *To Mam and Dad, Mr & Mrs Taylor at 16 Marsh Lane Miss you all, and I want to come home. Love, Lizzie* and went to stand next to Maggie as they ceremonially threw the bottles into the canal waters and hugged one another.

'They will get home; I know they'll get home,' Maggie said as she stood and watched them bobbing there, hardly moving on the still waters of the canal.

'They're not going anywhere, Maggie. That was a daft idea and now look, a barge is coming. They're going to get broken and sunk.' Lizzie sighed as a barge filled with coal started to chug its way past.

The husband and wife team on the barge looked at the two children on the bank and waved at them both, and then they noticed the two bottles bobbing in the water just ahead of them and the husband slowed the barge down and steered for the bank.

'Don't you be going throwing your rubbish into the canal, especially glass; it'll hurt the swans and birds that live upon it. You take your rubbish home with you,' the rough-looking man yelled at them both and swore as he pulled up a long pole with a net upon it and started to fish the two bottles out of the cut.

'Sid, hold your noise. They're only playing,' his wife said as she noticed the fear on the two girls' faces. 'Is that right girls, you were only playing?' The woman who was as rough and as dirty with coal dust as her husband jumped from the barge to the bank and stood next to them both.

'We were sending messages home to our mams and das. A message in a bottle,' Maggie said quietly and hung her head as she heard Lizzie start to sob, thinking that they were both going to get a good lugholing as the woman stood with her hands on her hips and looked at them.

'Well, they'll not last long in the canal; we'd have smashed them if Sid hadn't seen them first. Now, it sounds as if you two are a long way from home. From the Pool by the sounds of it? Like myself. Are you evacuees that are staying here? Better here than in any city at the moment, my loves.' The woman stared at the dejected girls.

Maggie and Lizzie looked up at the woman with the same accent as them and realized that she was going to be kind as she yelled at her husband.

'Sid, they're evacuees! They were sending messages home in their bottles. Don't lose your rag, they meant no harm.' She smiled down at them both. 'Now, why did you think your mams and das would get your messages? If the bottles did make it all the way to Liverpool, they'd float out to the Irish Sea, bobbing all the way down the Mersey, and be lost for ever.'

'Both our das work at the docks, sometimes even Stanley Dock, so they would have found them.' Lizzie for once had something to say after wiping her nose and stopping crying. 'I put my address on it so it could be given to him. Everybody knows Big Jack at the docks and he's my da.' Lizzie gazed up at the rotund woman dressed in shawls and long skirts.

'Never heard of him myself.' She shouted, 'Sid, have you heard of a Big Jack that works at Stanley?' Her husband walked from the far side of the barge to the bank. ''Cause this is his daughter.'

'Can't say I have but it'll depend on what he handles and there are that many dockers you only get to ken a few. Message in a bottle, eh?' he said and held both bottles up in his hands. 'To your fathers by the looks of it.'

'Yes, that's what we thought. We're allowed to write once a week but we hoped that they would get our messages this way,' Maggie said and blushed.

'Sid, I'll tell you what we'll do, we'll take these bottles to the dock's pay offices. They'll know both parents, they'll pass them on for you and then their fathers will have definitely got them. It's not out of our way,' the woman said and smiled at both girls. 'We come past here at least twice a month. Just look out for our tub *Rosie May* and that will be us. We're Molly and Sid Bryson,' she explained, glancing at the doubting face of her husband. 'We dock up at the locks just before the road, usually for a night, so look out for us there if you want to send another message home.' She turned to growl at her husband. 'These two lasses are missing home, you miserable devil, it's the least we can do.'

Sid shrugged his shoulders. He knew better than to argue with her. He needed her and the journey between the Durham coalfields and Liverpool was a long one not to be talking to your wife.

'Come on, let's be off. Stop your yattering, woman, we need to be at Burnley by nightfall,' Sid said and started up the engine.

'Your fathers will get their bottles but remember to look out for us. The *Rosie May*, we will be back in a fortnight,' Molly said, pulling up her skirts to board the heavily laden barge. 'Ta-ra, loves!' she yelled as the barge set off down the canal with its more than precious cargo.

'Well, I didn't think that would happen! Won't that be good if they do get our messages?' Maggie said as both girls climbed up the bank and walked back down the road.

'I don't know. All I said in mine was that I wanted to go home. I didn't think it would ever get there, so they'll be worrying even more about me now.' Lizzie sighed.

'They'll be worrying about us anyway, Liz, and they'll know we want to come home. Everyone does but Archie,' Maggie said, spotting him with Tom and his horses in the distance busy ploughing the field as they had been asked to do. 'He's as happy as a pig in muck.'

Both girls jumped as a car horn sounded along the road back to Gargrave and an open-topped car filled with two women and two men singing at the top of their voices passed them. Both men were dressed in the uniform of the RAF.

'I bet that's Michael, the son of them at the hall. They're expecting him. I'd better go h . . . I nearly said home and that it will never be,' Maggie said sadly.

'No, the vicarage will never be my home. If I never see another jar of jam or a bunch of chrysanthemums ever again, it will be too soon. They talk so posh and they look at me as if I should be something you sweep under the carpet. It's harvest festival apparently in another fortnight – another Saturday when I'm expected to decorate a church and smile.' Lizzie sighed. 'My mam will have plenty to say if she can ever get here.'

'We'll not be here for ever and at least now with Molly and Sid and the *Rosie May* we have more contact with home hopefully. See you Monday at school. At least there we fit in now.'

'Just,' said Lizzie. 'Yes, see you on Monday.'

Maggie slowly walked up the drive to Hawith Hall. She had been right: the flash-looking car was parked in the driveway.

Jeff Robinson was leaning over the garden gate of his gatehouse as she passed by. 'I see Michael is visiting, and his sister by the looks of it. There will be fun and games at the big house later. I'd keep to your bedroom tonight.' He smirked as he drew a long, cool breath after blowing cigarette smoke into the air.

'What do you mean?' Maggie said, feeling uncomfortable.

'No leaning over the bannister tonight, else you might

hear things that you don't want to hear,' Jeff said with slight menace in his voice.

Maggie decided to ignore him and get herself to the hall as fast as she could. She was beginning to realize that there were two sides to Jeff the chauffeur and she wasn't fond of either.

Chapter 11

'Oh, my dear, we weren't expecting you!' Rebecca said as she walked towards her daughter with open arms and a smile on her face, which disappeared as she glanced at her husband over her daughter's shoulder. 'How lovely for us to be all together. I'm so glad that you're here,' she said gushingly as she stepped back and looked at her errant daughter that now had her younger good looks.

'Michael said he was coming across with Philip, so I caught the train to Leeds and he picked me up at the station. Anywhere is better than in London at the moment. It's manic with all this worry of war. Besides, I start my new job with the Land Army next week, so I'll not get to see you for some time once I'm there,' Charlotte said, standing back and then flopping into the large leather sofa that took pride of place in the drawing room. 'It seems that he's been a sly dog as well, bringing the lovely Susan with him to meet you and not telling anyone.' Charlotte looked across at her older brother and his

155

girlfriend Susan and grinned. 'Lord help you, Susan. If you're to be part of this family, you need your head testing.'

'Steady on, Charlotte, we're not engaged or anything like that yet. We're just good friends,' Michael said and watched the woman he secretly loved blush with the suggestion of marriage that she had secretly hoped for.

'Just warning her, making sure she knows we're all crazy and to take everything that goes on here with a pinch of salt.' Charlotte smiled, her red lipstick making her lips turn up at the sides in a menacing way as her father passed her a glass of whisky in the hope of silencing her. 'What do you think, Philip? Are we not all mad?' She turned to ask Michael's oldest friend for backup.

'It's not for me to say, Charlotte. I am always made most welcome by your family and have the greatest respect for them.' Philip was dapper and handsome in his RAF uniform as he held his drink in his hand and knew that Charlotte was playing her family members against one another. 'You, I'm sure, will be made most welcome, Susan, just as I was.'

'Snake!' Charlotte said, glaring at him before taking a drink and glancing at her father, who seemed tired and worried.

'No bickering, Charlotte. Let us just have a quiet weekend all together, no arguments, please. After all, as you say, war is circling over our heads. Now, how are things in London? Are our boys in blue ready to defend our homeland?' Maurice said as the group sat down together around the fireplace.

'I shouldn't say this, Father, but this will be the last time that Philip and I will be allowed out of base for a while. All stations are on standby, waiting for the inevitable air raids that Germany is bound to send our way. I'd be lying if I didn't say it was worrying times, but we will do our best to defend this country of ours.' Michael squeezed Susan's hand as she put her head down and tried not to cry. Her dashing airman was going to be at the very front of the fighting and everyone knew it.

'I worry about you, my son. You should never have joined the RAF; you should have got a quiet job behind a desk. What I have done to deserve two such headstrong children I don't know.' Rebecca sighed. 'And your parents, Philip, they must be as worried as we are. These Nazis are showing no restraint in whatever they do. Lord help us if they do invade.'

'It'll not come to that because we won't let them, Lady Bradley. I should not say this but over at Linton there is talk of new aircraft arriving that will hold them at bay. Besides, it's the boys down on the South Coast that are in the direct line; we're relatively safe up here,' Philip said, hoping to soothe her distress.

'Now then, old man, you cannot say anything more. Remember!' Michael shook his head, hoping that Philip would not divulge much more about the operations that were supposed to be kept secret.

'Yes, I know, loose lips and all that. But we are with family,' Philip said and smiled.

'We'll not ask any more. We know you can only say

157

so much. We just worry, darlings.' Rebecca tried to keep her top lip from trembling; she loved her son and knew that his life would be on the line in the coming weeks.

'Well, down in London it is just fearful! Air-raid warnings keep sounding and barrage balloons are all down the Thames. Any day there could be an air raid. That's why I decided to join the Land Army: I'm not sitting in my apartment waiting for a bomb to fall on me.' Charlotte sighed. 'At least I'll be safe picking potatoes and feeding animals in deepest, darkest Norfolk.'

'I don't know why you just don't come home, dear. You know you would be more than welcome,' Rebecca said, looking at her daughter as she polished off her glass of whisky faster than any man.

'You know I can't do that – not yet. Besides, I'll be doing my bit and that is what counts.' Charlotte swirled the last dregs of her drink around in her glass and looked straight at her mother.

'Well, I've decided to see if the War Ag offices need me in Skipton. I need to do something more. As you know, we currently have two evacuees from Liverpool staying with us in the servants' quarters. Old Tom and his wife have just about adopted the boy and the girl is no problem; she spends most of her time with Alice and at school,' Maurice said as he went and stood next to the fireplace and regarded his family.

'How kind of you to take children into your care. How old are they?' Susan asked, finding the one thing that she could relate to within the family.

'In their early teens, I think. I can't really tell. Do you

like children?' Rebecca asked and peered at the pretty blonde-haired woman that had clung to her son's arm ever since she had arrived. She looked at the couple. Michael was smart and dapper in his sharp air force uniform and with Susan's fashionable but classy dress they made the perfect couple, Rebecca thought. Although if she had been as young as Susan, she would have dressed a little more daring and not quite so mumsy.

'Yes, I teach at Linton Primary School. They are all darlings and at least my class and the village's children are safe. It must be terrible to have to leave home and live with people that you don't know.' Susan hesitated. 'No matter how lovely the new home is.'

'We don't see a lot of them. As I say, the servants are looking after them and they live up in the servants' quarters. They want for nothing, though,' Rebecca said without a care.

'Still, they must miss their parents. I know I would and living in the country must be a big change to living in Liverpool, the poor things.' Susan glanced at Charlotte and knew that she had better say no more on the matter. She realized distantly that the two evacuees were taken into the Bradley family out of duty and no love would be shown them by Charlotte Bradley.

'They seem to have settled in, especially the boy, Archie. As Maurice says, he spends most of his days with Tom, our groom and groundsman, and the girl, as far as I'm aware, came with a friend who is staying at the vicarage, so they have one another.' Rebecca lifted her head as Baxter came to the drawing room doorway and announced

159

that dinner was about to be served. 'Thank you, Baxter. We will be with you shortly.'

'Baxter, you old coot, have you missed me?' Charlotte jumped up from her seat and draped herself around the embarrassed Baxter, flinging her arms around him.

'I have, Miss Charlotte,' Baxter said as he unfurled her arms from around his neck. 'I'm sure we all have.' He gave a wry smile and then made his way back quickly to the safety of the kitchen.

'He never changes, does he? Always droll and miserable,' Charlotte said and giggled. 'I'm sure that he dreads my arrival.'

Maurice shook his head. 'You should not tease him so much, the poor man. It really is time that you grew up, Charlotte, and stopped playing with people's feelings.'

'Oh, Daddy, you know I love to tease him. He knows me, does the old duffer. Besides, he likes it really.' Charlotte fluttered her eyelids at Philip as he just stood and watched.

'You are too old for suchlike now, and you have to think of your reputation, my girl,' Maurice said sharply.

'Rubbish! It's Baxter; he's known me since the day I was born. You worry too much, Daddy. Now, let's go and get something to eat, I'm famished.'

The family group watched as Charlotte wiggled her hips and headed out for the dining room. Charlotte never would know when to behave, it was not in her nature, but it would be her downfall one day, of that both her parents were certain.

* * *

160

Baxter slumped into the safety of the kitchen chair, looked at the cook who was red in the face from making the family's meal, and now watched as Millie and Alice, with the help of Maggie, washed the many dirty dishes and put them away.

'I don't know, Mrs Perceval, the girl gets worse. She knows no restrictions. First, she entwines herself around me and then she feels my bottom as I was bending over to serve her father,' Baxter said quietly. While feeling embarrassed to confess it to the cook, he knew she would listen to him without gossiping.

Mrs Perceval smiled and nearly laughed. 'She's having you on, Peter. You know what she's like and I bet she's been drinking whisky. You'd think her father would have more sense than to give her it. After all, it's not a lady's drink. She's a wild one is Miss Charlotte but I thought that she would have calmed down after the carry-on at the gatehouse.'

'Well, she hasn't. I dread to think what she'll get up to when she's working as a Land Girl. It will be a case of lock up your sons else there will be many a haystack fumble involving her, I may say.' Peter Baxter pulled a face. Charlotte was far too racy in his mind. He would always prefer a more down-to-earth woman, although she would have to have a mind of her own. Mrs Perceval would be his ideal candidate if she was not so stubborn.

'She will no doubt make the most of it and manipulate people into thinking her way. She always was a bit of a tinker when she was little. Not like Michael; he always has been a gentleman. I hope that he comes to no harm with Philip. They're both so brave. Is that a girlfriend on Michael's arm? She looks very bonny – a bit plain but bonny. I'm sure he could do better if you ask me,' Mrs Perceval enquired as she watched her girls plus Maggie tidy the kitchen and knew her biggest role for the day was over as night-time started to fall and Baxter got up to switch on the lights.

'Yes, she's a teacher from what I can gather. She's got no edge, unlike Miss Charlotte, and I don't know what she'll make of her. She's brave to be courting a pilot. Asking for heartbreak, I don't doubt.' Baxter sighed as he stood gazing out of the kitchen window. 'Here comes our new stable lad. He looks shattered but happy. Tom is keeping him busy but he's learning him a lot as well. It's a pity he'll have to return to his home in Liverpool eventually.'

'Aye, young Archie is as happy as a pig in muck, and he no longer looks like a waif and stray. But I can tell Maggie over there misses her home. Alice says she can sometimes hear her crying of a night, poor soul. She must come from a loving home, unlike this'en that will want to eat me out of house and home as soon as he comes into the kitchen.' Mrs Perceval shook her head as Archie came into the kitchen covered with mud from helping Tom to plough.

'There's some dinner for you under the cloth on the dresser,' she told him as he looked around.

'Ta, Mrs Perceval. I've had my dinner with Tom and his wife but I'm sure I can make room for it.' Archie grinned and lifted the cloth covering cold pork pie, cheese

162

and grapes. 'Just what the doctor ordered,' he said and bit into the pie as he sat down and winked at the cook, who he knew had a soft spot for him.

'I thought as much, Archie. I'm sure your legs are hollow but it is good to see a lad with a good appetite. Isn't it, Mr Baxter?' Mrs Perceval smiled.

'It is indeed and he'll not get any better food than yours, Mrs Perceval, that is a fact.'

'Tom's wife is a good cook; she makes a right good . . . good rabbit pie.' Archie hesitated and then added, 'But not as good as yours, Mrs P. Nobody's is as good as yours.' Archie was learning to hedge his bets. That way his belly was always full, he had found out.

'You are a grand lad and that's a fact, and Maggie is a grand lass. Just look at her helping out around the kitchen. We would have been taking you both on as staff if times were right. But this war and changing times have put a stop to all that. It's made a mess of everything and things are going to get worse yet.'

'It's not made a mess for me. I've never been as happy.' Archie bit into his pie. 'I've got everything I could wish for,' he said with his mouth stuffed full.

'Then I reckon that you are the only one, Archie. But strange things can happen in times of turmoil.' Mrs Perceval smiled at the two children that had been thrust into her kitchen and were both learning new skills and ways while miles away from home. She was doing her bit for the country even if she was not fighting on the front.

*   *   *

Charlotte stood with her heart pounding outside the gatehouse in the darkness of the night, waiting for the door to be opened by the man she truly loved.

'So, you've decided to show your face. I thought we agreed that you were to keep away. In fact, we promised your father as much.' Jeff Robinson opened the gatehouse front door and looked at Charlotte in the dim light of his oil lamp.

'I couldn't keep away. You know I couldn't. I needed so much to talk to you; I've missed you so much,' Charlotte said, trying to push past her ex-lover.

'I don't know if I want you here. It's all right for you. I need my job and I've already nearly lost that, and my reputation is shot in some places.' Jeff stood his ground and kept Charlotte in her place.

'Jeff, please, we've never had a chance to talk since that night, and this might be the last time I ever see you as I'm going to work in Norfolk as a Land Girl,' Charlotte pleaded. 'Please, we both still feel the same, I know we do. Just let me say goodbye properly.'

Jeff opened the door and looked at Charlotte. He had missed her. She was always on his mind, no matter how he tried, not even after replacing her with the charming Alice, who he knew loved him and would do anything for him. As for the love he felt for his dead wife, Maureen, who had died because of his and Charlotte's illicit love, that had disappeared a long time ago, ever since Charlotte had come home from her boarding school and had given him that look that she gave so well, just like her mother had years before. The one she was giving him now and that he couldn't ignore. He couldn't resist. 'Come in, quickly, before anyone sees you,' Jeff said, opening the door just wide enough for her to enter.

Charlotte squeezed past him, stopping as she did so, looking up into his eyes and kissing him eagerly on his lips. 'Oh, I've missed you so much,' she said in a low, sultry voice and then looked down at the bottom of the stairs in the hallway, where last time had lain the body of Maureen, Jeff's wife. She felt a shiver run down her spine.

'I have to live with that every day. At least you've got away and can forget sometimes,' Jeff said as he noticed Charlotte take a deep breath before entering his living room. 'I never will forget her body lying there and us two looking down upon her and wondering what we had done and the consequences of our actions.' He placed the lamp down and looked at the woman that he had risked everything for. The daughter of those at the hall, way out of his league, a woman that could make or break him and in the end had nearly broken him good and true by being the cause of his faithful wife's death. However, once again, as she stood in the lamplight, he didn't regret one minute of the love that they had shared together.

'I couldn't help it. She was pulling on my hair; I had to defend myself. I didn't hit her that hard, she just slipped on the edge of the carpet and fell backwards. You know that, you saw it. It was an accident.' Charlotte put her head on Jeff's chest and smelled the cheap aftershave that he thought was top-notch and felt his heart beating. He was her first true love and would always hold a special place in her heart, even though the accident had nearly put both of them in jail.

'Oh, stop it, Charlotte, you don't know what you do to me. Do you really know how hard you are to resist? I should hate you. You've ruined my life.' Jeff looked down at her and could not resist. He bent down and kissed her and kissed her again. 'I'd go to the gates of hell for you, do you realize that? I just wish you had kept away. You know nothing goes unnoticed around here.'

'Just one last night together. Hold me as you've never done before and then I'll leave and never return. This will be our final time. My parents will never know. Besides, my mother is a hypocrite. You of all people should know that. Father and I both know that she has something going on with that police inspector. Or whatever his rank is now. How can she lecture us?'

'Because she saved your neck through him and your father kept me in my job. I'm not that stupid not to be grateful to them both,' Jeff said, running his hand down Charlotte's face, then down her neck and to her pert breasts. 'For old times' sake, Charlotte, and this is the very last time,' he whispered as he took hold of her hand and led her up the stairs that had nearly seen both of them in more trouble than they could ever have envisaged. 'One last time and then we say goodbye and wash our hands of one another, no matter how much it hurts.'

'One last time, Jeff, but I'll never forget you,' Charlotte said as the bedroom door was opened and she entered, trying to forget the last fateful time they had spent in the very same bed and bedroom. One last night to lie in one another's arms until early light, then she must return to her room in the hall and act as if her heart was not hurting one little bit, even though it would be broken.

Chapter 12

Maggie lay in her bed. She had kept her window open and now in the dawn light, the crispness of the early autumn day was creeping into her bedroom as she tried to keep warm under her bedcovers. Along with that, she could hear raised voices coming from the garden seats along the terrace under her window. It was no good. If she wanted another hour in bed, she would have to get out and close her window. She shivered as she tiptoed across the cold wooden bedroom floor to close the window, but she hesitated as she made out the voices talking down below at such an unearthly time of the day.

'You've been with him! You just couldn't keep away, could you? No matter how much we've tried to protect you, you still insist on bringing this family's name into disrepute!' she heard Lord Bradley say crossly. 'I wash my hands of you! Your mother and I have done everything in our power to keep you out of trouble, but you have just thrown it all back in our faces.'

'But I love him, Father, you know I do. And you know his wife's death was an accident. I didn't mean to push her down the stairs. She was supposed to be at her mother's; we'd been so discreet up to that point. It was all a terrible accident.' Maggie recognized the voice of Charlotte that had echoed around the house all the previous day.

'An accident that could have got you both hanged if it had not been for your mother's contacts. To think of that poor woman coming home to find you in bed with her husband and then for her to be pushed downstairs without a thought,' Maurice said, making the listening Maggie shudder with fear.

'It was an accident, I tell you, Father! Please, last night was the last time. I told him so. He knows I'm leaving today and I'm going to be making a new life in Norfolk. It's over now,' Maggie heard Charlotte plead.

'I kept him in employment because he was a good chauffeur and at least I knew where he was, and I thought that you wouldn't dare attempt the relationship again, but I was wrong. He has had his chance and so have you. I'm loath now to keep him in my employment and until you have realized the harm that you have done to this family, I no longer want to see you and I'll withdraw your allowance. Let's see how you like to be a Land Girl with no money. Perhaps a taste of what life is really like will bring you to your senses.'

Maggie held her breath, not wanting to be noticed as she heard Lord Bradley open the main door and leave his daughter Charlotte weeping on the seat below her window. What a carry-on, she thought as she decided that she had heard enough and quietly closed her window. She felt shaken as she climbed back into her bed. All she could think about was that Jeff Robinson's wife had not died by accident; it sounded as if she had been pushed. No wonder he had told Maggie not to sneak about last night – he had been expecting Charlotte to call on him. And what about poor Alice? Did she know what was going on under her nose or was she so infatuated with Jeff that she chose to ignore it all? Maggie might only just be eleven but she knew that it was not right to love one woman and make out that he loved another as well. However, what was she going to do about it? Did she say something to Alice or keep her knowledge to herself?

Sunday morning was usually quiet, but not this Sunday. The house was busy, and the kitchen was bustling as Maggie made her way down to the breakfast table.

Archie shrugged his shoulders as Maggie looked across at him on the other side of the table.

'It's 'cause all the family are here. Mrs Perceval is in a right way with herself. She was crying as she cooked the bacon, thinking about the two that's in the RAF going to war. She keeps saying she's got to make them a good breakfast because it might be the last one she ever cooks them,' Archie explained.

'Let's hope not. I haven't met them properly, just seen them walking outside, but they're only young. Charlotte and the other woman are very pretty. They all look so handsome and beautiful; I hope nothing happens to any of them.' Maggie sighed and remembered her early-morning eavesdropping, but thought better than to talk to Archie about it.

'Tom and his wife wondered if you and Lizzie would like to come to them for Sunday tea, when the family say goodbye? He says it'll be a sad afternoon and that we are best out of the way of everybody.' Archie looked across at Maggie as she drank the tea that Alice had placed in front of her. 'She makes a really good trifle, but it'll probably be just egg sandwiches. That's what she usually makes at tea times because they always have plenty of eggs. Tom's hens are really good layers.'

'I'll come with you then as I think I am best not being here today. Everyone is busy in the kitchen and the Bradleys won't want us wandering about the place. I can't go and see Lizzie as she has to help in the church on Sunday, although she hates every minute. So yes, I'll come.' Maggie sighed. Archie was proving to be a good friend. She shouldn't have been so hard in her judgement of him when she first met him.

'What are you going to be doing after you've eaten your toast? Tom says that this is the time of year for hazelnuts. He showed me which trees they grow on and they aren't half tasty! Do you fancy coming with me? They grow in the hedges and are there for the picking.'

Maggie sat back and thought about it. The weather was decent and she had nothing else to do so she nodded and agreed. 'Go on then. I've never tasted a hazelnut before. My da brings peanuts in their shells home sometimes from the docks. Are they like those?'

171

'Dunno, never had a peanut, but you'll see when you eat one. I'll just go and tell Tom that there are two of us for tea and then we'll be off.'

'I'll wait for you on the big steps; I just want to finish my tea and toast.' Maggie watched Archie leave the kitchen and then waited as Alice went back and forward serving upstairs. Should she say something or not? Either way, Alice's heart was going to be broken. She thought better of it as she saw Alice smile at her. She couldn't spoil her day and, after all, she was half-asleep when she had heard the conversation so perhaps she had heard wrong. She was going to forget about it for the time being.

Maggie finished her breakfast then went and sat on the main steps of the hall. It was still quite warm in the autumn sunshine and she watched various butterflies making the most of the last of the summer's nectar in the late flowering Michaelmas daisies that ran around the border of the garden. It was a beautiful place to live but it would never be her home, she thought as she looked down the driveway to the village of Gargrave, hearing the church bells chiming to urge people to attend for the weekly sermon. She thought how poor Lizzie would be having to go along, despite her protests and those of her mother, made clear in the last letter that she had written to the vicar.

'Hello, you must be Maggie?' A man's voice startled her and she turned to see a man she knew to be Michael walking along the garden terrace in her direction. He was tall and looked extremely dashing in his blue RAF uniform. 'I used to sit there. It catches all the sun and you have such a good view across the valley.'

'Yes, I was just watching the butterflies until Archie comes for me and then we're going to look for hazelnuts. I've never done that before,' Maggie said and stood up to look at the airman better.

'Oh, Charlotte and I used to do that. Make sure you walk up that gill edge – the hazel trees are always the best there, they're always loaded with nuts. I wouldn't mind coming with you but we have to get back to our air base before dark and I have to drop my sister back off at Leeds station.'

'The gill?' Maggie questioned.

'Yes. Look at the small stream that runs down the side of that far field.' Michael pointed. 'There's always plenty of nuts on those trees; we used to raid them every year.' He stopped and looked at Archie as he approached them both. 'And you must be Archie? Tom's new apprentice, I hear.'

'That's me, Archie Brannigan. Wow! Just look at you! Do you really fly aeroplanes? Are you not frightened of crashing?' Archie gazed at Michael with his mouth open.

'I do indeed, Archie Brannigan. Next time I'll bring you a model of mine. I often whittle them out of wood while waiting to go on ops. And yes, I am frightened of crashing but hopefully I never will.' Michael grinned at Archie.

'You might if them Messerschmitts get on your tail. Tatatatat . . .' Archie said and ran around both Michael and Maggie with his arms outstretched, pretending to be shooting an enemy plane down.

'Then I will just have to be on guard, Archie, and keep those Nazi planes off my tail,' Michael said with a smile but Maggie could see a sadness in his eyes.

'Come on, Archie. Stop it. Let's go and don't be so daft,' Maggie said and watched as Michael turned to go back into the hall. 'You shouldn't have said that, Archie, you might bring him bad luck. You don't wish for anybody to crash while they're flying. I think he's awful brave and so dashing,' Maggie added quietly.

'It's only because he's in a uniform. My mam always says everybody loves a man in a uniform, but it's usually sailors from the docks she says that about. I have never seen a pilot before,' Archie said as he walked alongside Maggie with his hands in his pockets.

'No, I've never seen a pilot before but he told me where the best nut trees are at. Over there by the stream. He and his sister used to go there,' Maggie said.

'That's just where Tom said we had to go. He says to make sure to only pick them if they're toasty brown and to leave the ones that have fallen onto the ground because the squirrels will eat them if they haven't already. He's looking forward to us both coming to tea and Ethel, his wife, can't wait to meet you. I knew she would, seeing as you're a girl. She's been making you and Lizzie a posy bag each; she's always making something, either sewing or cooking. Tom plays heck with her because he says she should take it easy. I don't think she can be right well, the way he looks after her.' Archie nattered on as they made their way through the decaying long grass towards the gill edge where hazel trees grew in abundance. 'Look,

174

these are the nuts, they grow in ones or clumps of twos or threes, or even fours or fives if you're lucky.' Archie reached up as far as he could and pulled two nuts down from off the branch of the tree. The nuts were in their own tight green frilled jacket and Archie pushed and peeled them from out of it and then walked to the river's edge to pick up two flat stones. 'Here, smash it with this one and then eat the nut from inside but don't hit it too hard else you'll squash the nut.'

Maggie took the stones and sat down on the riverbank, placing the nut on the flatter stone and lifting the other one before banging it down on top.

'Go on, do it again. You've only cracked it a little, you weakling!' Archie grinned as Maggie lifted the stone up and smashed it harder, making the shell crack and reveal its creamy white nut within. 'Go on, pick the shell out of it and eat the nut. Tom gave me one the other day and they taste just grand.'

Maggie picked the fragments of shell out of the nut kernel and then popped her prize in her mouth. They were indeed just grand as Archie had said. They were tasty; sweet and fresh. They were as good as any sweets that she could think of and she quickly decided that she was going to fill her coat pockets and any other pockets she had with the free treats.

'Told you!' said Archie as he balanced on his tiptoes and reached for the next cluster, shoving it into his pocket. 'You want for nothing when you live in the country. I wish I'd have been born here.'

Maggie smiled. Archie was in his element. He didn't

miss home, not like her, although she must admit that when she looked around her and listened to the babbling brook and smelled the autumn air it was a lot more soothing than the busy streets of Liverpool.

'Now, isn't this just grand, Archie? I'm so glad you've brought Maggie with you; I've been longing to meet her, and her friend Lizzie. It's a pity Lizzie couldn't come. I suppose the vicar will have other ideas for her seeing it's Sunday,' Ethel Parker said, hardly drawing breath as she poured the tea out of her best teapot with matching cups and saucers.

Maggie looked around the homely kitchen and smiled at Ethel as she pushed the egg sandwiches under her nose. It was just the opposite of the hall; this was more like a real home. No wonder Archie liked it here.

'Yes, we've been gathering nuts up by the stream. Look, our pockets are full,' Archie said and pulled a handful of his plunder out of his pockets to show Tom and Ethel. 'Neither of us has ever done it before.'

'You should have come here and I'd have given you a basket and then we could have put them into salt and stored them in the loft, keeping them nice and dry to eat at Christmas.' Ethel smiled at Archie. He was the son that she had never had and she just loved to mother him and to teach him new things.

'I'll go and pick some more one night after school and then you can keep them. I bet Christmas will be special here. I can't wait,' Archie said and tucked into a sandwich.

'You'll have to see if you're still here. Your parents

might want you home by then and that's where you belong, with your families,' Tom said, noticing the disappointment on his wife's face as she thought that her adopted one might have to go home. 'What do your father and mother do, Maggie? Does your father have a job? It's been hard times of late.'

'He works on the docks, as Lizzie's father does, and my mam just keeps house,' Maggie said quietly.

'Nowt wrong with keeping a respectable home and your father must bring home a good wage, so that will be a blessing. Tom and me have a lot to be thankful for. We have a roof over our heads and his lordship is good with us, letting us have our own garden and hens. We're never short of anything. Now, come on, tuck in, my love. I've made the shortbread and the cake and there's a trifle to follow.' Ethel smiled and looked at her two guests. She could tell that Maggie had been brought up with manners, unlike Archie, but he was such a likeable lad.

'I have a brother as well; he works at the docks too. He's six years older than me,' Maggie decided to say as she helped herself to a piece of shortbread cut into the shape of a fan and covered with sugar. She bit into it and savoured each mouthful of the buttery crumbly biscuit as she looked at the kind couple.

'Aye, do you get on or do you fall out all the time? Me and my sister used to fall out constantly but in times of bother, we used to stick together. I remember once she was being picked on at school by a lad, so I learned her to box. The next time he pinched and kicked her, she turned around and planted him one on his nose. She

177

didn't half get into bother but nobody picked on her again.' Tom sat back and grinned, remembering the moment that must have been over fifty years ago.

'Aye, Tom, you'll be leading them astray if you're not careful. Just think about what you're saying,' Ethel said and glared at him across the table as she shook her head.

'Oh, Maggie can stand her own and look after herself. Lizzie and she were being picked on when we first came but she gave as good as she got, along with Mrs Perceval's help.' Archie sniggered.

Maggie blushed. 'I didn't hit her, though. I only said what Mrs Perceval told me to say and that shut her up.'

'Well, nobody has any right to bully anyone, so she did right. You must be missing your homes anyway without being picked on,' Ethel said and then placed the large glass dish of sherry trifle in front of them all. 'It's usually the ones with the most to hide that bully, just you two remember that,' she added as she dished spoonfuls of trifle into bowls.

Maggie sat back and looked around her. She could see why Archie loved being with Tom and Ethel; they were homely and kind. The kitchen was warm and full of love. She could quite happily have stayed there all day herself.

'Do you think we'll be sent home at Christmas?' Archie said on the walk back to the hall later that evening. ''Cause I don't want to go home, I've nothing to go home for. I never see my ma and I'd be back to going hungry. I don't even know my da. You're so lucky.' He hung his head and kicked a stone along the path home.

'I don't know, Archie. Hitler hasn't dropped a single bomb on this country yet. Perhaps we will be sent home,' Maggie replied and hoped for her and Lizzie's sake that they would be.

'I never want to go home. I hate Liverpool, and I'll run away if I have to go back there. My mam hasn't bothered getting in touch and Tom says that all our parents have been told where we are living. She can't write but she could have sent me something and get someone to write the address on it. She just doesn't want me and I ain't bothered,' Archie said. He wasn't going to admit that his mother had no idea where he was in the country.

Maggie put her arm around the lad. She felt sorry for him. 'But you've never written to her either. Never mind, I'll be your sister while we're here and Tom and Ethel dote on you.'

'I know. I wish you all were my proper family and that I could stay here for ever.' Archie sighed and tried not to cry. Scouse lads never cried.

Chapter 13

It was Monday morning and Rebecca Bradley sighed and looked out of the hall's window down across the lawn and to the gatehouse. The weekend had been fraught. There had been an atmosphere between Charlotte and her father all Sunday, one that she could have done without worrying about seeing that her son might not visit her again for quite a while. It wasn't until the family had returned to their working lives that Maurice told her that he had caught Charlotte on her illicit night with Jeff Robinson. Maurice had tossed and turned in his sleep all night and then had found the need to share his burden with her at first light. Charlotte would be the death of them; she was so headstrong and determined to have her own way, no matter who she hurt. How could she go with Jeff? Was she doing it on purpose to hurt her? Even she must admit she had been taken by the chauffeur's good looks, which had partly got him the job, and she had found him more than attractive as time had gone on.

Rebecca reached for her packet of Kensitas cigarettes and lit one, taking a long deep breath and then exhaling, watching the smoke disappear into the ether. She was missing her parties that had had to come to an end for the moment because of war restrictions but, most of all, she was missing her lover, Richard Stephenson, her charming police officer that was always there for her when Maurice was not. He would listen to her and give her the comfort that Maurice could not, but of late, since the incident at the gatehouse, he was not as free and easy with his time. The war and Charlotte were both to blame, she thought as she looked out of the window and wondered whether she should ring him. Maurice had gone into Skipton to arrange a meeting with the War Agricultural Board. If he was going to be working for them, she would have hours alone on her own – more reason to give Richard a ring. She walked over to the main door and looked around the hallway. All the servants were busy. She would not be disturbed, that was good. Sitting down at the telephone table, she did not need to look up Richard's number in the book she kept in the nearside drawer. She rang the operator and asked to be put through to Harrogate 247, extension 2 and held her breath, feeling her heart beating with the excitement of a schoolgirl.

'Harrogate police station, Detective Inspector Stephenson.' Rebecca held her breath and felt her heart warm at the voice she loved so much.

'Richard, I'm sorry I had to ring you. I am missing you terribly and I need to see you,' Rebecca said, gushing her love to the man she truly did love.

'Oh, Rebecca, it's wonderful to hear from you but I'm at work and I have told you not to ring at this time of day. The office is always busy in the morning.' Richard sat back in his chair and tried to muffle his conversation with the woman – the woman that at the moment he wished he had never got so deeply involved with – looking around at the busy office where he was stationed and hoping that nobody would hear.

'I'm sorry, Richard. I'm on my own and I am so lonely. Both children have stayed this weekend and Maurice has had words with Charlotte. She slept with *him* again, and Maurice found out. He's in a fearful mood and I just wanted to hear your voice and ask when will we be able to see one another?' Rebecca heard Richard pause.

'I don't know, Rebecca. I'm busy with work. Marjorie watches my every move and this blessed war that we are supposed to be in is curtailing everyone's movements. Perhaps it is better—'

'Don't say it! I'll say it for you . . . Perhaps it would be better if our little arrangement comes to an end?' Rebecca felt tears come to her eyes and a lump in her throat nearly stopping her from saying any more. 'I knew this was coming. I knew you'd lost that flame for me, and, of course, Charlotte's misdemeanours have not helped.' Rebecca breathed in deeply and waited for Richard's reply.

'I do love you, Rebecca, it's just that I can't compromise my position and Marjorie needs me as well as my children, and you forget they are not as old as yours,' Richard said, whispering down the phone, conscious of the people around him. 'I think we have run our course. We both have too much to lose. Surely you understand?'

'I understand, Richard, I understand perfectly. I'll not be calling you again,' Rebecca said sharply and tried to retain her dignity until he was off the telephone. 'Goodbye, but I will always love you.' She took another long deep breath and didn't wait for his reply as she put the telephone back down onto the hook. Her affair was over, not that it had lasted long, just over a year, she thought, remembering all the secret meetings and the secret messages given to one another and the thrill of lying in her lover's arms. She had loved him truly and deeply but she should have known she was just a passing fancy. In addition, Charlotte had not helped with her stupidity of going with the chauffeur and pushing his wife down the stairs. Rebecca sat with her head in her hands, only raising it when she heard Baxter open the kitchen door into the hallway.

'Is everything all right, ma'am?' he asked with concern on his face as he saw tears were in her eyes.

'Yes, thank you, Baxter. Just heard an old friend is not well, but I'm sure they'll soon recover.' Rebecca pulled her handkerchief out of her pocket and blew her nose. 'I'll not need a coffee this morning, Baxter. I think I'll go for a short walk and get some fresh air. It always makes one feel better.'

'If you're sure, ma'am. Take care and I'd advise a coat, if I may. There's a cool breeze this morning,' Baxter said and smiled as he made his way to the kitchen.

Rebecca watched him go and then returned to the

drawing room. She would go for a walk but first, she needed to cry. Another part of her world had just fallen apart. To the outside world, she might look to be a woman who had everything, but really she was living in a loveless marriage in a home she knew that her husband could not for much longer keep hold of. Even though he never told her so. With war looming, it was only going to get worse, she thought, as she looked at the first drops of rain run down the windowpane. Down the drive, she stared at the sight of Alice, the maid, running back to the hall. Where had she been? she wondered, and then held her breath as she saw Jeff Robinson call for her as he followed her up the drive with an umbrella in his hand. She watched as Alice turned and waited for him and then Rebecca gasped as she watched Jeff and Alice embrace before she ran quickly back to her work at the hall and Jeff returned to his home.

Rebecca shook her head. The dirty rat. Not only had he just slept with her daughter but he was encouraging the attentions of her maid. Now it was time for him to go and she was glad that Maurice had been talking of his sacking that morning. If she had to lose her lover, then she would not be on her own. She would take great delight in seeing the back of Jeff Robinson and telling Alice the truth about the handsome cheating chauffeur. He knew how to hurt and he was taking advantage of their past relations, going through the household like a dose of salts, without a care about her feelings.

*   *   *

184

'My, look at you, you're sodden to the skin! Go up and take those wet clothes off and change before you get your death of cold,' Alice said to Maggie as she burst through the kitchen door after attending school. 'Where's Archie? Is he not with you?'

Maggie unbelted her gabardine coat and shook it before Alice hung it up on the back of the chair in front of the kitchen fire. 'No, he's gone straight to Tom and Ethel's. Tom is going to show him how to make rabbit snares, and then he says he'll never have to go hungry again,' Maggie replied as Alice threw her a towel to dry her hair with.

'Aye, that lad, he's never away from Tom and Ethel's. He treats this place like a hotel. He should probably have gone to them in the first place. I do wish his mother would drop him a line; he never hears from her, unlike you. There's another letter awaiting you in your bedroom. I took it up this morning when the post delivered it. I thought it was better up there and out of sight than upsetting Archie.' Alice took the towel out of Maggie's hands and smiled at the big beam that lit her face as she heard the news of home. 'Go on then, put some warmer clothes on and go and have a read. Supper's at six. We've got trout tonight. Tom brought some in that he'd caught in the stream for the whole house – a right luxury.'

'Never had it! But I like fish,' Maggie shouted as she scurried up the stairs to her room. She couldn't wait to hear news from home.

Changed out of her wet clothes and feeling warm and comfortable, she lay on her bed and looked at the letter that her mother had lovingly written. Her finger lingered over the writing of the address before she tore open the envelope and read the contents, taking in every word.

14 Marsh Lane
25th September 1939

Hello, my love,

Well, isn't that strange? The other night me and your da were sitting eating our supper when there was a knock on the door and these two folks stood on the step. At first, I thought they were begging and then they mentioned your name and passed me a bottle with a note in it from you. Turns out that they have met you on their travels up and down the cut and they had tracked your da and Raymond down through the pay office.

Well, when we heard this we didn't half make them welcome. They had supper with us – thank heavens I had enough – and they stopped a good while. It was so good to hear that you looked well and happy and that you and Lizzie were still together. Now, I sent them back with some thicker vests, liberty bodices and jumpers because it's starting to get cold now autumn is upon us. They say that you have to look out for them in a fortnight's time moored in Gargrave. They'll be there for a day or two so you'll not miss them and can collect your clothes. Lizzie's ma has done the same. I knocked on her door as soon as they offered to do that for us. How thankful we both were. It saves us the postage because every penny, as you know, is always wanted in this house.

Your da and me are just grand. Da's busy at the docks, although he says there's not much coming in from Italy and them foreign countries. We've not had many oranges of late. The big news is your brother's news: he's started courting Mary O'Malley from near Albert Dock. I don't think she's good enough for him but your da says I've not to say anything about it.

As for any bombings, there's still been none; not that we want them. The Anderson shelter in the back garden is finished although I'll not look forward to spending any time in it with next door. We have put some water and supplies in there just in case the worst happens.

Annie is not happy at where Lizzie is billeted. I think she's written to that vicar and told him what she thought. I told her not to as they might take it out on Lizzie. You'll let me know, won't you, if she is ever upset? I've told Annie as long as you've got one another you will be all right.

Well, I've your da and Raymond's snap tins to make up for work tomorrow so I'll finish my writing. It was so grand to see that couple from the canal. We can get in touch and send stuff often now so you are not that much on your own.

We all miss and love you.

Lots of kisses,

Mam, Da and Raymond

Maggie lay back in her bed and held the letter close to her heart as she brushed a tear away from her cheek. She missed home but at least she had another way to reach her mam and da now that Molly and Sid Bryson had made themselves known to both her and her parents. The clothes that her parents were sending her would be more than welcome. She only had her summer clothes and those that the Bradleys had bought her. The days were getting colder and there was no heating in her bedroom at the top of the hall. She shivered and decided to pull her bedcovers over her as she reread the letter and thought about her brother courting Mary O'Malley. That would not sit well with her mam. She was the oldest of ten and had a reputation for being a bit too fond of men. Maggie closed her eyes. The warmth of the covers and the knowledge that all was well at home, apart from a lack of oranges, made her feel content as she closed her eyes and thought of home.

Rebecca looked at her husband and for the first time, she noticed how drawn and old he appeared. His face showed the worries of the world upon it and since he had come back from Skipton, he had hardly spoken. Something was wrong, she could tell, but would he eventually get around to telling her? Her worries could wait, she thought, as she watched him taking forty winks in his chair. Maurice always kept his troubles to himself and was not one for deep conversations, but this time he hadn't the need to say anything. His whole attitude had changed since his return. Things at the War Ag offices must have gone wrong, but how wrong and would he admit it to her? How she wished she still had her Richard to run to but those days were now gone.

Chapter 14

As Maurice picked up his best walking stick and made his way down the home field towards the home and smallholding of Tom and Ethel Parker, his heart was heavy. The trip into Skipton had been a fruitful one, with him acquiring a place on the War Ag Board, but it had also been one of great worry as he had called into the bank on the manager's request to discuss the mess that his estate was in.

The news had been bad: the bank was no longer in a position to cover any more of his outgoings unless he could lessen his accounts with them. Indeed, the manager that he had known all his life had been sympathetic with him but he had said it as it was and had told him unless he sold some of the estate's property and cleared some of his outgoings, they would have no option but to step in and declare him bankrupt. Maurice had hung his head in shame. Hawith Hall had been in his family's hands for centuries; his ancestors would be turning in their graves. However, since the Great War, society had changed and servants cost more, taxes were high and he could no longer sit back on his laurels and play lord of the manor. He'd no choice but to sell off Tom's home and the gatehouse and then he might just be able to keep the hall if nothing else. He thought of his father and mother as he stood on the doorstep of Tom's home and felt physically sick as he heard Ethel singing as she busied herself in the kitchen. His parents would never have done anything like this to loyal staff like the Parkers.

'Oh, sorry, sir, I was just singing to myself and didn't hear you knocking for a while,' Ethel said quietly and just about curtseyed to the man they owed their living to.

'No problem, Ethel. It was good to hear you in such good voice. Did I recognize the airs of Nellie Dean by any chance? One of my mother's favourites, if I remember rightly,' Maurice said and smiled at the red-faced woman. 'May I come in and is Tom about? I'm afraid I need to talk to you both.' Maurice bent his head down to enter the doorway of the sixteenth-century farmhouse.

'Aye, sir, he's just chopping some kindling sticks out back. I'll go and get him.' Ethel felt worried. Lord Maurice never asked to talk to them both. Something was wrong, she thought, as she walked through the house and out of the back door to stop Tom chopping the kindling sticks for the fire that now needed to be lighted every morning to warm the house through.

'His lordship is here. He needs to talk to us both, and he doesn't look that happy. Have you been encouraging Archie to skive off school because he would do anything that you said and not think twice about it?' Ethel scowled as Tom dropped the axe down and looked at his wife's worried face before joining her to enter the house.

'Nay, I tell him to get his arse to school. It's no good having no brains in this day and age. There must be something else afoot,' Tom said and wiped his brow of sweat. It had been hard work chopping the kindling and he was in his vest and shirtsleeves as he picked up his jacket from the woodstock, putting it on quickly to be dressed properly as he talked to his lordship.

Maurice looked around the homely kitchen where, just like Archie, he had spent a lot of his youth. The Parkers had always made him welcome and now he was going to ruin their lives.

'Now then, sir, what brings you on this visit? I hope all is in order with my work.' Tom stood up until Maurice beckoned for him and Ethel to sit and be at ease.

'Of course, Tom. I never have any problems with your work, nor did my father. You are always to be relied upon for everything.' Maurice hesitated and looked down at his hands, not knowing how to tell the lovely couple that they would shortly have to find a new home when he put the cottage and few acres around it up for sale.

'Spit it out, lad. Your father was just the same, could never deal with telling anybody bad news. Because I take it that it is bad news, else you'd not be here,' Tom said, trying to put his boss at ease.

'I'm sorry, Tom. If there was any other way to solve my problems, I'd do it. However, times are hard and I'm struggling to make ends meet at the hall. I've been advised

192

to put this cottage, the acres around it and the gatehouse up for sale, I'm afraid. It is the only way to stay solvent and it breaks my heart to have to tell you that.'

Ethel pinched her pinny and let out a sob. The lovely home that she put everything into was about to be sold from under her nose and she and Tom had nowhere else to go. It was time to put the plan she and Tom had been hatching for quite a while into action and hope that Maurice Bradley would accept it. However, it was still a shock to find out that in a few weeks they could be homeless if they didn't act fast.

'I'm sorry, Ethel. I really don't want to do it, but I've no option,' Maurice said and felt like the heel that he must be in their eyes.

'Nay, I understand, lad. You inherited a lot of debt and work from your father and things have got worse with every year of late. That wife of yours takes some keeping happy and all, not like my old lass,' Tom said, patting Ethel on her knee and smiling at her. 'Keeping up appearances is an expensive do and thy family have been doing that for centuries, just like mine have been scratting and saving and making a living on the land for as long. I knew this day would come someday and I've been preparing for it,' Tom said wistfully.

'That's very understanding of you, Tom. I thought you'd take it harder than that and, to be quite frank, I was dreading having to tell you. I will, of course, give you time to find another property and I don't expect you to be leaving before Christmas,' Maurice said as a tear rolled down Ethel's cheek. 'I'm so sorry.'

'Nowt to be sorry for, lad, but before you go back to the hall, can I ask to come and see you in the morning when I've had a word with my Ethel? Around ten when I've fed all the stock and mucked out the horses; would that be all right with you?' Tom asked, noticing the surprise on his wife's face for being so forthright in his proposition.

'Yes, of course, Tom. You'll need a clearer idea of things, no problem at all,' Maurice said and stood up ready to go.

'How much will this homestead be up for sale for? It's a bad time for you to be selling it. Half of our men are off to war and nobody has any brass,' Tom asked as he walked with Maurice to the kitchen door. 'You might be waiting for months to sell.'

'I don't know yet, I know what I want but that's another matter. I'll let you know in the morning, and keep my fingers crossed that a buyer comes soon for my sake.' Maurice reached out his hand for Tom to shake as a sign of no bad will, which Tom took firmly.

'Aye, somebody will have their eye on it, of that I'm sure. I will see you, sir, in the morning. Are you going to the gatehouse now to tell Jeff Robinson the same?' Tom asked as he turned and looked at Ethel crying in her seat.

'No, one lot of bad news for me to give out is enough for today. I will tell him towards the end of the week and I will be getting rid of him then as well, but please keep that to yourself, Tom. He's not welcome any longer in my employment,' Maurice said and put his trilby back on his head.

Tom watched as Maurice walked back across the field towards home and whispered, 'It's about time that bastard went but you won't be getting rid of us, not just yet, not if I have my way.'

'Now, Tom, I know I upset you yesterday with my news and I knew that you would want to see me here rather than distress Ethel more. It must have been a shock for her and I'm sorry that I was the bearer of bad news. You do know that I have to sell and it is with a heavy heart. I will try and find a buyer who will take you and Ethel as sitting tenants if possible and then you won't be losing your home.' Maurice looked at his faithful stableman from behind his desk and quickly put the papers from the bank to one side.

'Aye, I know, things have not been right for a while; I recognized that something was wrong a long time ago. You forget, sir, that I've known you since you were a bairn and in those days you had not a care in the world, unlike your parents who always had worries but never let on. The world's changed, and not for the better, may I add.' Tom kept standing. 'Now, you might think I don't know my place in the world but may I sit down? I need to talk a bit of business with you and help us both out of our pickle.'

Maurice looked across at Tom. What could he do to get him out of the situation? But he was willing to listen.

'Of course, Tom. Sorry, I was forgetting my manners. Please sit down and tell me what's on your mind.' Maurice looked at his groom as he pulled the chair out across the opposite side of the desk from him. He clearly had something on his mind.

'Now, you might think that I'm full of blether, but me and my old lass would like to buy Hawith Farmhouse. It's been our home for the past fifty years and I had hoped that I would only be carried out of it when I was in my box, as did my old lass.' Tom gazed across at Maurice and saw a picture of puzzlement on his employer's face. 'Aye, I know what you're thinking, that I'll not have the brass, but don't you fret about that. Just give me a price and I'll see if I can match it.'

'But Tom, are you sure? It would please me so much for you to own it but we are talking a lot of money here,' Maurice replied, puzzled by how Tom had come across enough money to buy his home from him.

'As I say, name your price and we will start from there. The house and garden and the twenty acres that surrounds us, and not forgetting the two Clydesdales, because you'll have no use of them after my day.' Tom kept a deadpan face as Maurice picked up the bank's estimate and looked at the suggested price given by them, although a valuation had yet to take place.

'The bank is suggesting three thousand five hundred for the house and garden and eight pounds an acre, but that's just a suggestion. They've not looked around the property yet. It is a lot of money, Tom.' Maurice looked at the man who had taken him by surprise.

'Aye, it's a good bit. They're quoting southern land prices at eight pounds an acre; some of that land is hardly worth nowt, so I'd be offering six pounds an acre. As for the house, I'll make you an offer of three thousand because as both thee and me know, the roof's in a bad way, the water supply I put in myself and there is many a job needs doing. Four thousand two hundred and I can pay you as soon as tomorrow if you still hold the deeds, or do I need to negotiate with the bank?' Tom leaned back in his chair and looked at the surprise on his master's face.

'No, no, I'm still in charge of the sale. But are you sure you can afford that, Tom? I didn't realize that you had that sort of money.' Maurice couldn't help but ask and was in shock at the offer from a man that always dressed tidy but didn't appear as though he had that sort of wealth.

'Never you mind that. Just be content that I can put my money where my mouth is and it's as good as any other man's or gentleman's. Have we a deal or do I go home and disappoint my Ethel? Are you as good a man as your father was?' Tom looked hard at Maurice and counted the seconds until the moment he had waited for all his life.

'I couldn't wish for the farm to go to anybody else, Tom. I'll accept your offer and you have my very best wishes, no matter what the bank says. As for the horses, they are yours, no charge, and you can keep them in the stables until you see fit to move them. I was thinking of getting one of those Ferguson tractors seeing as the War Office is lending them out to landowners that have decided to plough some of their land at the moment.' Maurice stood up and offered Tom his hand.

Tom stood too, took Maurice's hand, and shook it firmly. 'I'll tell my bank that it's going to be a bit lighter in the next few weeks. But, by God, I am glad that you've accepted my offer. It will make Ethel's day. She didn't think we had enough and she had set her heart on decorating the place and getting things that she had wanted for a while and I wouldn't let her, even though it was her money that helped us. Her aunt in Australia left her some brass and I've watched every penny I've spent all my life, that's how we have managed it.' Tom's mood lightened, knowing Maurice would not go back on his word now he had shaken his hand.

'Well I never! Well done, Tom. Has anyone ever told you that you'd make a good poker player? You can't be judged one way or another with that unflinching face of yours.' Maurice smiled and shook his hand more warmly.

'No, and I don't believe in throwing my hard-earned money away. Thank ya, Mr Maurice, you've made our old age more assured with you accepting this. What with us being able to buy the house and land and having Archie nearly living with us, our life is only just beginning. My Ethel has taken to that lad and I must admit I have too. To think he is out of the middle of Liverpool, yet he's willing to learn and hasn't a bad bone in his body.'

'I see you've taken him under your wing. You'll be the making of him. I don't think he comes from a good home from what I hear and his mother never writes to him nor him to her, poor lad. But he'll have to go home one day,' Maurice said and looked down at the bank's proposal of sale of Tom's farm, wishing he had asked just for a little bit more now he knew Tom had the money.

'Do you have his home address? I'll get him to write to his mother. It's only right that he should. She's bound to be worried about him; after all, he's her son,' Tom said and looked worried.

'Yes, it is here in my drawers. It would be good if he would. As you say, she must be worried about him.' Maurice reached for the folder containing the details of Maggie and Archie, wrote the home address of Archie's mother down and passed it to Tom. 'He's learning things with you that he could only have dreamed of in Liverpool.'

'Aye, and he's giving Ethel and me a new life. We should have had bairns of our own but daren't because of her health. Never mind, good things come to those that wait, as they say.' Tom smiled and put the address in his jacket pocket. It had been a very fruitful morning and it had not finished yet.

Chapter 15

Rebecca watched as Tom Parker closed the study door and for the very first time in his life left by the main entrance of the hall. Something was going on and it was time that Maurice told her exactly what, she thought as she closed the door to the morning room and crossed the hallway to her husband's office.

'Ah, Rebecca, I was just about to come and see you and give you the news.' Maurice looked at his wife and knew that she had gathered there was something afoot.

'I've just seen Tom Parker leave by the front door with a grin on his face for the first time ever. What is he doing here and has he forgotten his position?' Rebecca asked and then noticed the many letters from the bank strewn across the desktop.

'I've been trying to protect you from the situation that we are in but it is time for you to know the truth and for you to take measures to curtail spending.' Maurice looked at the shock on Rebecca's face. 'I'm afraid, dear, we are in dire straits. There is very little money in the bank and we are not making enough income to keep everyone paid.' Maurice sighed.

'No money, what do you mean? Of course we have money! We own the hall and all its properties and what has happened to your father's inheritance? Surely it can't be all gone?' Rebecca was shocked. She knew Maurice had been watching every penny of late but she hadn't realized just how bad things were.

'Father left his own debts and then there were the inevitable taxes, wages to be paid and, let's face it, dear, we both know how to party. I'm afraid the bank wrote a month ago to ask me to account for our spending and to amend the situation with them. I've had no other option but to look at selling some of the hall's property. That is why Tom Parker was here this morning, my dear. I told him that I was putting his home and surrounding land up for sale, to my sadness.'

Rebecca, deflated, sat in the chair opposite Maurice. 'Oh, poor Tom. And I had no idea that things were that bad for us. Why sell the farm? Why not the gatehouse? That would get rid of the problem we have with Robinson. At least the Parkers have always been faithful to us.'

'I'm afraid it gets worse, dear, because I aim to sell both. Jeff Robinson is going to get a visit from me shortly and I will not be too afraid of giving him a piece of my mind as well as telling him that he's homeless. However, do not worry about the Parkers. To my amazement, they are in a position to be able to buy their farm.' Maurice shook his head as he could not completely believe that his stable hand had that sort of money, unlike himself.

'So, that is why he left by the front door? He thought himself just as good as us for once,' Rebecca exclaimed. 'The gatehouse as well, Maurice? I wanted rid of Robinson, but not that house. We must be in a terrible mess.'

'We are rather, my dear, but Tom has paid near enough the price the bank was suggesting and once the gatehouse is sold we will be clear of debt. I also secured three days a week of work with the War Ag, working in the offices in Skipton, so that will bring money in too. It's best that we get ourselves clear of debt; the next few years are going to test us yet again, not that everyone didn't already go through enough in the thirties.' Maurice looked at the headlines of the local newspaper showing the mounting attacks by the Luftwaffe on British warships and the brave defence of the ships by the RAF. He prayed under his breath that Michael, their son, was safe. Money was nothing compared to the safety of his family.

'Do you know, I don't think I can cope with all this. I worry about our children: the very thought of people thinking that we cannot even pay our bills and the gossip that it's going to cause if the truth ever comes out about Charlotte and that terrible Robinson. At least he'll be gone from our lives. Why did you not tell me all this earlier, Maurice? I'm not a child,' Rebecca spat and put her hand to her brow.

'Because it would have achieved nothing, except a few more weeks of worry for you.' Maurice sighed.

'Things will calm down a little now with the bank. I'll put the gatehouse up for sale at the weekend and Tom says he can pay straight away. That will keep everybody happy.'

'Oh, Maurice! What a pickle! I need a drink,' Rebecca said, making for the study doorway.

'Of course you do, dear. It has been a shock,' Maurice said quietly. Any upset in Rebecca's life was remedied with a drink and it had been that way for some time now. 'You go and have a drink and a lie down. I'll see to things, don't you worry.' Maurice watched as his wife left him at his desk filled with worry. Tom Parker was a lucky man: his wife stood by him no matter what, come hell or high water. Rebecca would be having a long drink and then picking up the telephone to call her lover in Harrogate, although he had not heard them of late secretly talking, unaware that they could be heard by him. Perhaps that had come to an end as well? Hopefully it had.

'Well, go on, Tom, is it ours?' Ethel Parker hadn't been able to rest for thinking about the business that was taking place in the hall between Tom and his employer.

Tom walked into the kitchen and could barely keep the smile from off his face as he looked at the woman he had loved for the past forty-five years.

'Aye, we've done it, lass. I've to sort the money out and pay the Bradleys but this is now our true home and our own land.' Tom, a man of few emotions, grinned and held his wife tight and gave her a sloppy big kiss on her cheek. 'Hawith Farm will soon belong to the

Parkers and his lordship has given me the two Clydesdales. He's no use for them; I'll have to do up the stables because I can't expect him to keep them in his stable now. They're both long in the tooth so I'm glad he's agreed for them to be in my care.'

'Aye, never mind the hosses. The house is ours! I never thought it would be.' Ethel wiped a tear from her eyes; she'd not been able to spend a penny of her inheritance and had made do with very little over the years. Now every brick, window and door would be theirs, along with twenty acres of land, which they could farm as they wanted. She couldn't believe it as she patted her eyes dry. 'The things I want to do now I know it's ours . . . I saw some lovely wallpaper down in Gregsons' window, it was cream with red roses on it, and I thought how grand it would look on our sitting room wall.' She smiled and breathed in deeply.

'Now, take it slowly. Don't you be spending owt until we've settled up and have the deeds under this roof. Not that I doubt Maurice, he's a man of his word if nothing else,' Tom said and sat down, picking up a cold mug of tea that had been waiting for his arrival. 'I've summat else and all. I've got the lad's home address. I thought he should write to his mother, seeing the little devil keeps putting it off. I'll have a word with him over it or we'll write for him.'

'Aye, I've taken to Archie. Do you know, from what he's told us, I would be surprised if his mother would write back to him anyway. Poor lamb, he's never had any love spent on him. That's the only thing we're lacking now, a child of our own.' Ethel sighed and looked at Tom.

'Aye, well, that gate's well and truly shut, my old Dutch, but we can't have everything.'

'No, I suppose not,' Ethel said and thought about the babies that she would have loved to have held and nurtured.

Jeff Robinson stood in his garden at the gatehouse, considering the many apples that hung on the laden tree. He'd promised Alice that he would help her pick them and take them back to the hall for keeping over the winter months but it was a job he was not keen on – too much back-breaking involved, he thought as he pulled on his jacket to walk to the hall to polish the Ford that his lordship had started using instead of the Rolls. He turned and looked as he heard the garden gate opening and felt a slight wave of panic come over him as he saw Lord Maurice approaching with his face set in a grimace.

'Good morning, your lordship. I was just on my way to service and polish the Ford. Or will you be using it this morning?' Jeff said. He knew straight away the visit was not a social one. Maurice did not offer him his hand to shake, nor did he wish him the 'good morning' that he usually did.

'Robinson, I need to talk to you and you can take your jacket off because I've no need of you at the hall today.' Maurice walked straight into the gatehouse without even asking Jeff's permission. It was his house and in another fortnight he would be out of it anyway, he'd make sure of that.

Jeff followed him into his main living room and stood by one of the chairs as Maurice looked out of the window, not even turning to look at him. 'Is everything all right, sir? You don't seem yourself.'

'No, everything is not all right, Robinson. It has not been all right since the very day my intolerable daughter caught your eye. The only reason that I have kept you on here since the *incident* was because at least it would allow any gossip or suspicions to look unfounded if you stayed in my employment.'

Maurice turned and stared at the chauffeur that had caused so much upset in his life.

'I know my headstrong daughter was with you the other night, you need not try to deny it. You both knew that your staying in my employment was on the under-standing that you left one another alone. So, I've come down here today to give you your notice, and I require you to be out of this house before the end of October.' Maurice stood tall and resolute in front of the man that at first, he had thought to be a boon to the family but now, he could not bear to look at for any length of time. He had brought worry and shame to his family and it was time for him to go.

'You can't do that, you can't just throw me out upon the street! And I need more time. And when it comes to your precious daughter, it is her that does all the running to me, not the other way around,' Jeff said angrily and ran his hand through his hair, staring at the lord of the hall who had always been a fair employer if he was to tell the truth.

'I can. You have a month to get gone and if you ever dare to dirty my daughter's name, I will see that every move you make will not go unnoticed. I've turned a blind eye to the petrol bill at Pratt's garage being more than it should be and the odd packet of cigarettes going un-accounted for when you deliver them to the hall but believe me, that will not be happening from this day onwards. I want you out and you can think again if you want a reference for another employer,' Maurice said and patted his riding crop against the side of his leg as he watched Robinson's face darken.

'You at these big bloody houses rule our lives, while we little men mean nothing to you snobs. Your lass is besotted with me. I'm her bit of rough, the one that keeps her satisfied, unlike the ponces that come and court her at the hall,' Jeff spat. He saw the anger on Maurice's face as he lifted his riding crop to hit him, but Jeff caught it in his hand and pushed Maurice back, nearly making him fall.

'Is that what you did to your wife, Robinson? Pushed her just a little, so that she conveniently fell to her death, and then blamed it on my daughter?' Maurice said, his eyes blazing with anger and hatred as he gained his balance.

'No, you know I didn't. You know it was your easy-living daughter that pushed her down these stairs. You know that else you would not have saved my neck,' Jeff said and shook his head. 'Leave me. I'll be out of your bloody house by the end of October, with a full month's pay upfront, I hope, else I might be tempted to go and pay the coppers at Skipton a visit.' Jeff smirked. 'It wouldn't look good, lord of the manor and Chief Constable cover for his murdering daughter and her lover. I can just see it as the headline on the *Craven Herald*; it would ruin you and your family.' Jeff grinned. 'In fact, thinking about it, let's make it a year's wage and then I'll be gone before you can blink.'

'You are a cad, sir, one of the lowest kind,' Maurice said and felt the blood rushing to his cheeks. He couldn't afford to pay him a year's wage, but he would manage it somehow, just to get him out of his property and his life. 'I'll pay you what you're asking but I'm damned if I'll be giving you a reference.'

'Makes no difference to me, there's plenty that will need my services.' Jeff grinned as he watched Maurice walk into the entrance hall. He was planning to leave anyway before he got caught up in being recruited for the war that was rumbling all across Europe.

'Right, a fortnight and I want you out. Call for your wages at the hall, but other than that I don't want to see your face anywhere near my property,' Maurice said and looked at Jeff with disdain. Time the man went and the sooner the better.

Chapter 16

Maggie sat upon the church pew next to Lizzie. Neither wanted to be there but Maggie had agreed that if she helped Lizzie with the task in hand, they would have more time that Saturday afternoon to do what they wanted. The church was celebrating the harvest festival and Lizzie had been given the job of threading ripe red rosehips onto a string and then draping them at the ends of each pew to brighten the church up with all things autumn. The church smelled of polish, and candle wax, and the altar and windows were filled with fruit and produce from the villagers of Gargrave. The women of the WI and churchwardens were arranging blooms to show the church off at its best and to celebrate the year's harvest.

'I hate doing this, it makes my fingers sore,' Lizzie said as she pushed the darning needle threaded with green string through the centre of the seed-filled hip. 'And the seeds inside make you itch.'

'Never mind, we've nearly finished. There are only the last two pews then we can go, I hope!' Maggie said as she looked up at the do-gooders that were discussing if there was enough foliage under the main stained-glass window. 'How are you anyway? Did you catch it with the vicar when your mam wrote and said what she thought in her letter?'

'No, he just read it out in front of me, said I was an ungrateful child and then screwed up and placed Mam's letter in the bin, but he must have written back to her because I noticed a letter to my mam and da on his posting pile in the hall,' Lizzie said quietly. 'I nearly thought of pinching it and reading it but then I thought better of it. It's been posted now, so no doubt my mam will have had something to say if he's said anything bad to her.'

'Oh, Lord, my mam will be hearing all about it. She said your mam was not at all happy with you being at the vicarage. I bet if she could, she would take you back home,' Maggie said and picked up her length of threaded hips to make sure it was long enough before tying it to the two hooks used every year on the pew end.

'Yes, she said in this last letter that my father had heard the Yanks calling this war a phoney war as nowhere in England has been bombed yet by the Nazis. I'd walk back if they both said I could, never mind taking the train. I'd just like to be home.' Lizzie sighed and hung her string of hips alongside Maggie's and then started on another string before they both earned their freedom for the afternoon.

* * *

'It'll be another week before the Brysons are back on their barge. I wish they would hurry up, I could do with my winter coat and some jumpers that Ma says she's sending with them,' Maggie said as she leaned over the canal bridge and looked down into the murky waters of the canal, shivering in the cold autumn wind.

'Yes, they're bringing me some clothes as well and a hot water bottle, because I bet my bedroom will be freezing come winter. Not that I want to be still there then. Just imagine if we have to spend Christmas without our mas and das. I'll not be able to stop crying,' Lizzie said and looked down into the murky waters. She used to be so sure of herself but of late her assuredness had disappeared, worn away by her life at the vicarage and by not liking country life, and now all her thoughts were for the worse.

'It'll not come to that. We'll be back home by then. Like your da says, it's a phoney war so we'll be going home soon.' Maggie hoped that she would be right as she put her arm around her best friend. 'Come on, we'll go and play on the swing and collect some conkers from under its branches. I've seen the lads at school playing with them on shoelaces and Archie, the cheeky devil, was swapping things for them the other day because he knew that the village lads are not allowed on the estate.'

Maggie linked her arm through Lizzie's and tried to cheer her up as they made their way to the horse chestnut tree that the swing hung from and which was providing Archie with a new income from things that only boys cherished and carried in their pockets.

Maggie shuffled her bum onto the weather-worn seat of the swing and smiled at Lizzie. 'Bagsy I go first. You push me and then I'll push you and then we'll look for conkers.'

'Don't you think we're getting too old for going on swings? We should be acting more ladylike now,' Lizzie said as she grabbed hold of the ropes and pulled her friend back before pushing her forcibly.

'You're never too old for a swing, Lizzie. It's lovely to feel like you're flying.' Maggie motioned her body back and forward, making herself go higher and higher. Lizzie stood back under the other side of the conker tree watching as Maggie made the tree shudder, causing its orange and russet leaves and fruit to fall to the ground.

'You're making the last of the conkers fall,' Lizzie said as she rushed and gathered the prickly cases of the chestnuts up and peeled back the outer case to reveal the shiny smooth conker within and placed them in her pocket. She and Maggie could perhaps trade with some of the boys in their class for a sweet or something else that might be of use to them, she thought as she ran about picking more of them up as they fell to the ground.

'Woah, I can nearly see to Skipton!' Maggie yelled as she swung back and forward and looked down at her friend and across to the gatehouse where she could see Jeff Robinson digging in his garden. She had not seen him lately in the hall and she was glad after what she had overheard from Charlotte and her father when they were standing under her bedroom window. 'It's lovely up here, Lizzie. I'll stop now and then it's your turn.' Maggie leaned back and put her legs in the air, the last push before she changed over for her friend to have a go on the swing that the children at the hall had enjoyed for years.

'All right but then I'll have to go back to the vicarage. You can take care of these conkers until school tomorrow else *she* will only throw them out.' Lizzie suddenly turned as she heard Maggie let out a high scream that echoed around the park. She watched as if in slow motion as Maggie fell from the swing and slumped to the floor.

'Maggie! Maggie, are you all right?' Lizzie rushed over as she heard her hit the earth underneath the horse chestnut tree and her friend's crumpled body lay for a moment deadly still with the rope of the swing hanging frayed and broken above her head.

'Oh, I hurt. What a fall, but I don't think I've broken anything,' Maggie cried and slowly uncurled from the position she had landed in. 'My ankle hurts and my head feels as if I've been in a boxing match with Bridget. Although she'd not win.' Maggie looked up at the worried face of her friend. 'Bloody swing.' Then she grinned. 'Give me your hand to get me up on my feet.'

'Stay as you are. You might have hurt yourself more than you know,' the voice of Jeff Robinson shouted as he looked up at both girls from next to his garden gate. 'I'm coming.'

'Don't let him near me, please. Lizzie, give me your hand. I'm fine,' Maggie whispered and pulled herself up against the tree trunk and reached for Lizzie's arm to lean on. She didn't want Jeff Robinson anywhere near her. His hands were the hands of a murderer or a murderer's accomplice at the least. 'Ow! That hurts,' she said and tried to smile at her best friend as she offered her the arm that she needed so badly to rest on.

Lizzie looked at Maggie as she tried to put her weight on her ankle but struggled. 'He can get you back up to the hall,' Lizzie whispered. 'You might have broken your ankle.'

'No, I don't want him anywhere near me. He's a bad man, Lizzie, and I know he is. He killed his wife.' Maggie winced as she tried to put more weight on her ankle.

'What do you mean?' Lizzie whispered but Maggie could not reply as Jeff came running across the field to join them.

'Are you all right? You shouldn't have been playing on the swing; it should have been taken down years ago. The rope is rotten.' Jeff gasped as he stood in front of the two girls. 'Here, let me have a look at you. Do you hurt anywhere? Can you walk?' he said with concern in his voice to Maggie as Lizzie watched on.

'I'm all right, thank you. Just a little shaken up,' Maggie said and glared at Lizzie, hoping that she would not say anything to the contrary.

'Let us see if you can walk. You dropped from quite a height,' Jeff said, standing in front of her meeting her eyes and studying her reactions as she stumbled and yelped with pain when she put weight on her ankle.

'All right, eh? Looks like you've busted your ankle. I'd better take you up to the hall and they can get a doctor to look at it. Here, wrap your arms around my neck and I'll piggyback you there. You look as if you weigh next to nothing and the hall is not that far away,' Jeff said, crouching down for Maggie to cling to his back to be taken home.

'No, I'll manage. Lizzie will give me her hand and I'll walk there,' Maggie said and looked at Lizzie for her hand and backup. However, she hesitated, knowing that Maggie would struggle and not understanding why she wouldn't let Jeff Robinson help.

'Nonsense. If you won't climb on my back, then I'll just carry you. You can't put any weight on that foot until you know what you've done with it and besides, you might have damaged yourself elsewhere for all we know.' Before the girls could stop him he lifted Maggie into his arms and adjusted her weight for a second before starting up the drive to the hall.

Maggie resisted at first and then held on with her arms around his neck. She daren't tell him to put her down as he might lose his temper. He struggled to get his breath as he carried her up the drive and to the front of the hall and then took her to the back kitchen entrance, with Lizzie following in his tracks.

Lizzie rushed to open the kitchen door as he urged her to do so. Alice and Mrs Perceval gasped as he entered the kitchen and managed to put her into one of the Windsor chairs next to the large table.

'Lord above, what's been happening now?' Ada Perceval exclaimed and looked at the three of them.

'The rope on the old swing across from the gatehouse

broke and she's hurt her ankle, if not more. I've just carried her back. Lord, she's more solid than I thought.' Jeff bent double and caught his breath and shot a worried look across at Alice. She knew that he was supposed to be staying away from the hall.

'Are you all right? You don't feel dizzy and you can see straight?' Ada Perceval asked and bent down to look more closely at an ashen-faced Maggie. 'I'd better tell Lord Bradley to send for the doctor; better safe than sorry.' She turned to Alice. 'Can you tell him what's happened and I'll make her a hot sweet drink, along with one for you, pet. It must have been a shock for you as well, young lady,' Ada said to Lizzie and before looking at both of the young girls, who were strangely quiet.

'It's just my ankle, Mrs Perceval. It can't take all my weight,' Maggie said. She felt the tears welling up in her eyes with the realization that she could have been a lot worse from the height that she had fallen.

'Aye, now don't take on so. That's the shock coming out, pet. You'll be all right, we just might need the doctor to look at you. Go on, Alice, go and get his lordship and then we'll know whether to send for a doctor or not. Don't just stand there gawping,' Ada added sharply to a worried Alice. 'Go on, get him.'

'I'll be off now, as long as she's all right,' Jeff said, watching as Alice made her way into the main house to get Maurice Bradley. He didn't want to be about for another round of conflict.

'I'll see his lordship thanks you for this, Jeff. She couldn't have walked back,' Ada said as she put the kettle on the stove and summoned Lizzie to sit down next to her best friend and hold her hand.

'Aye, whatever, it's nowt,' Jeff said and made a quick exit out of the kitchen door, not wanting to stay any longer and to have to be pleasant to Maurice Bradley.

Lizzie held Maggie's hand tight and smiled at her best friend as she wiped her tears away. 'You'll be all right. If the doctor comes, he'll soon tell you what's wrong with you.'

'I've never had a doctor look at me before. My ma says we can never afford one and she always knows what's ailing us anyway,' Maggie said and then took a long sip of the tea that Mrs Perceval had put under her nose. It contained more sugar than the sugar canister itself, she thought as she felt the warm liquid bring life to her.

'Now, young lady, what have you been up to? That swing has claimed you as a victim, I hear.' Maurice Bradley walked quietly into the kitchen and bent down and looked at Maggie. 'You look a bit pale, my dear, but I understand it's your ankle that has been damaged. Now, let me have a look at it and if I think we need the doctor, then we will send for him. Is it the right one?' Maurice sat down in the chair that Ada Perceval gave him and lifted Maggie's foot onto his knee. He pressed on it, making Maggie wince.

'It hurts, doesn't it? It's a little swollen and you obviously can't walk on it. I think we had better send for Doctor Swainbank. It could well be broken and then it's a case for the hospital at Skipton.' Maurice stood up and looked at Maggie. 'Now, there's no need for tears; bones are soon set. But you might find it difficult getting about for a while.' Maurice sighed. 'I suggest I help you upstairs to your room and then you can rest in your bed and are out of the way of the kitchen staff.'

'I don't think it is broken,' Maggie sobbed. 'It doesn't hurt that much.' She was frightened. What if the doctor said it was broken and they had to chop her foot off? She'd seen some of the old sailors at the docks limbless and she didn't want to limp along like them.

'Better safe than sorry! So the doctor will come. We don't want your parents to think that we don't look after you while in our care. Now, let me help you up the stairs rather than you putting any weight upon it. How did you get back here? The swing is quite a few yards away.' Maurice offered Maggie his arm and took her full weight as she leaned heavily on him.

'Jeff Robinson carried her here, milord. It's a good job that he did if her ankle is broken,' Ada said and held the back stairway door open.

'Did he now?' Maurice said. 'There, can you manage to put your nightclothes on or would you like Alice to help?'

'No, I can manage, thank you. They're just here under my pillow and I don't have to stand, thank you,' Maggie replied, suddenly realizing how exhausted she felt.

'I'll send your friend up from downstairs, just until the doctor comes. She can keep your spirits up. Unless you don't want her, that is?' Maurice said kindly and looked at the evacuee that he and his wife had hardly spent any time with. She had flourished in looks in the few weeks that she had been with them, he thought. Country life was doing all the town children good health-wise, if not mentally.

'Yes, please do send Lizzie up. She'll be worried about me and I need to talk to her,' Maggie said, smiling. She felt thankful that she could rest her leg on the firm mattress.

'Very well. Doctor Swainbank will be with you as soon as he can and I'm sure Alice and Mrs Perceval will see to any needs you have.' Maurice hesitated for a minute. 'Do you have a pen and paper so that you can tell your parents what has happened or would you like me to write to them?'

'Oh, no, sir, there is no need for you to write. They would fear the worst. I'll write to them once I know what's wrong,' Maggie replied, thinking of the look on her parents' faces if a letter in Lord Bradley's handwriting fell through the letterbox.

'Very well. Now, keep your chin up, you are in good hands. It will probably be nothing more than a sprain and you'll just need to rest it,' Maurice said. He dipped his head as he left the servants' quarters that he rarely visited, swearing under his breath at the cost of a doctor's visit that he could ill afford and the fact that Robinson had come to the hall despite him being banned no matter what the cause.

'I told you that you were going too high. You could have broken your neck, never mind your ankle,' Lizzie said as she sat by the side of her best friend as she lay in bed feeling sorry for herself.

'I didn't know the rope was rotten, else I wouldn't have gone on the dratted thing,' Maggie said and lay back on her pillow. 'I'm frightened, Lizzie. What if I've broken my ankle or, even worse, what if I have to have my foot chopped off?'

'Don't be daft! Lord Bradley said downstairs that he thought it was just a bad sprain, that he was just getting the doctor to be safe, seeing you were in his care. He looked quite worried and sounded a bit angry, but I don't know why.' Lizzie sighed. She was going to be without her best friend at school for a while and she was going to miss her.

'It was when Mrs Perceval mentioned Jeff Robinson. He hates him,' Maggie replied.

'So do you, accusing him of murder. You've been listening to too much gossip.' Lizzie shook her head. 'The poor fella nearly dropped you because you were protesting so much about being carried and he was only doing you a good turn.'

'You didn't hear what I heard early one morning when I got out of bed to close my bedroom window. There was Lord Bradley and his daughter talking about when Robinson's wife died and it sounded like Robinson and Charlotte had killed her by pushing her down the stairs. As my mother says, there's no smoke without fire.' Maggie sighed and closed her eyes. 'Her father had caught Charlotte coming back from seeing him and they were having a row under my window. I tell you, it was no accident. The gossips are right.'

'Well, it's nothing to do with us. We can't do anything

about it and anyway, you might have been half-asleep and only heard what you thought you heard.' Lizzie then started to think about what she had heard from people visiting the vicarage. It might be a place of God but it was also a place of gossip and village affairs.

'I tell you, I heard every word and Charlotte is as guilty as him, but they covered it up.' Maggie yawned and felt her eyes going heavy. She had been shaken somewhat by her fall and now she needed a minute's peace.

'I'll go, Maggie, you look tired. Don't worry, I'll come after school on Monday. Tomorrow is harvest festival so I won't have time. I'm sure you'll be all right, though,' Lizzie said quietly, standing up and looking at her best friend. Would she have ever told her of the secret that she had kept to herself until now if she had not fallen from the swing? It was not like Maggie to make things up, so it must be true.

'Are you sure? But the doctor might be ages yet. I'm hoping that he'll be too busy to see me.' Maggie yawned and looked at Lizzie. 'You'll not say anything to anybody about what I've told you, will you? It happened before we came here and it really is none of our business, but Robinson's wife has had a great injustice done to her.'

'I'll not say a word. My lips are sealed. Now, you have a sleep before the doctor comes and you do need to see him,' Lizzie said firmly. 'I'll see you after school on Monday and I'll tell them what has happened to you as well.'

'Thanks, Lizzie, you're a good friend.' Maggie winced

as she moved her foot and felt the pain again as it throbbed when she repositioned herself under the covers.

'And you are too,' Lizzie said as she closed the bedroom door and sighed. If Maggie had broken her ankle, she would be off from school a long time and she did not enjoy the prospect of days there without her best friend by her side.

Maurice Bradley looked at Doctor Swainbank as he joined him in the study. 'Well, Roger, what's the damage? Has she broke her blasted ankle? It looked to be swollen and she could not put any weight upon it.'

'No, I don't think so, just badly sprained. I have told Mrs Perceval to put ice on it to bring down the swelling and I have left some aspirins by the side of her bed and told Maggie when to take them with a swig of water. If it does not improve in the next day or two, then she will have to go to Skipton Infirmary for an X-ray but I don't think there will be a need. She's got a bump on the back of her head which I was a little concerned about but she doesn't seem to be any the worse for it after I examined her.' Doctor Roger Swainbank sat down in one of the chairs. 'She'll be all right, so don't worry your head over her. Which is more than I can say about you. You look terrible, man. Are you still not sleeping and are things getting on top of you again?' Doctor Swainbank observed his close friend and felt sorry for the man that was trying to hold his estate and family together.

'I'm all right; things are straighter than they have been for a while. I've sold Hawith Farm to Tom Parker and his wife. They made me an offer when I said I was about to sell it and payment has just gone through, which has made the bank happier, and I've given Jeff Robinson his notice. I'll be glad to see him off my premises, although I'll miss his services.'

'So will your daughter,' Roger said quietly with a wry smile on his face.

'Aye, well, that's why he's going, she can't keep away from him, plus the money I get from the sale of the gatehouse will make me solvent at the bank.' Maurice walked over to his whisky decanter and poured himself a drink and offered Roger a glass.

'Not for me, old man. There's a baby due over at Malham so I need my wits about me. In addition, Rebecca, how is she?' Roger asked, watching his friend as he swigged the glass of whisky straight back.

'Quiet at the moment. In fact, I rather think her big love affair has come to an end, which I'm thankful for. Although if it hadn't been for her having an affair with that terrible man and you being a good friend of mine and covering my back, I'm sure I would be visiting my daughter and Robinson in prison.'

'Well, there's been plenty of gossip down in the village, as you probably know. Folk won't be sorry to see the back of Jeff Robinson and it is just as well Charlotte is out of it now and has joined the Land Girls. But people have long memories so the longer she is away from here, the better.' Roger Swainbank rose from his chair. 'Any news of your Michael? I hear that our boys in blue are busy protecting our shipping and keeping the Hun at bay.'

'No, he's not allowed to tell us anything. We just pray that he keeps safe and hope that we won't be the recipients of bad news,' Maurice said and looked down at his feet. 'You'll make sure that you send me the bill for today's visit?'

'I will not. A few aspirins don't cost the earth and, after all, she's not your family. Call it my contribution to the war effort, old man.' Roger Swainbank patted his good friend on the back. 'And if the ankle doesn't get any better, let me know, but she should be up and putting her weight on it by the end of the week.'

'Thank you, Roger. I don't know what I'd do without you,' Maurice said, patting his lifelong friend back.

'You'd manage, I'm sure, and we only do what friends have to do for one another and cover one another's backs. Old school rules, remember,' Roger Swainbank said before he left, thinking that he was lucky to have such a faithful friend.

Chapter 17

Tom and Ethel Parker looked up from their early morning breakfast as they heard the postman come through their garden gate, whistling as he did so. He put his head around the ever-open kitchen door as he delivered the mail.

'Morning, Tom. Morning, Ethel. I see the gatehouse is up for sale. So where's that cocky bugger going to go now that Lord Bradley has had enough of him?' Robin West said and put the letter that he was delivering down on the sideboard as Tom got up from his seat.

'Don't know; don't care as long as he's far enough away from here. I noticed the for sale board go up the end of last week, although Lord Bradley had told me before that he was selling it, along with here,' Tom said dryly and looked at the postman who missed nothing.

'What, you are losing your home and all? Where are you two going to go?' Robin asked, shocked. 'It must be true then, that those at the hall have hit on hard times if they're selling everything up. Like, they'll not be the first; all these big houses are struggling. Malham Manor is up for sale and all.' Robin took his postman's cap off his head and brushed his hair back, thinking that Tom seemed quite calm seeing as he was going to be homeless soon.

'Nay, I think they'll be all right now. Ethel and I have bought this place, so we're not going anywhere soon unless it's out in a box. And I'm hoping that will not be for a while yet for either of us.' Tom grinned and glanced at the letter that both Ethel and he had been waiting for and wished that the postman would get on his way.

'Bloody hell! Well done, Tom. Now, that is good news. It would have been a shame for you both to leave here; you've been here for as long as I have ever known you. I bet that went down badly with his lordship, his stable man buying his property off him?'

'He was the perfect gentleman, Robin. He and his father have been good to us over the years and I will not have a bad word said about either,' Ethel said sharply as she rose from the table and started to clear the break-fast dishes.

'Nay, I wasn't saying owt bad about him, just that it would hurt him a bit, thinking that he had to sell everything off. These last few years and the war coming now is hurting everybody where it does hurt. Times are bad!' Robin said, aware he'd put his foot in it with Ethel and Tom who had always been loyal to their employer. 'I'll be on my way now. It's good to hear some good news for a change and I'm happy for you both.'

226

'Aye, grand, Robin. Thanks for delivering the letter. You take care now,' Tom said, watching as the postman mounted his push bike and made his way up to the hall. 'Well, that will give him some gossip for the day; everybody in Gargrave will know that we've bought here by nightfall.' Tom grinned and picked up the envelope. 'He'll have another bit to spread about the village the next time he comes if I can persuade Lord Maurice that the lad should come and stay with us for the time being. I'll away and see him after we've had our dinner, lass, because I know that's what would make your life just perfect.'

Lord Maurice looked at Tom after hearing that Tom and Ethel had decided that young Archie would be better living with them. That would bring around a big change in the elderly couple's life yet again. 'Are you sure, Tom? Neither you nor Ethel is getting any younger and he's only nearly eleven.'

'Aye, we're both sure. It would save you having him staying here and it would give my Ethel someone to look after and fuss over. Besides, he's a good hand with the horses. As you said, we're not getting any younger and we could do with some young about the place.'

'That's what I'm worried about, Tom. Perhaps you're being rather hasty.' Maurice looked at the ageing old man who of late he had seen in a whole new light.

'Well, he just about lives with us now apart from on a night. As I say, he'll be one less for you to worry about and I hope that you'll know that we will give him a good home. I don't think he's come from one by what he's

227

told us.' Tom looked hard at Lord Maurice. 'I take it all's going through with the sale of the farm? I took my cheque down to your solicitor the other day and he said he'd hand over the deeds on Friday.'

'Yes, all is in order, Tom, don't worry about that. There's no problem whatsoever with the sale. You'll have seen the sale board up at the gatehouse. Robinson will be leaving us this month. He's been given his marching orders,' Maurice said and nodded at the man who he couldn't help but respect. 'Now, I take it you'll still be working some hours for me or are you going to be a man of leisure now you own your own farm?' Maurice asked, hoping that he was not going to have to employ somebody to maintain the grounds and few acres that he was going to be left with after the sale.

'Nay, sir, I can't leave you high and dry. I'll still do the work you expect me to do. I'm a better man than that and now I'll have a helper anyway.' Tom grinned. 'How's the lass? I hear she fell from the tree swing. I should have taken it down myself, but I didn't think there was anybody here to play on it.' He shook his head regretfully.

'She's on the mend. Just a bad sprain, as the doctor thought, thankfully nothing broken. She's able to make her way downstairs on her own now, so she must be improving.' Maurice breathed in. 'Now, back to Archie Brannigan. Do you want to tell him the news that he can now go and stay with you or should I? He will be home shortly from school so you might as well tell him here and now.'

'Aye, I'll tell him. I want to see his face,' Tom said and

looked across at Maurice. 'You are a good man, sir. We owe you a lot.'

'You owe me nothing, Tom Parker, and I'm glad that the farm is about to be placed in your safe hands, along with the lad for now.'

Tom sat at the top of the hall's steps that ran down to the lawn, guarded on either side by the stately stone lions that had been there for as long as he could remember. He looked out at the gardens that, along with the horses and land, he had kept immaculate after the gardeners had been made redundant. He had turned his hand to many a job around the hall and now it was beginning to pay off, he thought as he enjoyed a puff on his pipe and watched as Archie ran up the drive, eager to get back to his new life at the hall.

'Now then, young man, have you done your best at school today? Not been in any trouble?' Tom stood up and joined the smiling Archie on the drive. He looked ten times healthier than the nit-ridden, bedraggled urchin that he had first seen.

'I have. I beat everybody at conkers, with Lizzie's conkers. I did what you said, I soaked them in vinegar. I asked Mrs Perceval for some, so I didn't pinch it from the kitchen. This one's a sixer!' Archie pulled a large shiny conker from his pocket, attached to a piece of string, and smiled at his prized possession.

'That's a grand lad,' Tom said and put his arm around his shoulders. 'Now, I've summat to tell you and I hope that it will sit well with you.'

'What? I've not done anything wrong, have I? There's nothing up, is there?' Archie looked worried.

'Nay, lad, I hope that it's just the opposite.' Tom hesitated. 'I've just spoken to his lordship and said how much time you were spending with me and Ethel and I asked him if it would be all right if you came and stopped with us both instead of living at the hall.' Tom looked at Archie's face.

'I can't believe it! You mean I can really come and live with you and it will be all right? I don't know what to say. I'd have my own bedroom and be able to look after the horses every day with you.' Archie gasped and looked up at the man that was changing his life.

'Aye, just while you're billeted here, but you write to your mother and if you ever want to go back home, Ethel and I won't stand in your way. Not that we would want you to leave.' Tom tousled Archie's hair and looked at him and smiled. 'Things sometimes change for the best.'

'I've got to go and tell Maggie! I can't wait! Can I come tonight? Stay with you, and go to school in the morning from your house?' Archie asked.

'Aye, lad. Pick up what belongs to you from your room and come tonight. There's a rabbit pie and carrots on the go for your supper and the missus has aired the bed and made ready for your coming. She cannot wait for you to be living with us.'

Archie wiped his runny nose and eyes and grinned. 'I can't wait to tell Maggie. She'll never believe it!'

'Go on then, get on with it. Tell Mrs Perceval that

there will be one less to feed from now on and remember, get everything that's yours and leave what belongs to the hall where it is. I'll wait here for you.' Tom sat across on the mounting blocks outside the stable and closed his eyes. There was no going back now. The lad had been told and the cheque had been signed. Both he and Ethel owned their own home and now had the responsibility of the lad as well. They must want their heads examined, he thought as he took a long drag of his pipe and waited for his new dependant.

Archie burst into the kitchen and looked around at everyone as he shouted, 'I'm going to live at Tom's! He's got me a bedroom and everything and his lordship says that it's all right, I can stop with him as long as I want.' He stood with a beaming smile and looked at the surprise on everybody's faces.

'Oh, Lord, Tom must have had a turn! Whatever has possessed him to take you on? But then again, you've just about been living with them anyway,' Mrs Perceval said and then glanced at Maggie as she bowed her head at the news.

'I've just come to pick my things up and then I'm off,' Archie said, running through the kitchen and up the stairs to his bedroom, where he quickly began to put his few belongings into the bag that he had been given by his mum as she had waved him off.

'Are you all right, pet?' Mrs Perceval said to Maggie, noticing that she was looking a little bit glum about Archie's announcement.

'Yes. I'm glad for Archie; he loves living here and it's doing him good. It's just that I have a home and I want to get back to my mam and da and I miss them so. They're all I've thought about since I hurt my ankle and I can't do a lot to take my mind off things. Never mind, I'm starting to put my weight on it now so I can at least go back to school next week and stop worrying.' Maggie sighed. She could have burst into tears but her pride didn't let her.

'Never mind, pet, you'll not be here for ever. I bet you're sent back home before long. There doesn't seem to be any danger as of yet of us being bombed. This war might all come to nowt if Hitler decides to keep over that Channel and not bother us,' Mrs Perceval said and turned to Alice for support.

'Yes, don't worry, Maggie. Your ankle is getting stronger, you can get back to school next week, I bet, and even if you are still here at Christmas, I'm sure your parents will be able to visit you.'

Maggie looked down at the newspaper that lay on the kitchen table reporting on the fighting in Europe and the dog fights that the RAF were having with the enemy. There would be no way she would be back home for Christmas unless her parents sent for her or if the war ended. How she wished that now she was on her own at the hall she could return home.

'Right, I'm off.' Archie bounced back into the kitchen with his few possessions tucked under his arm. 'Thank you for looking after me,' he said and then made for the door, stopping for a second to look at Maggie. 'You'll be all right, Mags. I'm only down the lane.' And then he was gone and the kitchen felt already quieter and lonelier even though Archie's departure had no effect on anyone but Maggie.

Ethel stood at the farmhouse doorway and held her arms out as Archie walked as proud as punch next to Tom through the garden gate and came up the pathway.

'Now then, what do you think of that? Wish hard enough and your dreams do come true, young man.' Ethel wrapped her arms around him and kissed the top of his head. 'I've made your bed and there's all you need in the back bedroom. I've even been down to the paper shop and got you one of those comics that you lads seem to like reading. You'll be all right living here with me and Tom, but you must always say if you want to go home or see your mam,' Ethel said and held Archie close.

'I'll never do that. This is going to be my new home and my mam won't miss me for a minute,' Archie said, looking up into Ethel's tear-filled eyes. This was the home he had always dreamed of and he was not going to lose it for anybody or anything.

Chapter 18

'You're still limping. Does it hurt?' Lizzie said as she stood next to Maggie in the playground.

'No, it's not so bad now,' Maggie said, sitting down on the top of the wall and looking at the rest of her classmates talking and walking or playing Jacks, conkers or tig. 'It aches when I've walked on it a lot but when I'm sitting down at my desk it's all right, and at least I can stand on it now.' Maggie sighed. 'I needed my mam when I first did it and I still could do with her now. She'd be there for me and make sure I'm all right. Them at the hall keep asking me if I'm managing but they're not really bothered, and why should they be? I'm not related to them and they have no ties to me.'

'I know what you mean. They act as if they care about us but they don't really. That is, apart from Archie and he's just fallen lucky. I hate it at the vicarage and my mam's made it worse because of her writing telling them not to drag me to their church or else she'll come and knock their blocks off. I can't believe that she would write that in a letter. She never takes any rubbish from anyone does my mam but she doesn't think sometimes. She's not the one living with them.' Lizzie sighed.

'I never thought that your mam would say anything like that. But she always does speak her mind, especially when in a bad mood.' Maggie smiled and looked at a frowning Lizzie.

'You don't know her that well then. She once was so mad with my da that she hit him over the head with the frying pan all because he had a few in the Dog and Duck after work. She's fearful when she's pushed.'

'She only does it because she loves you. My ma is the same. She once told Mrs Semple that lives two doors down the street to keep her nose out of her business and to look at her own family. When our Raymond made a noise with some of his mates coming home late one night, she argued in front of everyone on the street. I could have died with embarrassment.' Maggie grinned.

'We'll walk back by the canal if you're up to it tonight? Molly and Sid might be moored up along the bank, although I looked for them all last week and there was no sign of them, which was a good job seeing that you could hardly walk,' Lizzie said. 'I could do with my warmer clothes and all; they never light the upstairs fires at the vicarage, and it's getting to be a bit cold.'

'Yes, it's getting to be a bit parky at the hall as well. The warmest place is the kitchen but I only get in the way if I sit in there all day. When it comes to winter, I don't know what we're both going to do if we don't get our warmer clothes. It was all right when we first came, they couldn't do enough for us, but now they don't think twice about us. I thought Alice was going to be looking after me but she seems preoccupied at the moment. She'll be worrying about where her lover boy Jeff Robinson will be going. She's bound to know what's going on,' Maggie said, noticing the questioning look on Lizzie's face.

'Did you truly believe what you said about Jeff Robinson when you hurt your ankle? Do you think he is a murderer?' Lizzie asked and waited.

'If he isn't, Charlotte Bradley is. But we can't say anything, they would never believe us.' Maggie sighed as the bell was rung for the end of the afternoon break and for the last hour of school to begin and she looked at Lizzie as she shook her head in dismay.

'What a place we've come to live. I do want to go home,' Lizzie whispered as they entered the classroom and sat down at their desks.

The rain had been threatening all day and as both girls walked out of their lessons, the heavens opened and the cold rain started to pour down upon them.

'I wanted to go and look for Molly, Sid and the barge, but we're going to get wet even going home. I need my clothes and things from home and a letter to read to cheer me up,' Maggie said as they both stood in the stone-carved arch of the school's doorway while the rain bounced off the pavement and road.

'But we'll get sodden and Reverend Brown and his

wife will play heck with me for being late home,' Lizzie said, while at the same time feeling tempted to do as Maggie suggested.

'Tell them that you had to help me home as they can't complain about that,' Maggie said and pulled on Lizzie's arm. She stood in the pouring rain with her hair flattened and sodden almost as soon as she stepped out of her shelter. 'Come on, because I bet they're here, in their usual spot under the road bridge. I'm already wet and nobody will miss either of us yet for another half hour.'

'I don't know. I'm supposed to go home and arrange the church flowers with Mrs Bridges, one of the church-wardens. She always tries to get me to join her and show me how to do arrangements, not that I'm interested.' Lizzie hesitated. She knew that she should go home but also wanted to join Maggie as she watched her limping slightly down the road in the opposite direction to both their homes.

'Come on, we won't be long. They might not even be there. We can walk the length of the canal that meanders behind the village and still be on the right track home even if they aren't under the road bridge. Take my hand and then I can walk faster with your help.' Maggie reached for Lizzie's hand and grinned. 'I need my coat; look, this thin thing isn't keeping out the rain.' Maggie turned up the collar on her washed-out gabardine raincoat that had once been her brother's and now was showing signs of its age. She was already soaked to the skin, as would Lizzie be. She debated not letting her friend down and finally put an arm around her waist and walked down the road to where it spanned the canal by a wide bridge where barges made use of the overhead shelter.

'You shouldn't be walking this far, you'll damage your ankle more,' Lizzie said as Maggie limped beside her and wiped the rain away from her face.

'I won't. It looks worse than it is, and anyway, it's not that much further.' Maggie winced but didn't want to show Lizzie her pain. 'Look, look, there's smoke rising from under the bridge from a barge's chimney. Please let it be them,' Maggie exclaimed as they got within a hundred yards of the bridge and the first lock onto the canal at Gargrave. 'It is! It's them, the *Rosie May* – that's the barge's name. I remember seeing it last time.'

Both girls quickened their pace and smiled at one another. The rain didn't matter now because on board that canal barge were letters from home and parcels for them both as well as news of their parents that they missed so much.

'Hello, hello, is there anybody there?' Maggie shouted as both girls descended the steep steps down to the flat canal towpath. The dark smoke of the barge's chimney hung in the air and Lizzie coughed as the taste of tarred coal hit the back of her throat. The barge doors were closed but along the dark green paintwork were pictures of other barges in bright colours and lavish flowers that brightened the coal-bearing barge on brighter days. Maggie and Lizzie looked through the small-paned windows and could see that both Molly and Sid were inside and watched as Molly made her way down the length of the barge and opened the cabin hatch to greet them.

'Girls, what are you doing out in this weather? You'll be to bury. Come in, come in and share a pot of tea,' she said as she put her head out of her snug cabin and looked at the two washed-out waifs, ushering them into their cramped living quarters.

Maggie struggled to climb on board the wooden-decked barge and Molly held her hand tight as Lizzie stood behind her and followed in her steps.

'What on earth have you been doing? You're struggling to come down our few steps into our cabin?' Sid asked as his wife gave both the girls a towel to dry their hair with and put a blackened metal kettle on the small stove that heated their living accommodations.

'I fell off a swing and twisted my ankle. It's a lot better than it was,' Maggie said as she sat down on a small bench at the side of the barge and rubbed her hair.

'She was showing off and going too high and the rope broke,' Lizzie said and grinned at her best friend as she dug her in the ribs with her elbow. 'You were and you know it!' Lizzie said and then gazed around the small space that Molly and Sid lived in. It was full of colourful pottery and ornaments reflecting their lifestyle on the canals. There was everything within that you would ever need to live your life on board: a table, two long benches on either side of the barge and shelves that secured plates, cups and other crockery. The stove kept everywhere warm and through a small hatchway Lizzie could see there were sleeping quarters. All was kept immaculate and felt homely.

'Did they take you for an X-ray? It might be broken,'

Molly asked as she passed Maggie and Lizzie each a colourfully painted mug filled with warm tea and urged both of them to drink.

'No, but they did call the doctor to see me. It's all right, it's mending now. It can't be broken else I wouldn't be able to walk.'

Molly and Sid looked at one another. At least Maggie had seen a doctor and that would have been expensive. 'They've been looking after you both, I hope? Your parents are worrying about you,' Molly said and leaned forward to look at both of the children.

'Yes, we're all right, but we miss home,' Lizzie said quietly and wiped a tear away from her eyes. 'It's not home but we're making the most of it.' She reached for Maggie's hand to squeeze.

Maggie and Lizzie took long drinks of the strong tea that they had been given and felt their stomachs churning as they thought about their packages from home that they knew Molly and Sid had for them. They needed to smell the odour of home on their clothes and read the loving words written by their mothers – anything that brought them closer to their parents and the busy city streets of home.

'Aye, well, we saw your parents and they have sent you both a parcel and their love. They miss you as much as you miss them. I think half of Liverpool is regretting sending their children away seeing as up to now there has been no need. Not a single blooming bomb dropped. A lot of fuss about nowt.' Maggie sighed and then stood up and made her way into the sleeping quarters.

Sid shook his head. 'That's my lass talking. She only knows this canal and to keep her family close to her. There's fighting over those seas and it will come here eventually, nothing's as sure. The government wouldn't be doing all it's doing if there wasn't any threat.' Sid lit his pipe with a spill from above the open stove and filled the cabin with the smell of strong tobacco as he sat back and puffed away.

'Stop frightening these lasses with your war talk. Now, this will be what you've come for. There's a parcel for each of you and a letter and I've spoken to your mams and I've promised them to make sure that you're all right every time we come through Gargrave.' Molly passed them each a brown paper parcel wrapped up with brown string and love and watched both their faces light up with delight. 'We are here for you. We've promised that to your mothers and fathers so don't be afraid to visit and ask us for anything. I wouldn't be able to stop worrying if my two lasses were living with strangers miles away from home. It's a good job that mine are both grown with families of their own and living up north.' Molly was worried as she looked at the faces of the two girls and knew that as soon as they got home, if not sooner, they would be opening their parcels.

'Thank you. We couldn't wait for your return. We've been watching most days for your barge.' Maggie held her parcel tightly. She didn't want to seem ungrateful but she now wanted to go home and read her letter and see what her mam had sent her.

'Have you finished your brews?' Molly asked and took

the cups away from them. 'Sid, give them both a bit of that toffee that I made and then they'll want to be on their way.' Molly pointed to a tin on the shelf with her other ornaments.

'It'll have your teeth out will this stuff. Mother's toffee is good but blinking chewy,' Sid said as he let both girls take a piece from the tin and watched as they both struggled to talk as well as eat the well-proportioned pieces of home-made toffee.

'Thank you, it's a real treat,' Lizzie said and nearly dripped some saliva out of her mouth as she chewed contentedly on the creamy syrupy mixture. 'But we had better go now. Nobody knows we're here and both houses will be wondering where we've got to.'

'We know, and the nights are drawing in, so you're best back where you belong. Now come and see us again if you can. We'll be here another day and then we'll be back on our way to Leeds. We'll return when we have another load to deliver in about a fortnight. Look out for us then if you need anything taken to your parents.' Molly smiled as she watched the two girls hug their parcels close to them and knew that she and Sid were doing right by the two homesick evacuees. They said their goodbyes to the girls and Maggie and Lizzie thanked them again before making their way off the barge.

'I've got to get home. Them at the vicarage will be wondering where I'm at,' Lizzie said, hearing the church clock chime four thirty and knowing she was going to be questioned as to where she had been till that time, especially now the nights were drawing in as Molly had pointed out.

'Then you go. I'll manage to walk up to the hall. They'll not be worried about how late I am, I can take my time,' Maggie said and tucked her parcel under her arm. 'I think I might tell them that we've made friends with Mr and Mrs Bryson and then they know what we're doing. They'll not be bothered anyway; nobody seems to be bothered about anything at the moment except what's going on at the farm and why the gatehouse is up for sale.' Maggie sighed. 'You will be all right, won't you?'

'Yes, but I'm going to run and I'm going to hide my parcel in the porch under my coat. I daren't tell them that we're friends with barge owners and that they're in touch with our parents. I'll be in bother enough with not helping with the church flowers.' Lizzie tucked her parcel under her arm and left Maggie to make her way back home, watching her limping slowly along the towpath as she took the road and sped back to the vicarage.

Lizzie quietly opened the porch door into the vicarage, hung her wet coat up on the coat hooks, and then quickly hid her parcel behind a huge terracotta pot that housed an aspidistra within it. She then tried to make her wet hair look respectable before she turned the door handle to enter the vicarage and tell her tale of helping Maggie home. Her legs felt like jelly as she passed the study next to the porch and realized that Reverend Brown, Dorothy, his wife, and Mrs Bridges were sitting waiting in the near darkness for her.

'So, you've decided to return, have you? Just where do you think you have been and why have you kept Mrs Bridges waiting when you knew that she was waiting for you?' Reverend Brown stood up and glared at Lizzie.

'I'm sorry, I was only walking Maggie home as she's struggling with her injured ankle,' Lizzie replied, blushing and hanging her head.

'Since when has your friend Maggie lived on a canal barge?' Reverend Brown towered over Lizzie and looked down at her, while Dorothy Brown shook her head and sneered. 'Mrs Bridges saw you both climb down the bank and board one of those deplorable canal barges. What business had you there? I will not have you associating with water rats or lying to me.'

'We did not. I just walked Maggie home by the canal just for a change, honest. We didn't go anywhere near a barge,' Lizzie stammered and didn't dare look at her accusers.

'But I think you did otherwise Mrs Bridges would not have said anything. I think you're lying, like all those of your religion do. I have tried to teach you better ways while you're with us, kindly and with patience, but I can see I have been too lenient.' Reverend Brown got hold of Lizzie's arm and escorted her out into the hallway. 'Go to your bedroom and expect me up to see you shortly. I expect an explanation or it will be the worse for you.'

'I might have been wrong,' Mrs Bridges said loud enough for Lizzie to hear as she felt tears welling up in her eyes. This was not how she had expected to be treated in a religious household. There had not been one ounce of love and compassion shown to her since her arrival and now it sounded as if she was going to be in for worse. The only thing that kept her spirits up was the parcel hidden by the front door and she prayed that it would not be found before she could retrieve it.

Lizzie's heart hammered as she heard Reverend Brown stomping up the stairs and she held her breath as he marched into her room. 'I will not be lied to and shown as a fool! Do you think that I would believe a snivelling waif from Liverpool over a trusted churchgoer and friend? We should never have agreed to take you in, especially knowing that you've been brought up Catholic. Well, I'll teach you that lying is the devil's way. Hold your hand out!'

Lizzie sobbed and held her hands behind her back defiantly as she shook her head and watched the vicar take a ruler out from his back pocket.

'Hand out now, or it will be worse!' Arthur Brown said in a low, hard voice, glaring at the young girl who he wished he and his wife had never taken into their home.

'No, I'll tell my mam and da and they'll come and sort you out!' Lizzie said, frightened to the core but determined to stand her ground.

'Very well then, you give me no option.' Reverend Arthur Brown grabbed hold of Lizzie and roughly sat down on the edge of the bed with her laid over his knee. He pulled her skirt up and her knickers down and started to cane her bottom with the ruler as she sobbed and screamed. Ten times the ruler went down, leaving welts and marks where he hit her before ordering her to stand up and make herself decent as he combed back his hair and stood up. 'You'll not be lying to me again and you can forget any supper tonight. Stay in your room until you repent. I don't want to see your face again this evening.'

Lizzie sat crumpled on the edge of her bed. She hated the vicar, she hated his wife and she hated the tell-tale Mrs Bridges. She wanted to go home and be with her proper parents, her parents that loved her, and she would not stay in her room. She had her parcel to retrieve before it was found and a letter to write home.

'You're late back from school? Did you struggle with your ankle?' Alice asked as Maggie entered the kitchen and took her sodden coat off before putting her parcel on the table and sitting down in the chair to rest her ankle.

'I did struggle but that's not the reason why I'm so late. Lizzie and I have become friends with an elderly married couple that travel up and down the canal from Leeds to Liverpool. They're moored up under the road bridge and we stopped to have tea with them,' Maggie said quite openly and watched as Alice, too busy with her own worries, just smiled at her.

'That's nice for you. Have they given you that as well?'

'Yes, and they gave Lizzie a parcel too. I'm going to go upstairs and see what's inside,' Maggie replied, glad that Alice went no deeper with her questioning as she went into the pantry. 'I'll see you at supper time, Alice.'

'Yes, all right. Mrs Perceval is having a lie down before supper; she's been busy all day. Tom butchered one of the pigs this morning, so the kitchen has been busy preparing the cuts. Sorry, I don't have the time to sit with you,' Alice yelled from within the pantry as she salted the flitch of bacon that Tom had placed in a large zinc brining bath.

'It's all right, Alice, I'm tired anyway.' Maggie rose from her chair and tucked the parcel under her arm; she couldn't wait any longer to see what was inside and to read news from home. Besides, nobody cared what went on in her life, even though she had told Alice what she had been doing that afternoon, she thought as she climbed the stairs with difficulty, sat on the edge of her bed and looked out of her bedroom window. The rain was lashing down and the leaves were blowing off the trees with force; it was grey, cold and miserable and there was little warmth in her room. Thank heavens she had news from home to cheer her up and a warmer coat hopefully, if her mother had remembered to send it. As she unwrapped the parcel, memories of home flooded over her and she held her woollen coat with velvet collar close to her as she pulled it out of its wrapping. She could smell home on it: her father's pipe and her mother's baking from when it was hung on the coat hooks between the kitchen and the small hallway. It was a stark reminder of how much she was loved and how much she missed her true home. Inside the coat was a pair of blue knitted mittens that her mother had made for her and a pixie-style hat that matched. Then she picked up the letter which included a three-penny bit inside it with the words *get some toffees* written right at the bottom. Then she read about the continuing romance between her brother Raymond and the girl her mother had no time for, her father's work at the docks and how food stocks were starting to be affected by the war, that Brenda Mathews had run away with the milkman and that the baker on the corner was being stingy with his bread loaves. But it was the last couple of lines that made her think and feel happy as she read, *Annie and I have become good friends with Molly and Sid Bryson. If you need anything at all, you just have to ask them. They will do whatever is needed to keep you happy if they can.*

Bless her mother, Maggie thought. If only she knew how good it was just to hear news from home through Molly and Sid and to know that they had not been abandoned by families that cared not one jot for them.

Lizzie waited until the vicarage lay still and sleeping and then quiet as a mouse she dared to sneak downstairs and rescue her parcel from behind the plant. She curled up with the bed-sheets around her and unwrapped her parcel, revealing a new warm cardigan, mittens, bag of sweets and the longed-for letter. The ink ran as her tears wet the letter and she sobbed as she remembered the look on the vicar's face as he had caned her and compared it to the kindness of her father's face. Her father had never hit her, ever. He might have threatened it but he never would have carried it out. The threat, he knew, was enough. She read the words of love within the letter and knew she had to go home, no matter how she got there.

In the next-door bedroom Reverend Brown lay awake in his bed. His thoughts were troubled. He had enjoyed spanking the young evacuee a little too much. He only hoped that Mrs Bridges would not report him to the diocese for the hard words that he had given to the young Lizzie, otherwise his leadership of the parish would be reviewed yet again. Why could people not see that if you gave the devil an inch, he would make a mockery of your life? Damn the girl; damn his temper and his urges. He must fight them with all his might.

Chapter 19

'What on earth is that coming up our driveway?' Rebecca Bradley said as she sipped her morning tea and looked out of the window.

'I think it's a tractor, ma'am, and it looks like it's his lordship driving it,' Baxter said as they both stared out at the view of the huge-wheeled green tractor coming up the driveway towards the hall.

'It's ploughing the driveway up with its wheels! Look at the trail it's leaving behind it!' Rebecca put her cup and saucer down and ran out onto the patio and down the steps to go and talk to her husband as he drove the monster of a machine towards her and stopped the engine. Throwing his leg over the gearstick, he jumped down from the seat and smiled at the expression on Rebecca's face.

'Well, what do you think? There's six of these just been delivered to the Skipton War Ag offices, brand new from off the Fordson production line for use by farmers in the area to make their land more profitable. The Fordson N in forest green so that any planes in the air can't spot them as well as the earlier orange model. She's lovely,' Lord Bradley said and stood next to the still-warm engine. 'She can do in an hour what it takes two horses a day to do. You should see when it's ploughing. I've already watched Dick Fawcett plough two of his fields with it this morning. He's planting them with kale to help feed his stock.'

'I can never understand why men get so excited over engines and machines. You've obviously not seen the mess that the tracks have left coming up the drive,' Rebecca said curtly.

'That's nothing, my dear; just think what we can do with this beauty on the land that we have left. Old Tom and the lad took ages ploughing the few acres that have already been dug up by his horses but this will save us all time this coming spring and we'll be helping the war effort. All the farmers in the district are going to be offered the use of one and the help of a man that can drive it if they can't. It's a new farming revolution, my dear.'

'It's noisy, smelly and makes a mess.' Rebecca turned to go back inside.

'Our Charlotte will be learning to drive one and she'll have to learn to repair it as well if she's going to survive in the Land Army. Women are going to have to learn men's jobs, Rebecca, if we are to win this war,' Maurice said sharply.

'What war? I have not heard a German plane go over our heads, nor has anywhere been bombed yet. We're

251

safe on these shores.' Rebecca stood defiant in her knitted two-piece and pearls hanging around her neck.

'Now, you know that's not true. Why do you think Michael isn't writing like he used to? Nor does Charlotte come to that. They're both busy doing their part for this country, fighting one way or another to keep the Hun from invading our shores and to keep us fed. Just because we live in this quiet backwater does not mean the war will not affect us,' Maurice said with feeling.

Rebecca walked back into the house, lit a cigarette, and watched as her husband came in and sat in his usual chair. She was tired of his continuous working and the lack of attention he had shown her of late, plus he had taken his time to tell her exactly how bad the family finances were. Life was tedious with no parties or friends visiting.

'I think I might take some time away and visit my sister in London. I'm bored and you're wrapped up in the war effort,' Rebecca said and looked at Maurice who crossed his legs and sighed.

'Really, Rebecca, London! Have you any idea what the capital is like at the moment? It's in chaos! Air-raid warnings are sounded at every minute of the day, the museums and art galleries are closed and their exhibits are taken to safety. There are barrage balloons throughout the city, ordinary people are hoarding food and there is a lack of it in most shops, and you want to go there!' Maurice sighed and stared at his wife. 'Is this all because I've put a stop to our social life? Because if it is, then you should count your blessings and realize just what you have.'

'What I've got! That's just it, I have nothing. I have a husband who doesn't give me the time of day and a house that the bank owns. Then there are our two children, one of whom is so wild no one can control her and a son who cannot be bothered to even write to his mother who worries about him every minute of the day.' Rebecca stubbed her cigarette out and folded her arms. 'I'll catch the last train from Skipton and telephone my sister to tell her I'm going to be staying with her for a while. I need a change of scenery. I'll get Robinson to take me to the station in the Rolls rather than bother you.'

'Rebecca, don't be so stupid. You don't want to go there.' Maurice got up on his feet and grabbed Rebecca's arm, which she pulled out of his grasp.

'I'm going, Maurice, and then you can play all you want with your tractors and suchlike. I'll only be gone a week or two, just to get some taste of life, the life that no longer happens here. Now, I'm going to pack.' Rebecca took a long glance at Maurice and noticed the hurt in his eyes. She didn't care as her love for him had long since died and now was the time to go back to the life she had left behind in London all those years ago, war or no war.

'Catching the late train down to the big smoke? Does his lordship know?' Jeff Robinson asked Rebecca as he opened the back door of the Rolls that she had sent Alice to tell him to drive for the first time in a while.

'I am, not that it's any business of yours, Robinson,'

Rebecca said and climbed in the back seat as he placed her suitcases in the boot.

'So, you've had enough too? I'll not be far behind you. I aim to be gone by next week, so that will suit him.' Robinson looked in the rear-view mirror at Rebecca as he drove off down the drive. 'Bit of a bad time to go to London, though. I think I'll be heading north – less chance of being found and having to join up.'

'At least there will be some life in London, Robinson. There's nothing here for me any more.' Rebecca sighed as she sat back in her seat.

'Not like there used to be, when I first came to the hall. We had some good nights together.' Robinson smiled and looked back at the woman who was his mistress in more ways than one.

'Those days have well and truly gone and you got greedy and wanted a younger model, like my daughter,' Rebecca said sharply.

'Aye, and you made yourself available to that strutting cock in copper's uniform. The games we play, milady. We are both selfish, callous buggers but the world would be lost without us now, wouldn't it, Lady Bradley?'

'Most definitely, Robinson. I wish you luck and if the army does catch you up, keep that bonny head down and safe,' Rebecca said, giving a wink to her shared lover.

'Aye, I don't know. Her ladyship's gone and caught the train to London. London, for Lord's sake! Doesn't she know there's a war going on?' Mrs Perceval said as the kitchen staff and Maggie sat down at the table.

'She gets bored. His lordship is a little steady,' Alice said and smiled at Maggie as she looked sullen while she ate a jam sandwich that Alice had quickly given her on her return from school. 'What's up with you then, Miss Sunshine? You look as if you've lost a sixpence and found a ha'penny.'

'Lizzie hasn't been at school today. I'm just hoping that she's all right,' Maggie said and looked down at her feet. Lizzie wasn't the only worry on her mind. She had walked along the canal bank back home and had realized that the *Rosie May* had gone, along with Molly and Sid.

'Did you not call on her on your way back home to make sure she was all right? The vicar wouldn't have minded,' Alice asked, concerned at the glum face of the usually cheerful Maggie.

'No, he'd not have wanted me to. If she's not there tomorrow, I'll call. She was all right yesterday but we both got wet through so perhaps she's caught a cold or chill,' Maggie replied before finishing her two small squares of jam sandwich that just helped fill her until supper time.

'You were sodden too, and what were you telling me about a canal boat? I'm afraid I was a little busy yesterday with the pig-killing.' Alice smiled as she sat down next to Maggie. 'Can you smell the black pudding being baked in the oven? It smells lovely and when you eat it you tend to forget that it's made from the pig's blood.'

'Oh, it doesn't matter about the canal boat, it's gone now. Is black pudding really made of pig's blood? I don't think I want any, thank you.' Maggie pulled a face and hoped that she would not be made to eat it.

'It's an acquired taste but Lord Bradley says mine is the best made in Yorkshire. He likes big pieces of fat in it and plenty of pearl barley and sage. Puts hairs on your chest!' Mrs Perceval said as she listened in to the conversation. 'That and my savoury ducks; you can't beat those: little patties of pig cheek, liver and onion, wrapped up in the pig's caul. Gorgeous they are.' Cook laughed as Maggie pulled a face. 'You'll not be pulling a face like that once you've tried them.'

Maggie didn't know what a pig's caul was but she wasn't going to ask. It was like a cannibal's feast in the kitchen and she had seen and heard enough as she stood up from her chair, wincing slightly as she put her weight on the still-fragile ankle. 'I'm going up to my room and I'm going to write to my mam and da, tell them that my ankle is mending and that I'm back at school.'

'All right, my dear. Supper at six, with a special big portion of black pudding just for you.' Mrs Perceval laughed and Alice shook her head, knowing the cook was having her fun with the young girl.

Maggie limped up the stairs and sat on her bedroom chair next to her washstand. She pulled the writing pad out of the small drawer. She was worried about Lizzie not being at school, especially after they both were late back yesterday and carrying parcels sent to them from home. Surely she couldn't be in that much trouble that she would be kept from school for those two things?

Maggie picked up her pen and started to write. It would have to go in the hall's post now or wait a fortnight to go back with the Brysons on their barge. It was best that it got posted, she thought as she chewed the end of the pen thoughtfully.

Dear Mam and Da and Raymond,

Thank you for sending me my coat and lovely hat and gloves. I'll be warm now because it is freezing here. Lizzie and I had tea with Mr and Mrs Bryson inside their canal barge. It was full of pots and pans and really homely. It was nice to talk to someone who knew you. They have gone on to Leeds now but we will see them on their way back.

I fell off a swing last week and hurt my ankle. The doctor that Lord Bradley got said it was just sprained but it still hurts a little. I didn't go to school all last week because I couldn't manage to walk there but I'm all right now, so don't worry. Lizzie wasn't at school today so I hope that she is all right. I don't think the vicar and his wife are used to children and Lizzie is not liking living there. Her mam will have probably told you.

Archie, who came and stayed at the hall as an evacuee just like me, has gone to live with Tom, the stable and odd-job man, instead of living here. I don't think he had a good home but Tom and his wife love him, even if his mam doesn't.

I'm on my own now here at the hall, and Lady Bradley has just left to go to London for some nightlife, whatever that is? Sometimes I get lonely

and I wish I was back home. I miss you all so much.
But don't worry, I'm all right.
   All my love,
   Maggie xxx

Maggie sniffed as a big tear dropped on her kisses, making them smudge on the paper as she folded it to place it in the envelope. She was terribly lonely and her ankle hurt, Lizzie was not at school and all she wanted was her mother's arms to hold her and comfort her. In her past letters, she had tried to sound chirpy but it was hard.

Lizzie heard her bedroom door being opened and looked around to see Dorothy Brown standing with a supper tray in her hand. A boiled egg was covered with an egg cosy and a slice of toast was next to it, along with the customary pot of tea.

'Now, Lizzie, have you calmed down any? Reverend Brown says that if you have, you can go back to school tomorrow. He couldn't let you go today because he thought you were hysterical from being reprimanded last night for lying.' Dorothy put her tray down on the small table next to Lizzie's bed and stood with her hands on her hips.

Lizzie said nothing. She didn't want the boiled egg, she didn't want anything from the Browns, and she wanted to go home.

'If you go back to school tomorrow, you must promise not to say anything about the words and actions that Reverend Brown had to deliver to you.' Dorothy Brown sat down on the bed next to Lizzie and tried to smile and put Lizzie at ease. 'I do hope that you realize that we could not possibly have anyone that lies under our roof. That is why I'm afraid he lost his temper. He is usually such a mild-mannered man, as I am sure you know.'

Lizzie hung her head and said nothing. Her buttocks hurt where the side of the ruler had caught her and she wasn't about to forgive the vicar or his wife for giving her a punishment that even her parents would not have given her for telling a little white lie.

'Promise me, Lizzie, that you will not say anything to anyone about the incident. Please promise me and then you can perhaps return to school tomorrow. You must be missing your friend Maggie.' Dorothy reached for her hand but Lizzie pulled it away from her grasp.

'Lizzie, promise?' Dorothy said firmly and glared at Lizzie, wanting her answer. 'Promise, Lizzie, otherwise Reverend Brown will be angry with us both.'

'I promise,' Lizzie said in a whisper and realized at that moment that Dorothy Brown was as scared of her husband as she was, regardless of him being a man of the cloth.

'Good, then that is that. Now, eat your supper before it goes cold and let's not hear another word about our little misunderstanding. School it is then in the morning and remember, not a word.' Dorothy Brown stood up and smiled. 'You can come down and join us for breakfast as usual in the morning. I'll make you fried bread; I know you like that and I have some crusts to use up.'

* * *

Lizzie sat silently and did not dare look at the vicar; he sat back, read the paper, and ignored both Lizzie and his wife, as she made sure Lizzie had her lunch with her and her usual coat on her before going to school.

Lizzie hadn't dared take her winter coat out from under her mattress where she had hidden it after her mother had sent it to her and so was sent off to school cold and fretful about her secret being found.

'Now, you'll remember what I told you? Don't say anything to anyone,' Dorothy said as she opened the front door for Lizzie to go to school.

Lizzie nodded her head and said nothing. She wanted to go to school to see Maggie and tell her of her ordeal no matter what Dorothy Brown said. She wanted the comfort of her friend and for her to understand that she could no longer stay at the vicarage.

Maggie was standing at the school gates watching for her best friend. She was lost without her at school. There were local children that she mixed with but nobody was as close to her as Lizzie, so when she saw her walking up the road towards the school gates she was relieved.

'Oh, Lizzie, I thought that you were ill, or even worse. Are you all right? Why weren't you at school yesterday?' Maggie asked and looked at Lizzie with love and care.

'I'm all right. I couldn't come yesterday, and the vicar didn't let me,' Lizzie said, feeling like crying.

'What do you mean, he wouldn't let you?' Maggie asked, concerned for her sad-looking friend.

The school bell sounded as Lizzie was about to answer

and she put her head down, whispering to Maggie, 'I'll tell you later. We'd better get on with our lessons and I don't want anyone else to hear.'

All through that morning, Maggie kept glancing at Lizzie. She was worried about her. The spirit that her best friend had always shown back home had gone. She had been the one that was going to relish a life in the countryside but it had not happened. Neither had enjoyed the open countryside as they would have wanted to. Finally, the break-time bell went and Lizzie got up from her seat and summoned Maggie to join her.

'What's up, Liz? Did they play heck with you for being late home the other night? Did you have to tell them that you've had a parcel from home, although I notice you're still in your old coat?' Maggie said as Lizzie slipped her arm through hers and made her way to the block of toilets along the school wall.

'It was worse than that, Maggie. Mrs Bridges, who I promised to help with the church flowers, had seen us going into the barge to see the Brysons and she'd told the Browns. I made it worse by lying but I wasn't going to tell them everything.' Lizzie opened the green-painted wooden door into one of the whitewashed toilets that smelled of disinfectant and just had room for one person within it but Lizzie pulled Maggie in behind her.

'What are you doing? You know we should never share toilets,' Maggie said and looked around her as Lizzie shut and bolted the door.

'I know, but I want you to see how bad my bottom is after he hit it. Not that I'm supposed to tell anyone,'

Lizzie said as she pulled her pants down around her ankles and bent over to show Maggie the red marks where Reverend Brown had hit her with the ruler.

'Lizzie, he didn't, did he? I mean, he shouldn't. Oh, he's walloped you. Not even our fathers would have done that.' Maggie looked at the redness of Lizzie's bottom and the diminishing marks where the ruler had been laid on more heavily. 'Your mam and da would go mad if they knew. I think you should tell the teacher because he can't do that.' Maggie breathed in and thought about what her best friend had gone through and shook her head. 'Tell the headmistress. She keeps in touch with the evacuation board. She might be able to get you rehomed or even sent to live with me now Archie has left the hall.'

'No, no, I can't do that! I promised that I wouldn't say what he'd done and he'll be even angrier if he finds out I've said something. Please don't say anything, it'll only make things worse.' Lizzie started to unlock the toilet door only to find her teacher standing outside.

'What do you think you girls are doing sharing a toilet? You know the rules, one at a time,' Miss Sanderson said sternly to the two of them.

'I'm sorry, Miss Sanderson, but Lizzie was upset and wanted to show me the marks left on her bottom from the vicar hitting her with a ruler on Monday evening. They're still there if you want to see.' Maggie pushed Lizzie forward and looked with concern at Miss Sanderson.

'Is this true, Lizzie? Has the vicar been reprimanding

you with such force? Surely not?' Miss Sanderson said with kindness but shock in her voice.

'I promised him I wouldn't say anything, but yes, he has, Miss Sanderson. He hit me with a ruler ten times on my bottom just because I was late returning home from school after calling at a friend's,' Lizzie replied and was near to crying.

'Dear me, that is quite disconcerting. I cannot quite believe it of Reverend Brown; I will have a word with the headmistress and see what she says.'

Maggie suddenly said, 'She's not happy living there with the vicar and his wife. She could come and live at the hall with me, now Archie has gone to live at the farmhouse with Tom.'

'Archie is living at the farmhouse now? I don't think anyone has informed us here at the school and as for Lizzie going to live at the hall, that would be for the authorities to decide. I'll go and see the head now and tell her all this. Lizzie, if she needs to see you, I will let you know.' Miss Sanderson walked off shaking her head. The evacuees were more of a problem in every school within the Dales than the everyday local children. It was never-ending.

'Miss Sanderson, do you think that Reverend Brown would hit a young girl across the bottom with a ruler? The girls are telling you anything so that they can be together.' Mrs Butterworth, the headmistress of Gargrave School, sighed.

'But they said so and I have no reason not to believe

them. Lizzie Taylor does seem very upset and she's struggling in the classroom at the moment.' Miss Sanderson hoped that the head would ask to see Lizzie and at least see if there was any sign of her being abused.

'It's a load of tosh, Miss Sanderson. These city children have a vivid imagination and will do anything to get what they want. The poor vicar. He's such a meek and mild soul. He wouldn't lift a little finger to hurt them.' Mrs Butterworth shook her head and started to look through the many exercise books that she had yet to correct.

'I'm sorry, Mrs Butterworth, I should have known better. I'm sure you're right,' Miss Sanderson said and walked towards the door. 'Do you know that Archie Brannigan is no longer living at the hall? That he's living with Tom Parker at the hall's farmhouse?'

'I do. Archie brought a letter in from his lordship saying that it had been arranged with his mother and that she was happy for him to do so. That is the problem, Miss Sanderson, Maggie wants someone at the hall with her. Mark my words, Lizzie Taylor is as happy as Larry living with the vicar. Now, go and ring the bell to summon the end of playtime. They've already had five minutes too long because of this waste of my time,' Mrs Butterworth said sharply. She dismissed Miss Sanderson, who closed the door behind her.

'She doesn't believe us,' Maggie whispered to Lizzie as Miss Sanderson shot them a glance and then asked everybody to open their reading books. 'They think we're lying.'

'It doesn't matter. I'm glad. I didn't want to show my bottom to Mrs Butterworth and it would only have caused bother anyway.' Lizzie sighed. 'I'm going to tell them that my winter coat and things my mam sent me came posted to you at the hall. Is that all right? Else I will have to wear my old Mackintosh all winter.'

'Yes, but if he wallops you again, you say,' Maggie said and looked with sympathy at her best friend.

'I will, I promise. Thanks for being my friend, Maggie; I don't know what I'd do without you.'

'We'll get through this, Lizzie, as long as we stick together,' Maggie assured her.

Chapter 20

Maurice Bradley sat back in his easy armchair and swirled the warming glass of brandy around as he read the letter from his wife. She was, despite the signs of war being all around her, having the time of her life. Wining and dining with her friends in high society regardless of the working classes going hungry and fearing for their lives. That was Rebecca to a tee, he thought as he got to the crux of the letter that had been sent from a classy penthouse in Chelsea and belonged to her old friend Charles Seymour.

I am afraid, my dear Maurice, I feel that any love we ever had for one another has well and truly gone. I wish for you to grant me a divorce, as I know that you are probably as unhappy as I am.

The truth was that she was not prepared to live with a working man with little money. She had always been one for enjoying life to the fullest and now she had decided to look elsewhere for her lifestyle to continue. Charles Seymour had always been lurking in the background with God knows how many other lovers and suitors but he was the one that she always ran to when her luck was down or she felt unwanted. Well, this time she could stay with him, because Maurice too had come to the end of his tether in a marriage where he had always been the faithful one and had turned a blind eye to her wanderings. In a way he was thankful all was coming to an end and perhaps now, in his fifties, he could find a bit of peace in his life. He put the letter down and sighed. She could have a divorce and she could have what money she could get out of him. It would be a relief. The past few months had made him look hard at his life. He might be the lord of the manor, but he was a lord with no money and it was time to adjust that. The sale of Hawith Farm had gone through without a glitch and now with Rebecca about to leave him the next step could be carried out without any complaint or annoyance from her. It was time to put it into action. However, he loved the woman and always would, no matter what she did or how she hurt him.

Jeff Robinson packed the Austin car that he had bought on the cheap at a garage in Skipton to the gunnels with the household items and personal possessions that he had accumulated over the years. He was leaving under the cover of the night; he wasn't going to say farewells to people he knew were glad to see the back of him and he had no time for. He was glad to close that chapter in his life and start a new one in his new position over the border in Dumfries as a chauffeur to an elderly woman who hadn't even asked for a reference, thank the Lord. He wandered through the house where so many memories had been made: the death of his wife, who he had never really loved; the times he had spent with both Lady Bradley and her scatter-brained daughter. Both were desperately in need of love and a real man. Aristocracy might have the property but that was all they had, or at least it was in the case of Maurice Bradley. Ignorant, arrogant fool that he was. He placed his chauffeur's cap on his head and took one last look at the house he had at one time been happy within. Time to move on, he thought as he locked the door and put the key through the letterbox. If they hadn't got a spare key up at the big house, it was their lookout. They'd have to break the door down.

'Are you right, lass? Have you got everything?' Jeff said and smiled at Alice as she nodded. 'Let us be away then. A fresh life for us both,' he whispered, kissing her on the cheek before opening the car door for her. 'Scotland here we come.'

'Yes, my love, a new life as husband and wife, away from anyone who knows us and away from any scandal.' Alice smiled as she climbed in the car and then sighed. Tomorrow morning there would be hell to pay when they all realized that she had run off with Jeff, but she didn't care. A whole new life was in front of her with a man she knew loved her and would look after her. The only one she felt guilty about leaving without a goodbye was the little evacuee, Maggie. She would have nobody at the hall now to look after her. Still, that was not her problem and never had been. She would have to take her chances like the rest of the evacuees. 'Let's go. A whole new life, and hopefully a happy one.'

'Yes, let's put this place and the scandal behind us. To Scotland, my love, and to hell with the lot of them.' Jeff turned the ignition. It was definitely time to move on but how long he would be with Alice was another matter.

The shock of finding Alice not in her room and the fact that she had left a letter saying exactly what she thought of the running of the hall and treatment of her beloved Jeff had been met with disdain in the hall's kitchens.

'Well, I always did think there was something between them. The little hussy. You'd have thought butter wouldn't melt in her mouth but I knew she was a deep one.' Mrs Perceval sat and looked across at Baxter as they both enjoyed their morning break of ten minutes before starting preparing for lunch and dinner for later in the day. 'But I'd have thought that she would have known better than to run away with that cad. He's a chancer, that's what he is. He'll break her heart,' Mrs Perceval said and drank deep into her cup.

'He's more than that, Mrs Perceval. He's a home-breaker and I always think that his wife's death was more than suspicious. Why was Miss Charlotte involved and why did they get in Lady Rebecca's friend in the police force when our local bobby was capable? I've never said anything before but things were highly suspicious,' Baxter said, watching the growing horror on Mrs Perceval's face.

'You're not suggesting . . . ?' Mrs Perceval exclaimed.

'I think Miss Charlotte had a lot to do with it, but it's not for me to say, especially if we need to keep our jobs,' Baxter said and shook his head. 'There was just something not right about the whole carry-on.' Baxter sat back in his chair and looked peeved. 'I never thought that I'd be going around with a feather duster rather than greeting people and serving. Times are strange. The days of parties and entertaining have well and truly gone, just like our deep-thinking Alice.'

'Aye, they have. I don't make or bake half that I used to do. Which is a good job because some food is becoming scarce with this war. The days of cooks and servants are disappearing, I don't doubt. Let's hope that Lady Rebecca returns shortly as she always brings life to this old hall,' Ada Perceval said with a sigh.

'Well now, I don't think she will. She sent a telegram this morning to his lordship requesting most of her clothes to be sent to her down in London. I've to pack and see to them this afternoon. Something is afoot and it will only be bad news, I have no doubt, for you, Millie and me. She's never sent for all her belongings before. I fear the worst. We are a dying breed, Mrs Perceval, a dying breed.'

'You're not saying that you think she's left his lordship, are you? She would never do that, surely?' Ada Perceval looked shocked.

'She likes the good life does Lady Rebecca. She'll be bored up here now. Both children have flown the nest and, to be honest, I don't think his lordship is exactly rolling in it.' Baxter shrugged his shoulders. 'It wouldn't surprise me if his lordship calls it a day and leaves here. After all, both you and I know this place requires some money spending on it. Plus, would you pay for staff that you don't need and keep heated rooms that are very rarely used?'

'Dear God, I hope that you're wrong. I still need my job. Just another few years and then I've got my eye on one of the almshouses in Long Preston. My sister lives there and I've always fancied living near her.'

'Well, Ada, I must admit, I've been a bit of a dark horse and I've been saving for that rainy day. After all, I have lived here for the past thirty-five years and have had the chance to save enough to buy myself a nice little cottage if it comes to having to leave. I've been a butler long enough and I want my own life when I'm in my dotage.'

'Heavens, the stuff that's been going on around here is nobody's business of late! Everything's changing. Although when Tom told me he had bought the farm and some of the land, I did wonder what was going on. I haven't seen anyone looking around the gatehouse yet, but it wouldn't surprise me if that Jeff had been putting off the viewers just to get his own back. Spiteful, that's what he could be. Alice won't be with him long, he'll just be using her, poor devil,' Ada said and looked around the kitchen at her empire for many a year.

'Yes, I'm personally glad that he's gone. I once caught him sneering at me in that way that he had and I've never liked him since. Anyway, never mind, let's go about our business with decorum and support Lord Maurice no matter what the future holds.' Baxter pushed his chair back.

'Too true, Mr Baxter. We will mind our own business and carry on until we're told different. Now, would cold tongue sandwiches with a touch of mustard be to your liking for lunch?'

'Certainly, Ada, couldn't wish for anything better,' Baxter said and lightly touched her hand with his. He had always admired the straight-talking cook but had never dared show his affection for her. Perhaps it was time to do so, he thought as he picked up the duster and shouted for Millie. He was far above dusting and polishing; that was the maid's job, no matter how short staffed they were.

Maurice stood in the kitchen of the gatehouse and looked around him. He had picked up the key from the tiled floor and memories of the night when Robinson's wife had been found dead at the bottom of the stairs flooded over him. That was the start of the end of his life with Rebecca; he had known there and then that she had been unfaithful to him as she wormed her way around her lover of a detective. She had never been faithful in all fairness. No matter how wealthy or what property he owned, it would never have been enough for Rebecca. She was a society girl, even though now her looks were declining and age was against her. Well, this time it was over. He would send her wardrobe of clothes down to

London and his solicitor would draw up divorce proceedings. Along with the spare house key, Maurice picked up Robinson's daily newspaper, which he had not cancelled in his haste to leave or perhaps intending to leave the bill unpaid. He would soon find out once he walked down to the newspaper shop in Gargrave. He picked it up and looked at the headlines. U Boat attacks HMS Nelson while Winston Churchill and Charles Forbes on board. It had been a near-miss but could have resulted in disaster. The war was escalating, there was no peace in sight, and Maurice had been there once before and had never quite recovered from his time leading men to fight in the trenches of the Somme. He still had nightmares, seeing the young soldiers' faces that he had sent over the top to their deaths when he was in charge of a battalion. Now, he queried the sense in it and was racked with despair reading of Hitler's rages of war and his hatred of the Jews. Did the world never learn? he thought as he went into the main living room of the gatehouse and looked around him. Possessions and status meant little to him, unlike Rebecca. It was time to make changes to his life. He would talk to his son Michael and hope that he would keep safe while flying in the RAF, and buy the wayward Charlotte a home of her own, to hopefully settle down within. He only hoped that they would all listen to him.

Chapter 21

'I don't know what's going on at the hall, but Alice wasn't about this morning,' Maggie said as she and Lizzie sat on the school wall together. 'Mrs Perceval was in a real bad mood and all and she had forgotten to make my breakfast. Not that I was bothered, I can feed myself nowadays.'

'She's perhaps just gone into Skipton on the bus or something,' Lizzie replied, not really worried about what Alice got up to. She was more concerned that she had been cross-questioned again and again by the Browns about exactly how she had come about the winter coat that she was now daring to wear.

'No, the bus doesn't go that early,' Maggie said and kicked her feet against the wall.

'Do you think I'm bothered about Alice? All you think about is what's going on in the hall,' Lizzie said with a sharpness in her voice that took Maggie by surprise.

'I'm only telling you what's happening,' Maggie said and looked at her friend.

'I'm sorry, it's just that all I do is worry about if I'm doing this right or doing this wrong, did I say something I shouldn't. And since I told them that my mam sent my coat to you at the hall, I'm frightened to death that they'll find out the truth and stop us from seeing the Brysons. It's the only proper contact I have with home because I'm sure that he or she opens my letters from Mam and Da. They're never sealed as they should be and they always act harder towards me every time a letter arrives.' Lizzie stopped herself from crying even though she could have burst into tears so easily. She was living on her nerves all the time and it was starting to show.

'I'm sorry, Lizzie. I twitter on about everything and it is all nothing compared to your worries. Is the vicar no better with you? I can't understand him being so hard.'

'No, neither he nor his wife are. I'm so scared that the teachers will tell them what we said. My heart goes into my mouth every time I see one or the other of them go past the school, just in case a teacher catches them and tells them.' Lizzie sighed.

'They're not going to do that. They didn't believe us anyway. The Brysons are long gone and they'll probably be back in Leeds by now, but they'll soon return. Did your mam put in your letter that they'll bring and take anything from us each time they pass through this way?' Maggie asked and then looked up as she saw Archie making his way to them both from the other side of the playground.

'Yes, she did in the one the Brysons gave me, but with the ones that she posts to me there's always a line or two crossed out in her letters and I can't make out what she's written. That's another reason why I think my letters are being read. But shush for now, I don't want Archie to know else he'll only tell everyone.' Lizzie lifted her head to look at the boy.

'Hey up, you two!' Archie sniggered. 'I bet that there's fun and games at the hall today!' Archie shouted, sounding more and more like Tom.

'What do you mean, Archie?' Maggie said as Lizzie gave a big sigh.

'Well, Tom and I were wandering back into the house before it was even light after setting some rabbit snares and we saw all that was going on at the gatehouse. That Jeff was loading a car that he'd got from somewhere with everything he could possibly push into it. Then running down the road comes Alice with her bags packed too. They've done a moonlight flit together. I bet you Alice hadn't told anybody at the hall that she was off.' Archie grinned and then felt in his pocket for a humbug that he had forgotten about and was covered in fluff as he placed it in his mouth.

'She can't have! Alice can't have gone? She never said anything to me and how could she run away with a rat like Jeff Robinson?' Maggie said, looking upset. 'There's only Alice that ever listens to me. There's nobody at the hall that I can talk to now.'

'Well, she's buggered off and you'll not be seeing her again. Which is quite a pity, unlike seeing the back of Jeff Robinson. Tom and Ethel say that he's a right wrong'en and that it's good riddance to bad rubbish.'

'There hasn't been Lady Rebecca about of late either. That big hall with hardly anybody living in it, and it's so cold now as they hardly have any heating. I'd give anything to be back in my mam and da's little terrace,' Maggie said and felt a wave of homesickness come over her. Alice and she had bonded out of everybody at the hall so she thought that at least she would have said goodbye to her.

'Aye, well, from what we know at Tom and Ethel's, she's buggered off to London and she's not likely to be coming back. It's all gone to pot since I left. I'm glad that I'm where I am. All warm, fed and looked after so well by Ethel, I never want to be anywhere else but with them two.' Archie looked at the crestfallen faces of his two friends and knew that just for once he had been the lucky one. 'Right, I'm off. I'm going to have a game of marbles with Jim Todd before the bell rings, but I thought I'd come and tell you the news first.'

Both girls watched as a more confident Archie walked across the schoolyard with his hands in his newly made pair of corduroy trousers and a striped V-neck pullover that Ethel had knitted for her young lodger.

'At least he's happy,' Lizzie said and squeezed Maggie's hand knowing that the news of Alice leaving would have upset her friend.

'All's wrong with the world,' Mrs Perceval growled as she waited for the potatoes to boil. 'Look at that pan. I used to have to make ten times the amount. There's nobody here to cook for.'

Maggie had come back to a kitchen up in arms. Poor Millie, who never did have much to say, was hiding out of the way from Ada Perceval, whose face was as red as a beetroot after finding out that Alice had well and truly left, as well as Lady Rebecca, leaving Maggie to wash up the few dishes that had already been used.

'Nobody gives a damn about here in the kitchen. We're always the last to know anything. If it wasn't for Baxter, I'd know nothing. I'm like one of those mushrooms there, always in the dark and surrounded by you know what!' She pulled out a perfectly cooked chicken and mushroom pie that could feed half of Gargrave. 'Well, everybody will just have to have chicken pie for two nights on the trot, because I'm not wasting it!'

Baxter came back into the kitchen with an empty soup dish and stood at the side of Mrs Perceval after serving Lord Maurice alone in the dining room with the first course. 'Please, Mrs Perceval, don't get so stressed. I can hear your voice in the hallway.'

'Well, it is all going to the dogs, Mr Baxter. I'm just a little bit annoyed.'

'I know, but you losing your temper is not going to sort anything. There's a lot worse happening in the world. We're lucky in this little backwater, believe me. Now, is the main course ready? His lordship is waiting and he too seems a little agitated. It must be because of Alice and Robinson leaving.'

'It is and once he's had his dinner, we can have the same for our supper,' Mrs Perceval said, placing plain boiled potatoes, broccoli and carrots from the garden in a tureen and slicing the pie onto a plate ready for serving. 'Good enough for the King of England,' she said and licked the serving spoon as Baxter took the tray and walked with his usual elegance up the stairs to the dining room.

'Stuffy old devil. He always looks after himself; I could complain about him many a time.' She grinned and smiled as she watched Baxter leaving. He always looked after her in his own way, she thought, as she started to stir the custard for his lordship's dessert.

'Did Alice not say anything about her leaving, even to you, Mrs Perceval?' Maggie asked and started drying the few dishes that she had washed.

'Not a word, not a single word. To think I got that lass her job and she didn't even have the courtesy to tell me she was off. Did she think that I could have given a damn if she'd told me she was running off with that blaggard Robinson? I might have told her that she would live to regret it, but that's all I would have said,' Mrs Perceval moaned and stirred her custard. She was hurt more than surprised when she had found the cutting note left on her bed-sheets. 'The things she said about us all were beyond belief, calling me a dragon and Millie a milksop. If I ever see that girl again, I will give her a piece of my mind.'

Maggie got on with drying the pots and kept quiet. Alice had been right but the truth hurt and there was no need for her to say it.

Mrs Perceval looked up at Baxter as he came back in the kitchen. 'The custard isn't ready yet, he'll just have to wait for his pudding. He must have fair gulped down his dinner.'

'He's not ready for his dessert quite yet. However, he would like to see all of us after he has finished his evening meal,' Baxter said, looking quite shaken and his complexion going grey. 'I fear it will be bad news, Mrs Perceval. I hoped that I had read the signs wrongly but alas, I'm going to be proven right.'

Maggie watched as Mrs Perceval pushed her pan of boiling custard to one side and wiped her hands on her apron. 'He what? He wants to see us all? All of us in the dining room? Oh, my Lord, what is he going to say? I feel sick just wondering.' The wind and bluster faded from out of Mrs Perceval's sails as she sat down in the kitchen chair.

'Maggie, bring her a drink of water. I think she's going to faint,' Baxter said and went to the aid of Ada Perceval, grasping her hand and holding it tightly. 'It might be just to tell us about Alice and Robinson, nothing more, so there's no need to panic.'

Maggie passed Mrs Perceval the glass of water and looked at the elderly couple who were worried about what their master was going to tell them. She watched as Baxter patted the old cook's hand and tried to calm her down.

'Can you go and find Millie for us, please? I think she was watering the plants in the master's study the last time I saw her.' Baxter tried to smile at Maggie. It wasn't just his staff this was a concern for. It was also a worry for the poor evacuee that had arrived among them when times were changing. The evacuee had rarely been given any time or attention since her arrival, apart from when she had sprained her ankle, which she was still limping with, he noted as she climbed the few stairs up into the main hallway.

'No matter what he says, it will be all right, Ada, I'll make sure of that. Now, come on, put your brave face on. Serve him his pudding and coffee and then we'll see what he has to say.'

'Aye, my heart's pounding so fast, Peter, I don't know if I can serve him his pudding. What's he wanting with us? What's he going to say? I hope to God that you're wrong. I have nowhere to go!' Ada wailed.

'We don't know what it's about so stop your fretting. He may only be going to tell us about Alice and Robinson. Now, dessert and coffee and then we will all attend.'

Maggie made her way into the study. She had only been there once when she had first been shown around the hall with Alice and she had been astonished by the amount of books that furnished the walls and the smell of Lord Bradley's cigars that were kept on the grand oak desk. She opened the door with hesitancy and peered into the room, hoping to see Millie straight away without entering Lord Bradley's inner sanctum. However, she could see nobody watering the array of plants that filled the bay window and she was about to close the door behind her when she noticed a foot poking out from behind the huge wing-backed brown leather chair that had its back to her.

'Millie? Millie, is that you? Lord Bradley needs to see you,' Maggie said quietly and then walked towards the chair as she got no response.

'Millie, wake up, you're wanted,' Maggie said and shook the sleeping young parlourmaid on her shoulder. 'Wake up, Millie, Lord Bradley needs to see you all.'

'Eh, what? Oh Lord, I must have fallen asleep! I'm so tired. Don't tell Mrs Perceval, she'll have my guts for garters.' Millie yawned and then jumped to her feet and rubbed her eyes. 'Lord Bradley wants to see us all? Do you know why? I expect it's about Alice, Robinson and their carrying-on. You must have been blind if you hadn't seen what they were up to. It didn't surprise me.'

Maggie looked at Millie with surprise. She hardly ever said anything to anyone but she must have noted everything that happened within the hall and kept it to herself. 'I don't know what it's about. All I know is that Mrs Perceval and Baxter are worried, so you had better get a move on.'

'Right, right, don't tell them I was asleep,' Millie said and then picked up the small watering can that she had been carrying and quickly left Maggie on her own.

Maggie looked around the study. It was a wonderful room; a room that she could only dream of ever owning. The walls held paintings of past generations of the Bradleys and where paintings did not hang, the walls were filled with books. Leather-bound, illustrated and beautiful. She sat down in the chair that Millie had dozed in and picked up a book that lay on the nearby table, *A History of Hawith Hall,* and turned the pages, reading that the Bradley family had built the hall and had lived in it for centuries. No wonder there was upset in the kitchen. The hall was an institution, an institution that was on its last legs compared to the history that she flicked her way through, reading of its great past.

Mrs Perceval, Baxter and Millie stood in front of Lord Bradley as he sat at the head of the long dining table and sipped his coffee, looking seriously at his three staff. He too could remember when there were more staff than family; however, those days were well and truly gone. There was a knock on the dining room door and Tom from the stables entered the room and all servants looked worriedly at one another.

Maurice Bradley stood up and walked across the room to stand in front of his staff and looked at all of them knowing that what he was going to say would affect their lives deeply.

'You will all know that Alice has left with Jeff Robinson, and that was highly regrettable. However, it saves me from telling her what I am about to tell you all.' Maurice cleared his throat and looked at his faithful staff. He hated what he was going to tell them but it could not be helped.

'I've decided to sell the hall. It's been in my family for generations but since my father's death, I have been struggling to keep solvent. He left debts and, of course, on his death, the government wanted their share too. Also, Lady Rebecca has decided that she has had enough of being married to a pauper and has asked for a divorce, therefore I have no option but to sell the hall and move on.' Lord Maurice hung his head and steadied his voice; he could see the shock on everyone's faces.

'Tom, you are safe in your own home and I'm glad that worked out for you. Mrs Perceval and you, Baxter, I'm afraid I will have to give you a month's notice but I will pay you until the year's end when you leave. Millie, I am going to be moving to the gatehouse so will need a maid and a cook some evenings, so I am to keep you in employment.' Maurice looked at the relief on Millie's face but also noticed the tears running down Mrs Perceval's. 'I'm sorry. You have worked for me and my father and have been faithful to both of us but times are changing and these grand houses are no longer viable to run. I have not made this decision lightly, believe me, especially with war also hanging over our heads.'

Baxter stepped forward and cleared his throat. 'I think we all completely understand, Lord Maurice, and we thank you for making clear the situation. However, may I say on behalf of all of us that it is an honour and will continue to be an honour until the day we go to have served you and your family.'

'Aye, that it is, sir, and thank you for letting me buy the farm. You can be sure it's in good hands,' Tom said and shook Lord Maurice's hand.

'Mrs Perceval, I'm so sorry. What will you do now?' Lord Maurice asked with concern.

'I don't know, sir. Perhaps move in with my sister, if she will have me, as I'm not getting any younger, or hope that an almshouse near her comes up for let soon.' Ada

Perceval sobbed and wiped her nose with her handkerchief.

'Well, I wish you all the very best,' Maurice said and hung his head. 'Now, I'm sure you have much to discuss and sort, as I have, and once again, thank you for your service.'

Back in the kitchen, Ada sobbed as she sat in her favourite chair and looked around the kitchen. 'I knew this day would come but I just hoped for another year or two more. I don't know what I'm going to do.'

Baxter sat down beside her and took hold of her hand. 'Mrs Perceval, we have worked together for the past thirty years. I don't know if you feel the same way about me as I do you, but perhaps it is time for me to say what I should have said at least twenty years ago.'

Tom and Millie looked at the elderly couple and could not believe what they were seeing.

'Mrs Perceval, I know I'm not the best catch in the world; I'm long in the tooth, cantankerous and set in my ways. However, I'm trustworthy, not short of a bob or two and I must admit to having had affection for you for some time now. With that in mind,' Baxter said, holding his breath as he then quickly said the words he had wanted to say for years, 'will you honour me by becoming my wife, Ada?'

Ada put her handkerchief down on her lap and looked at him with tear-filled eyes. 'You silly old devil, you're only feeling sorry for me.'

'Believe me, I am not, Ada Perceval. Marriage is not

something to be taken lightly, as we have just witnessed. I want you to be my wife,' Baxter said and held both her hands tightly.

Ada looked at the man who might as well have been her husband for all these years. She had grown fond of him and after the death of her first husband, he had always been there for her, giving her help and advice. 'Peter Baxter, I must need my head tested but yes, my answer is yes! Aye, what a day! I don't want another of these in a hurry.'

Tom and Millie clapped. At least some good had come out of the day.

'Oh, I'm sorry, I'm not supposed to be in here. I was sent to look for Millie and then I saw this book and started to read,' Maggie exclaimed. Placing the book that she had been lost in for the past half hour down, she apologized to Maurice Bradley as he caught her sitting in his chair and reading the book that he had been reading previously.

'No, there's no problem. Please sit down. I also need to talk to you because my decision affects you too,' Maurice Bradley said quietly and pulled up a standard chair to sit across from the girl that he had hardly paid any attention to regardless of her staying under his roof.

Maggie felt nervous as she looked at the man whose family she had just been reading about, of how they had been loyal to both kings and queens of the country and had justly been rewarded by them.

'There's no need to worry, but I am about to put my

home, this hall, up for sale and therefore I will not be able to keep you housed here. I'm afraid you have descended on the Bradley family when it is in decline and not flourishing as in days of old,' Maurice said gently. 'However, this doesn't mean you'll be homeless. I'll contact the board and they will get you rehomed, hopefully nearby so that you can still continue to be schooled down in Gargrave, or at least Skipton.'

'Oh, I see. I'm sorry,' Maggie said quietly and felt her heart beat fast. She did not want to go and live elsewhere. She might not have had a lot of love spent on her but she had not been beaten, gone hungry or uncared for like some.

'I'm sorry. I have no option. Now, perhaps Mrs Perceval will tell you what you need to know. And as I say, don't worry, I'll see that you get a good home,' Maurice Bradley promised as he rose and went to look out of the window across the grounds that he had loved so much and was going to miss keeping in order.

'I understand. I've enjoyed staying here, Lord Bradley, thank you for having me,' Maggie said, standing up from the chair.

'Don't worry, it will be a week or two before you will need to leave. Now, you'll need some time to think about things and I have some letters to write.' Maurice Bradley opened the door for Maggie to leave his study.

'Thank you,' Maggie said and, feeling dejected, she walked back to the kitchen, dreading to see the faces of the staff she had begun to know so well.

Instead, she was met with smiling faces.

'We have a wedding! Mrs P. is marrying Baxter and I'm going to work for Lord Maurice at the gatehouse! All is going to be well.' Millie grinned, not thinking about Maggie's situation as she looked at the crestfallen lass and not bothering to ask what was to become of her.

'That's good, all's worked out fine then,' Maggie said and then turned to go up to her room. All was fine except for for her, she thought as she climbed the stairs to go and cry in her bedroom. She did not know where she was going or what her life would be like.

Chapter 22

Lizzie sat in the outside toilet; she was trying to keep out of the Browns' way. There was tension in the vicarage. She had heard shouting first thing and she was trying to keep her head down until school started. Dorothy Brown had scuttled around her like a church mouse as she had given her and her husband his breakfast. Her peace was broken abruptly by a braying on the door as she sat and waited until the last minute to leave.

'Lizzie Taylor, are you in there? Do I really have to tell you that it is eight forty-five and time you were at school?' Reverend Brown shouted and waited for the toilet door to be opened.

Lizzie opened it hesitantly; there was no privacy in the vicarage, not even on the lavvy.

'Sorry, I was about to leave for school,' Lizzie said and looked up at the vicar's angry face.

'I should think so, and mind your manners when you return this evening. We'll have important guests from the diocese here. I don't want any interruptions while I hold a meeting in the study.' Reverend Brown watched as Lizzie walked around the side of the vicarage without replying. If nothing else, the meeting today would be a way of finding her a new home. He had regretted taking on an evacuee as soon as she had entered the house and taken his wife's time away from doing Church business. Aside from that, he was not happy with his new assignment; someone had been gossiping to those higher within the Church. Things had been said about him, of that he was in no doubt. He had not been expecting to be moved to a new parish on the outskirts of Leeds; he was quite settled in the sleepy village of Gargrave. However, he could not argue with the bishop and his idea for him to bring succour and care to the industrial outskirts of the city. At least the people there would leave him to his own brand of guidance and he would be free of the countryside gossips.

'Blinking heck, Maggie, I'm glad I've come to school. Something is going on at the vicarage this morning. It's like walking on eggshells. I've been hiding in the lavvy for most of the morning.' Lizzie pulled her coat off and hung it up on the hooks in the school's hallway. 'He's in such a mood and she's scared of her own shadow and there's a meeting seemingly today,' Lizzie went on quickly as she watched Maggie hang her coat up, not noticing that for once it was Maggie who looked downcast. 'I don't want to go home tonight if they haven't changed their moods.'

'You never want to go home, Lizzie, so that will make no difference. Anyway, at least you've got somewhere you can call home. Unlike me,' Maggie growled and turned to her friend who always had so many troubles.

'What do you mean? You have a home at the hall so what are you moaning about?' Lizzie said, putting her arm through her friend's.

'I haven't for much longer. Lord Bradley is selling the hall, Alice has run away with Jeff Robinson, the chauffeur, and Baxter is to marry Mrs Perceval. How's that for things to worry about? Lord Bradley says he has to inform the evacuees' board and find me a new billet; I might be miles away from here and miles away from you!' Maggie moaned and then unlinked her arm from Lizzie's as the bell rang for lessons. 'I'll tell you more at playtime,' she whispered as they both walked to their wooden desks and sat down to take the lesson being drawn out on the blackboard by Miss Sanderson. School life at least was stable and for that they were both thankful.

All morning neither girl could concentrate on their lessons. Both were worried about the news at their make-shift homes upon their return from school, Lizzie not knowing what the unexpected guests were visiting the vicarage for and Maggie worrying that she may return to the hall to find her bags packed with a new address label tied to them. Since their arrival and after the first run-in with local children the school was their safe place as they listened to Miss Sanderson explain the rock formations that made Yorkshire what it was. Neither of the two girls took any of the information in and when the bell rang for playtime they were both thankful.

'You look worried, Maggie, tell me more. What exactly is going on at the hall?' Lizzie asked and held Maggie's hand as they walked outside to the shelter of the shed that was open to the elements on one side but at least kept them out of the rain that was pouring down, adding darkness to the already dark, damp day.

'As I said, Lord Bradley is to find me a new home. He's moving to the gatehouse, taking Millie the maid with him to keep house, and all the rest of us are to make our own way in the world. I think his wife has left him but he's not told me that. However, I overheard Mrs Perceval and she was saying that she's staying in London.' Maggie bowed her head and tried not to cry. 'I'd just got used to living there and was happy now that we could send messages back and forward with Molly and Sid Bryson.'

'Oh, Lord, they surely won't send you far away, will they? I don't want to lose you, and I'd never manage to stick it here, especially now the vicar doesn't trust me as far as he can throw me. He keeps looking at me strangely and she keeps asking and commenting that it was strange that my coat went to you, not to them. I'm sure he knows that I'm lying.' Lizzie gasped. 'What are we going to do?'

'I don't know, Liz, I just don't know. I wish we'd never come here. It's not like our homes have been bombed; we could still be living with our mams and das and have not come to any harm,' Maggie said and then saw Archie coming her way.

'I've heard the news. What are you going to do Maggie? Tom says Lord Bradley is trying to find you a family to live with in Skipton, but you'll not want to go there,' Archie said and looked at both girls. 'I'm sorry, I'm so happy now, not like you two.'

'Skipton? I'm not going to live in Skipton! I'd never see you, Lizzie.' Maggie tried her hardest to fight back the tears.

'I don't want you to go. Oh, Maggie what are we going to do?' Lizzie said as the school bell went, summoning them back to their lessons.

'I don't know, but we can't be parted. We won't be parted!' Maggie said defiantly.

Lizzie watched the visitors from the Bradford diocese leave from her bedroom window; they shook Reverend Brown's hand and then climbed into a black Ford car and drove off. As soon as the front door was closed she heard Reverend Brown talking loudly to his wife. He was not happy with whatever news he had been given and his wife was having to take his wrath. Lizzie went to lie on her bed and buried her head under her pillow. She did not want to have to go and sit and mind her manners and say prayers at the supper table. She wanted to be home, with her parents that never said a bad word to one another no matter what life threw at them. She had hated every day at the vicarage. It was not a home of peace; it was anything but. Even Maggie had it better than her. Nobody might give a damn about her but at least she wasn't living on her nerves all the time. Things, however, would get even worse if Maggie was to be re-billeted somewhere else. Even if it were only Skipton, it would still be five miles away and she would have no one to share her worries with at school. She hated the war, she hated Yorkshire and most of all she hated Reverend Brown and his wife.

Maggie woke up early. She had only slept for a few hours. The dark hours of the night had made everything seem ten times worse than it was, and her world was coming to an end, she had decided before sleep overtook her. Then just as she was waking up, somewhere between dreams and reality, her plan hatched. The plan would see both her and Lizzie safe and happy with the ones that they loved and who loved them. She hastily dressed and got ready for school but before going down for her breakfast she wrote the shortest note home that she had done since she had left.

Dear Mam and Da,
    Lizzie and I are coming home. We are going to ask for a lift back home with the Brysons. We can't stand staying here any longer. Don't worry, we will be with you soon.
    Love Maggie xx

That was what they would both do, she thought as she sealed the envelope and smiled. Lizzie and her should never be parted and besides, it would be good to be home for Christmas. Nobody had ever wanted either of them so they wouldn't be bothered once they discovered what they had done. She only hoped that the Brysons would return before she got sent to her next billet. Every day she would watch for that barge without fail; it was the escape plan for both her and Lizzie and they must not miss it.

'Well, I've found out what the arguing was about at the vicarage,' Lizzie said as she and Maggie met in their usual place in the playground.

'Oh, what was it?' Maggie asked, not interested in the affairs of the vicarage.

'He's being moved to another parish and she doesn't want to go. I heard her say it's because people have complained about his sharp manners, which doesn't surprise me. Although according to him, it's because this other place needs his help. However, I'm sure someone has complained about him, but we'll never know. I even heard her answer him back, which she never usually does.' Lizzie sighed. 'That means that I'm in the same situation as you because I don't know if they'll be taking me with them or not. It sounds as if they'll have packed up and gone by Christmas as well.' Lizzie grinned at Maggie. 'I really hope that they don't take me with them. Perhaps we could find somewhere to go together if we tell the board that is in charge of evacuees. Anywhere will be better than the vicarage.'

Maggie hesitated for a moment and then confessed to the letter that she had written. She hoped that Lizzie would not be mad with her and that she would agree to what she had scribbled so hastily when she thought both their worlds were about to collapse around them.

'We'll not be needing new homes, Lizzie. I decided when you were so unhappy and when I thought I was going to be moved on to Skipton that I'd write and tell Ma and Da we're coming home. I hope you're not mad at me but we're both so upset. Besides, Hitler hasn't dropped a bomb yet; he's all mouth and bluster,' Maggie said and looked at the disbelief on Lizzie's face.

'And how do you think we're going to do that? I'm not walking. It's miles and I don't even know the way and we can't afford the train back.' Lizzie couldn't believe what her friend had just said and that she had already put her plan in place by writing home.

'We go by the canal, and we get a lift with Molly and Sid Bryson on the *Rosie May*. They said they'd do anything for us and we know they're to be trusted. They should be coming back through Gargrave by the end of next week so we need to catch them and get home with them,' Maggie explained. 'We'll go sailing down the canal; nobody will be bothered that we've gone home because, let's face it, nobody wants us here.'

'But the Brysons might not want us either. They might worry that they'll get in bother for taking us back.' Lizzie couldn't help feeling excited about the idea of returning home but at the same time was scared of their actions.

'No one will know. We'll both leave a letter saying that we've gone home, but not saying how we're going. If we sneak out at night, we'll be down the canal at

Barnoldswick before anyone realizes that we've gone,' Maggie said excitedly and looked at Lizzie, hoping that she agreed.

'Oh, Maggie, it's a long way and what if the Brysons get fed up with us and leave us halfway, or are worse than the people we live with now? We don't really know them that well, do we? My mam will be having a fit at the letter you've written to your parents because your ma is sure to tell mine. You could have waited and asked me first.' Lizzie sounded vexed with her best friend but at the same time, she could just imagine her mother's embrace as she stepped off the Brysons' barge into her arms.

'Anything's better than being pushed from pillar to post. If it comes to it, we can always walk home, because I'm not staying here a minute longer.' Maggie said and looked into Lizzie's eyes. 'Go on, Liz, we'll both watch out for them and then ask them together. Let's go home. You know you want to.'

Lizzie gulped and wiped her eyes. 'All right then, we'll do it.'

Nancy Shaunessy thanked the postman and smiled as she opened the letter with Maggie's handwriting on it. She loved to hear from her daughter so she sat down at the breakfast table with her husband to take each word in and cherish them.

'Oh, my Lord, Dan,' she gasped. 'She's taken it into her head for her and Lizzie to get a lift home on board the barge with the Brysons! We don't know them that well; will they be fit to carry our children?' Nancy

Shaunessy couldn't believe the letter in her hand. 'That's all she's put, coming home with the Brysons and that they can't stand where they're living any longer.'

'That bloody lass of ours! We don't know them from Adam, but the Brysons seem decent enough souls. Something must have gone on else she wouldn't even think of coming home,' Dan said and shook his head. 'She's that headstrong is that lass of yours.'

'How come she's my lass when she does something wrong but at other times she's yours? But I must admit, it may be my fault because I put in my letter that she had just to ask the Brysons for anything and they would help her. I only hope their word was true and that our lasses will be safe with them. I'm not going to sleep of a night until they're home. I wonder if Annie has heard from Lizzie. I'm just going to pop next door and see.' Nancy put on her headscarf even though she was only going next door and left Dan sitting at the table thinking about the letter that his headstrong daughter had written. He knew that he couldn't get hold of anybody at Leeds docks to give the Brysons a message; by now they would be on their return journey and be somewhere in the wilds along the meandering canal. The girls were going to have to take their chance and he would be worried sick until they were back home safely.

'Well, I'll be glad when they're both home, but I must admit, I'm not keen on them coming back with folk we hardly know. There'll be no room on that barge and our Lizzie likes her privacy,' Annie Taylor said as she read the letter that Nancy had shoved under her nose. 'Our Lizzie is not happy with them heathens. I can tell she only tells me half a story but I know now that I should never have sent her away.'

'What do you think we should do, Annie? Leave it be and see if they come home or should we get in touch with the authorities?' Nancy said and looked at the letter again.

'Well, Jack has always said they were all right and we all met the Brysons, and besides, if they had a bad reputation, all the docks would know and shun them. Hopefully, they should be back in a fortnight at least. We could send the lasses letters and hope that they receive them before they leave, but I'd be frightened that they would be opened, especially by those at the vicarage. But I would like to tell them to be careful and if there's any funny business on the way back, to leg it and find somebody they can trust to tell and get them back home to us.' Annie smiled. 'Our lasses home, that'll be grand. Holy Mother of God, let them come home safe and sound and forgive me for ever sending my lass away.'

'Aye, I'll just send a letter and tell her to be careful. Oh, Lord, Annie, I'll not sleep a wink until they're back home under our roofs, safe and sound. That is, if Hitler still behaves himself. You can't do right for doing wrong.' Nancy sighed. Her lass was coming home and she wished that she could walk through the door there and then, safe and sound, laughing and smiling just like she used to do.

* * *

Every day for the next week Lizzie and Maggie watched for the gaily painted *Rosie May* to be seen on the canal and for it to be moored alongside the towpath. Then one Saturday morning as they were both peering over the canal bridge into the thick fog that clung to the canal, they saw the barge that they loved come chugging up the cut. The smoke from its engines added to the fog and shrouded it in cloud as Sid steered it on its true path.

'It's them, Maggie! It's them. They made it before we both had to leave!' Lizzie jumped up and down, grabbed hold of Maggie's coat sleeve and started to pull her towards the canal edge.

'Wait a minute, I can't walk that fast! I'm coming!' Maggie said and hung on to Lizzie's arm as they both walked down the canal bank, waving and shouting at both Sid and Molly as they sat on the deck with the barge low down in the water – filled to the gunnels with coal for the port of Liverpool.

Molly waved and both girls could see her tell Sid to pull up and moor on the canalside. They watched as the barge slowed down and a rope was thrown overboard towards them to be tied securely around the mooring post as Sid jumped from off the barge onto the canal pathway.

'Now then, what are you two doing out in this cold damp weather? It's hardly light yet, let alone warm,' Sid said as he rubbed his hands together and looked at the two young girls that had obviously been watching for his and Molly's return. 'Have you got a letter or something for us to take home?' he said as he watched Molly shout at them and tell them to come aboard.

Maggie looked at Lizzie as she took Sid's hand for support and breathed in deeply as she glanced at the elderly couple that she was going to ask a great deal from. She knew that they could both get in bother for doing as she asked.

'You look worried, lass. You'd better come in and tell us what's wrong with you both,' Molly said quietly, opening the small green-painted doors that led to the cabin where they had sat once before. There Maggie and Lizzie sat and felt butterflies in their stomachs as they told both Molly and Sid their predicament and how Lizzie had been hit with a ruler for her last visit to them and that nobody was showing care to either of them now that both homes had their worries.

'So, what are we going to do about all this? Do you want me and Sid to come and sort them out, because we will? They need telling that you both need some sort of care. Maggie, your ankle doesn't look to be mending that fast, you need to have your weight taken off it for a week or two, and Lizzie, the vicar wants to practise what he preaches, there's no two ways about that. Even if you get new homes, you'll both be split up and might end up worse than you already are,' Molly said as Sid shook his head, wondering what to do.

Maggie looked at Lizzie. 'I wrote to my ma and said we would like to come home and hoped that you would be able to help us. She sent me a letter saying that she was cross with me for even thinking of it, but if you were in agreement, then she would see you right with a payment once we were home.' Maggie pulled out the letter that her mother had sent by return out of her pocket and passed it to both Molly and Sid.

'Did she now? Well, we'll have none of that, you can tell her,' Molly said and looked hard at both the girls, whose faces dropped a mile. 'We want nowt for taking you two home; I was going to suggest we did that anyway. There's many a family back together at the moment. The war might be raging in Europe but he's not dared put a foot anywhere near England yet.'

Maggie and Lizzie's faces lit up and they both could have cried with joy.

'Now, if you're coming back with us, we'd better not stop long here in Gargrave. We'll make our way to the end of the village and then keep going; we'll wait for you at dusk down by the last locks. Is that all right, Sid?' Molly asked and looked at her husband's face, who was more hesitant about their idea.

'Aye, but they both leave a note saying that they're in safe hands and are on their way back home, but make sure not to mention us,' Sid said before walking out onto the deck. He wasn't happy with the idea but he knew if they didn't take them home, they could try to get a lift with someone disreputable.

'Never mind him; he'll be right once we have Gargrave behind us. Now, go and get ready and we'll see you after you've had your suppers when nobody will miss you before breakfast time. It will give us a head start just in case anyone cottons on that you're going home with us,' Molly said. 'Your mas and das will be glad to have you back and you'll be safe with us.' She watched as the two young girls made their way out of the cabin. She and Sid could have done without them – where they were going to sleep and what they were going to eat would be a worry – but she knew both girls had to be returned home no matter what. It was the least she could do for their worried parents in Liverpool. They would deliver them happy and fed if it was the last thing she and Sid did.

Maggie sat and ate her supper in silence. It had been made for her by Mrs Perceval but nobody had time to sit with her or bother about her. She looked around the kitchen. She would never forget her stay in the hall; there had been good times and bad times there. She had already written a note thanking everyone and had told them not to worry about her safety and had put it on the dressing table for them to find in the morning. Her bags were packed and it was time to go as she finished her soup and placed the empty dish in the sink. She made her way upstairs, only to come back down again five minutes later without anybody spotting her departure. She took one last look at the hall and ran as fast as her injured ankle would let her. It was time to put it all behind her. The only person she would miss would be Archie. At least he had found the life that he had always wanted and she was glad for that.

Lizzie kept quietly opening her bedroom door and closing it again. Downstairs Reverend Brown had a visitor and voices could be heard going from room to room as she tried in vain to sneak away and out of the back door. It was dark now; she should be on the barge and making her way home, she thought. She felt sick as she hoped that the Brysons and Maggie would wait for her.

At last, she heard the front door open and the vicar saying to his guest that God would take care of whoever had been visiting for advice and guidance. Then she heard the voices of the Browns as they sat down in their main living room and turned on the radio to listen. Now was the time to make her escape. She picked up her few belongings and sneaked downstairs as quietly as she could. Quickly she walked through the kitchen and opened the back door, just as she heard Mrs Brown ask her husband if he would like a cup of tea and open the living room door. She pulled on the back door but it was locked; the key hung up against the kitchen's fireplace so she dropped her belongings and prayed that she could get the key and unlock the door before Mrs Brown caught her. Her hands fumbled with the key as she hastened to unlock the door and pick up her belongings just in time. She quietly closed the wooden door behind her and heard Mrs Brown's footsteps on the tiled floor of the kitchen. She was free, she was going home as fast as her legs could carry her. Please let the *Rosie May* still be moored and waiting for her, she thought as she rushed through Gargrave and along the canal towpath to the very outskirts of the village. There, in the darkness, she could see the lamps aglow on the barge that was going to take her back home. They had waited. She was safe.

*   *   *

'She's not going to come, is she? The Browns must have caught her.' Maggie felt her stomach churn. She couldn't leave without Lizzie.

'Be patient, we can give her a bit longer. Keep looking out for her,' Molly said and glanced at Sid, hoping that she would be right.

'I can't wait all night. We'll have to be away soon,' Sid said as he kept the barge's engine just ticking over.

Maggie and Molly peered into the darkness and held their breath. Sid wouldn't wait much longer; he needed to leave soon if he was to take the girls back under the cloak of the night.

'She's here! She's here! I can just see her. Come on, Lizzie!' Maggie shouted as she just made the shape of her friend out in the darkness. 'We're about to go.'

'I'm coming, I'm coming. I couldn't get away. I thought that you would have gone without me. I'm so glad I've caught you,' Lizzie cried as she climbed aboard with all her belongings and caught her breath.

'No, we would never have gone without you, don't worry. Are you all right?' Maggie asked, looking at her friend.

'Yes, I am now. I can't believe we've done this.'

'Well, we have, Lizzie, we have. We're going home and no one can stop us! I can't wait to smell the sea air, eat my mam's cooking and to be shown love again.'

'Me too. Yorkshire is lovely but it's not home. Goodbye Gargrave and Reverend Brown. I'm going home to where I'm truly loved.'

Chapter 23

Ethel felt her heart beating fast as the postman handed over a letter with the Liverpool postmark on it and looked worriedly across at Tom.

'Looks like a letter from the lad's folks,' Robin the postman commented. He noticed the expressions on Tom and Ethel's faces and the horror on Archie's as he heard the words that he never thought would be uttered. It couldn't be a letter from his mother, it just couldn't. She couldn't write and she didn't give a damn about him anyway.

'Aye, it does. I've been expecting word coming from over there. Now if you don't mind, Robin, me and the lad have a bit to do today and I need to read this in private,' Tom said and just about pushed the nosy postman out of the cottage's kitchen. He'd get to find out about the news the letter contained when he was fit and ready to tell him it. Tom looked at Archie, whose head hung low. He was nearly in tears. 'We've been

306

waiting for this letter, lad, after we wrote to your mother,' Tom said as he started to open it.

'It can't be from her, she can't write. She never writes. And what do you want to write to her for? She doesn't care about me and please don't say that you're sending me home. I don't want to go home. Please don't say you're sending me home! Maggie might have gone but I don't want to go!' Archie wailed.

'Nay, lad, it was just the opposite. Ethel and I asked for your mother to give us permission to keep you, to make this farm your proper home and for us to bring you up as ours.' Tom handed over the opened letter for Archie and Ethel to read. In scrawling handwriting they both read:

I, Mary Brannigan, give you permission to adopt my son, Archie, until he is of an age to look after himself.
X

At the bottom was a signed cross as a signature by Mary Brannigan and there was a note from the next-door neighbour, Elizabeth Bell.

This is the best thing that could happen to Archie. God bless you for taking him in. Elizabeth Bell, neighbour

Archie couldn't believe his eyes and Ethel went and held him so tightly he could hardly breathe.

'You are our lad now, Archie Brannigan. There's no going back to Liverpool for you. Tha's a Yorkshire lad now, with a farm of your own after our day,' Ethel said and kissed his head.

'Aye, lad, that is, if you'll have us,' Tom said before slumping in his chair with the letter trembling in his hand.

'You don't even have to ask. I love you both, I love it here, I love Yorkshire and I will never ever leave. I can't believe that this has happened to me,' Archie cried and wiped his eyes.

'Well, it has, lad, and you have made our lives complete. This is one good thing the war has brought: a new life for you and us.'

'A new life in Yorkshire! I just can't believe it,' Archie shouted. Unlike Maggie, he would never have to see the back streets of Liverpool ever again. Yorkshire and a farm with a loving family: he had everything he could ever wish for and more. He only hoped that his two friends, Maggie and Lizzie, would keep themselves safe when and if bombs did start to fall on Liverpool, and fall they would. Nothing was more certain as the war intensified.

Maggie and Lizzie lay in the narrow bunk beds within the barge and felt safe, warm and loved for the first time in a long time. The steady chugging of the barge's engine had been comforting over the past few days and the open countryside was now giving way to the built-up fingers of Merseyside. Their flight in the darkness of the night had been stressful and fearful but they had not been followed and every minute shared with the Brysons had been filled with love.

'Come on, you two lasses, last breakfast aboard the *Rosie May*. There's sausages to be eaten before docking and you need both to have a wash else we'll be turning you both into water gypsies and your families won't be having that,' Molly said as Sid kept his hand on the tiller. She watched as both girls crept out of the hold and sat on the floorboards with plates of sausage and bread and metal cups of tea in their hands.

'I can smell the sea! isn't it lovely? Hello, seagulls. I love you! I never thought I'd say that. My da always calls them shite hawks,' Maggie said, closing her eyes and breathing in.

'Look, Maggie, look! There's the Liver Building in the distance. Look at it! Look at it!' Lizzie stood up, nearly knocking her tea over, and waved excitedly at all the other ships and boats that were making their way into port.

Maggie rose to her feet and smiled with a tear running down her face as she hugged Lizzie.

'We're home, Lizzie. We're finally home and I'm never leaving here ever again.'